Absolution

Absolution

A NOVEL

REGINA BUTTNER

SparkPress, a BookSparks imprint
A Division of SparkPoint Studio, LLC

Published by SparkPress, a BookSparks imprint,
A division of SparkPoint Studio, LLC
Phoenix, Arizona, USA, 85007
www.gosparkpress.com

Published 2020
Printed in the United States of America

ISBN: 978-1-68463-061-5 (pbk)
ISBN: 978-1-68463-062-2 (e-bk)
Library of Congress Control Number: 2020904736

Formatting by Katherine Lloyd, The DESK

For T. R. W.

Chapter 1

Erie, Pennsylvania, 1993

I was in bed, but it wasn't my bed. I struggled to surface from the depths of my drunken haze. I was freezing. My eyes cracked open and focused on an air conditioning unit whirring in the window. This wasn't my room. I was curled into a tight fetal position with my goose-pimpled arms clamped to my chest, and—oh my God, was I naked? I ran a hand over my stomach and down to my hips. Nothing.

The air blasting from the AC smelled of mildew, and the pillow under my head held the taint of cigarettes. I pushed myself up onto my elbows and felt a soreness between my legs. I inched my hand downward, and my fingertips touched a damp spot on the rumpled sheet beneath me. *Holy crap.* Beside me, my Early American Literature professor stirred and coughed, then rolled away from me, dead asleep.

I remembered going to Dr. Asner's office the afternoon before, prepared to beg him for an extension on my final paper. I'd been sick with mono for weeks, and I was behind in all my classes. Graduation was only a month away.

"I'm sorry you've been ill, Jeanie," he'd said. He had that upscale-outdoorsy sort of look in his ragg wool sweater, pressed jeans, and spotless L.L.Bean boots. "I wish you would have come to me sooner. I was going to recommend you for a scholarship to the graduate program, but now that you're in danger of failing, I'm not sure I can help you."

I tried not to cry. My financial aid had run out, my part-time job with Dining Services wouldn't cover the cost of an additional semester, and my parents couldn't afford it. Asner scooched his chair closer to mine and put a comforting hand on my knee. "We can talk it over," he said. "Someplace more comfortable." I can't believe I fell for such an obvious line.

We walked across the quad together, the spring air heavy with the fishy stink of hawthorns in full bloom. It was late Friday afternoon and the campus was deserted. I had to hustle to keep up with Asner's athletic pace; I was still weak from the lingering effects of the mono, and I fatigued easily. "How about a drink?" he said, and of course I agreed. I wasn't about to say no to the newly installed chair of the English Department.

We headed toward State Street, and for a delighted minute, I thought he was going to take me to the froufrou wine bar where the faculty liked to hang out, but then he turned left onto Fairview Avenue and pointed out his big brick house on the next corner. I glanced at his left hand, saw the gold wedding band. So, I'd get to meet his wife. She was probably in the kitchen fixing his supper right now, expecting him back from his office hours at any minute.

But no one was home except a sleek wisp of a cat that leaped from the windowsill and scraped itself against my legs. I preferred dogs to cats and nudged it away with my toe. Dr. Asner went over to a tall wooden wine rack in a corner of the living room. "Red or white?"

"Red," I said, thinking it the more cultured choice. I wasn't really a drinker and always stuck to the three-for-$5 Rolling Rock specials whenever I went out to the college bars with my roommate, Carla. I perched myself on the edge of the couch as he poured two glasses and handed one to me. The only kind of red wine I knew was the awful cheap stuff that came in a jug, so I was surprised by how good it tasted.

Asner dropped into the leather armchair across from me and propped his ankle on his knee. He was handsomer than I'd ever noticed before, and younger too. I wondered where his wife was. I fiddled with my backpack at my feet. "Um, Dr. Asner? About my final paper?"

"Don't worry about the paper, Jeanie. You can have till the end of exam week to turn it in."

"Thank you." I gulped my wine in relief and glanced through the archway toward the dark kitchen. "I suppose your wife will be getting home soon? I don't want to take up your time."

"No worries," he said. "She's away at a conference. Poetry Society of America."

I remembered now; his wife taught freshman English. She went by her maiden name, so I hadn't connected the two of them right off. Asner reached for my glass, refilled it, and passed it back to me. I'd eaten nothing but a granola bar all day, and I was already catching a buzz. I felt funny being alone with him now, knowing his wife wasn't around. I thought I should probably leave pretty soon, but I was afraid of seeming rude if I skipped out too quickly. I'd at least finish my wine.

Asner got up and put on the new Sting CD that I totally loved but couldn't spare the $16.98 for. The edges of the room started to grow hazy. The skinny cat jumped into my lap, and I laughed and stroked its narrow back. Asner was on the couch with me now, pouring us more wine, and Sting was singing about his barley and his fields of gold.

I'm not exactly sure how the kissing started, but I know I didn't resist it at first. I was flattered and amazed that such an accomplished older man could possibly be attracted to me. I didn't have much of a love life—boys seemed to overlook me for some reason. They always went for Carla, who was much prettier and far more outgoing than I. She was the one who sometimes hooked up at last call, while I trudged back to our dorm room, alone.

So, when Asner took me by the hands, tugged me up from the couch, and headed for the stairs, I was thrilled to follow right behind him, caught up in a strong current of wonder and desire. But when he steered me into his bedroom and pushed me backward onto his bed, it was as if I woke up all of a sudden and realized what I was doing. "No," I said, pulling away from him. "No. You're married."

"Never mind my wife. She's my problem, not yours." He'd kissed me again, hard. I had tried to push him off me, but he wouldn't let go of my arms. I remembered kicking and thrashing, my long hair tangled in my face, my head jammed into the pillows. I hadn't had the strength to fight. I'd felt the weight of his body on top of mine, pinning me down. After that, it was all a blank.

I slid out of the bed, groped for my clothes, and found my jeans and sweatshirt bunched on the floor. I yanked them on, staggered into the hall and down the stairs. I had to get out of there, fast. My sneakers were by the front door; I jammed my feet into them and ran outside. The sky was starting to lighten, but the street-lights were still on, and the grass was glistening from a recent rain shower. I paused, swaying, on the creaky front porch. I was still drunk. A jolt of nausea rose from my stomach, and I slumped over the wooden railing and vomited into the bushes. When I caught my breath, I realized I'd left my backpack in the house. I crept back inside and felt around in the dark entryway, then remembered I'd left it by the couch.

Footsteps sounded above. I whipped around, and there was Asner's dark outline hovering at the top of the stairs. "Jeanie," he called down to me. "What are you doing?"

My foot bumped the backpack. I grabbed it, slung it over

my shoulder, and made for the door, but I stopped short on the threshold. I should say something. Confront him. Tell him he was a jerk and he could go to hell, like Carla would have. I gripped the backpack strap with both hands and turned around to face him. Asner cinched the belt of his bathrobe and started down the stairs. "Wait a minute," he said, holding his hand out to me. "Don't go yet." I bolted for the door.

I scanned the sidewalk for early dog walkers and took off running up the street toward campus and the senior dorms. After three blocks I had to slow to a shaky walk. The wind kicked up, scattering flower petals across the pavement like blots of snow. Did we really, actually have sex? I couldn't remember, couldn't say for sure. The physical signs said yes, but my mind wouldn't let me go there. No way. I didn't do stuff like this. One-night stands weren't my thing, and I never got so drunk that I lost control of myself or couldn't remember what I'd done. I'd never even thought about sleeping with a professor. It was sleazy and stupid, so stupid! And it was all my fault for going to his house with him when his wife wasn't home. My fault for staying when I should have left, for drinking too much, for letting him get me into bed. I was a good girl, a *nice* girl. How could I have let this happen?

The wind gusted through the trees, and raindrops splashed my face. What if I wound up being pregnant? The thought was too much for me to process. I started to run again.

Chapter 2

The classroom windows were open wide, but no breeze came to cool the room. I hunched over my desk and filled in the last few bubbles on my Scantron answer sheet at random. I rubbed my sweaty palms on my jean shorts, unstuck my thighs from the chair, and wondered for the millionth time if I could detect the twinge of impending menstrual cramps in the recesses of my pelvis.

How late was I now? I couldn't remember the date of my last period. I'd never been very good about keeping track of that kind of thing, and my cycles had been irregular for months anyway, from being sick for so long. The days had slipped by, uncounted, while I burrowed my head in the sand of denial. I flipped my exam booklet over and ticked out a row of hash marks on the back cover. The thing with Asner had happened in April, and it was now the first week of May. My heart lurched. Nearly a month had passed.

I turned my answer sheet facedown and tried to focus on the essay questions: *Discuss the diplomatic goals of Richard Nixon's 1972 trip to China. Explain the political implications of the Iran-Contra scandal.* Modern American History was by far my least favorite class, but I needed the elective to graduate. I dug my fingertips into my forehead and started to write.

After a few minutes of incoherent scribbling, I let my pen fall to the desk. It was no use—all I could think about was the frightening likelihood that I was pregnant. I'd already blown my

Literary Theory final the day before, and my paper for Asner's class was only a quarter of the way done and due in his mailbox by five o'clock today; there was no way I could finish it in time and not a snowball's chance that I'd dare go anywhere near him to ask for another extension.

I might as well give up. This semester was a bust. My entire college career was a bust. Four long years of intensive reading and writing for my English lit major had come down to this pathetic failure, all because of my stupidity and bad judgment. I got up from my desk, handed my exam materials in to the proctor, and walked out.

I found Carla in our dorm room trying to cram her comforter into a black plastic garbage bag. "Hey," she said when I walked in. "I didn't think you'd be back for a while yet." She saw my face and let the comforter droop to the floor. "What's wrong?"

I had shaken Carla awake on that awful morning a month ago and blurted out what Dr. Asner had done to me the night before. She was incensed. Dr. Asshole, she called him. Conniving scumbag prick. We needed to call Campus Safety right away, she said. We had to report him for what he'd done.

I refused. He hadn't jumped me in a dark alley or held a switchblade to my neck. He hadn't forced me to go home with him or dragged me by the hair up to his bedroom. It wasn't truly a *rape*, not like the ones you read about in the newspaper. I was the one at fault anyway, for being there with him in the first place.

Carla argued with me, but nothing she said was going to change my mind. Think about how furious he'd be if I exposed him, I argued back. The questions and the humiliation I'd have to face. No one would believe my story over his anyway—he was too important of a figure within the college community. I'd be better off keeping the incident to myself for the few weeks that were left until graduation, then I could go home and forget about it.

I dropped onto Carla's bare mattress, covered my face with my hands, and burst into tears. "I'm pregnant, Carla, I just know it." My voice rose to a wail. "What am I going to *do*?"

She kicked the trash bag aside. "Hold on, just cool it a minute. We don't know that for sure yet."

I shook my head. "I'm screwed."

She squatted in front of me and crossed her arms over my knees. "There's still a chance you're not, Jeanie."

"No, there isn't. It's been too long."

"Then you've got to go buy a home pregnancy test and find out for sure. You can't keep putting it off."

"I can't. Not around here. Someone will see me." I hung my head and sobbed. "I just want to go home."

She watched me cry for a second, then got up and hugged me. "All right, we'll go home. I'll help you carry your stuff out to my car."

We stopped at a Rite Aid in the middle of nowhere, and we both went inside to buy the e.p.t. kit. I could feel the teenaged cashier's eyes on me as she rang it up. I wrapped the flimsy drug store bag around the box and stuffed it into the zippered pocket of my purse, and we continued the drive back to our hometown.

Adams Mills was a faded community of farmers, metal fabricators, and Wal-Mart shoppers in the northwestern corner of Pennsylvania. Parents raised their children with traditional family values in that part of the state, and many of the smaller townships still adhered to Prohibition-era laws that banned the sale of alcohol.

My parents lived on a quiet street of aging Victorians and enormous maple trees; Carla's house, where she lived with her widowed mother, was a block down from ours. We turned into my driveway, and I saw my mother's Chrysler in its usual spot beside our detached garage. My father's Ford F-150 wasn't there, which

I'd expected, since he supervised the four-to-midnight shift at the Alcoa plant.

Carla turned the engine off and pulled the keys from the ignition. "At least there's no sign of your sisters."

"Yeah, that's a relief." I had three older sisters—Eileen, Marian, and Debra. They were all married, and they had large families that tended to turn up at the house around dinnertime. I didn't think I could withstand their sisterly scrutiny today, particularly since Debra, the one I was closest to in age, was eight months pregnant. Her bulging belly was the last thing I needed to see right about now.

"You probably shouldn't come in," I said to Carla. "It'll only get Mom started, trying to feed you and all." Carla was five feet ten and naturally slender; she never had to worry about her weight, unlike us short, sturdy Flanagan girls.

She wrinkled her nose at me. "You don't really want to do that pregnancy test alone, do you?"

I puffed my cheeks out in a sigh. "I've got to deal with this myself, Carla, however it turns out. I'll wait and do it later tonight, when my mother's watching TV. I'll call you right after."

Diagnosis: Murder came on at nine. When Mom was settled in the family room with her cup of tea and her crochet bag, I slipped upstairs and locked myself into the bathroom. My hands shook as I opened the kit and carefully read the instructions. I peed, closed my eyes and counted to sixty, opened them, and stared in disbelief as a pink lined formed on the plastic stick in my hand.

The Out of Office reply to my e-mail informed me that Professor Steven Asner, PhD, was away on sabbatical until further notice. All inquiries should be directed to the secretary of the English Department.

Carla snorted when I told her. "No surprise there. His wife probably dumped him for cheating on her. I'll bet he seduced tons of girls at school and disappeared as soon as the semester ended, to avoid the consequences."

I climbed onto her double bed and sat with my back against the wall. Her mother had gone to the movies with her book club friends, so we could talk without the worry of being overheard. "I'm glad he's gone," I said. "It would be a huge mess if I had to tell him I'm pregnant. He'd demand a paternity test, and then I'd be tied to him forever. I don't think I could bear it."

Carla jumped off the bed and paced the room. "Let's go over your options." She hooked a forefinger. "You can keep the baby and raise it yourself. You could put 'father unknown' on the birth certificate, so Asner would never know."

"Yeah, right. I'd be labeled a tramp for the rest of my life in this town. I'd be a pariah."

Carla ignored me and hooked another finger. "You can have the baby and give it up for adoption. You could live that down, I think. People would forget about it after a while. Or you could move away. Get a job someplace where no one knows you, and start over like it never happened. I'd even go with you. I'd be glad to get out of Adams Mills."

"No. If I have it, I keep it." My sisters had already produced eleven children between them, like good Irish Catholic girls were supposed to, and Debra's baby would make it an even dozen. I couldn't imagine any of my nieces or nephews being given away to a stranger.

Carla stopped pacing and looked me in the eye. "You know what I'm gonna say next. You don't have to have it."

I punched my fist into her pillow. "Really, Carla? You think I would have an abortion? There's no way I would do that. You know my family and how old-school my parents are. It's been pounded into our heads since grammar school that abortion's a mortal sin. No. Not happening."

She made a grumbling sound in her throat. "All right, never mind."

Carla got it. The two of us had gone to Blessed Sacrament School together from first grade through eighth. We'd endured the sour-faced, yardstick-pounding nuns as we memorized the Ten Commandments and the Corporal and Spiritual Works of Mercy. We had faced the terrors of the confessional booth together and supported each other as we gave up eating candy and watching *Magnum, P.I.* for Lent. Growing up Catholic was a hard habit to shake.

I stayed at Carla's house until midnight that night, then walked home. Mom was reading a Maeve Binchy paperback by the light of her ruffled bedside lamp, waiting up as she always did for Dad to get home from his shift. She'd been a devoted housewife for forty-three years now and had never worked outside the home, except for a short stint filling in as parish secretary when Dad was laid off during the recession in '82.

"Hello, dear," she said when I paused in her doorway. "Come in and sit with me." She laid the book on top of the coverlet and folded her gnarled hands over it. *She's getting old*, I thought. More like a grandma than a mom anymore.

"Did you girls go anywhere tonight?" she asked.

"No. We just stayed in and talked."

She studied my face. "Anything the matter?"

"No, I'm just tired."

She patted my wrist. "Your father and I are so excited about your graduation coming up. First in the family! Have you heard back from any of those companies you said you were going to apply to?"

I couldn't look at her. I hadn't applied anywhere. My parents still didn't know I wasn't going to graduate. "Not yet," I said. "I'm planning to this week."

The back door slammed—Dad was home. I heard the familiar sound of his work boots clunking to the floor in the mud room, then the lamp in the front hallway clicked off, and he came creaking up the stairs in his socks. He grinned when he saw me. "Here's my best girl! How are ya, honey?" He pulled me to his broad chest, and his flannel shirt was soft and smelled of motor oil. I hugged him tight. He asked how my final exams had gone, and I tried to deflect the conversation away from me and onto the safer ground of my sisters and their doings. My spirits sank deeper and deeper into a purgatory of guilt. "I'd better get to bed," I said finally, and wished them both a good night.

In the bathroom, I let the water run as I scrubbed my face. I needed to do something about my dilemma before I broke my parents' hearts and ruined my life. Maybe the best thing really was to take the easy way out and get rid of it. *It*, like there wasn't a life growing inside me, cells dividing and differentiating each day. The beginnings of a human being. I turned the faucet off and stared into the streaky mirror. Could I do it? And live with myself afterward?

I searched the yellow pages, found a women's health clinic in a sketchy part of Erie, and drove up there with Carla two days later. Because I wasn't certain of the date of my last period, the doctor performed an ultrasound to make sure he was on the right side of the law, and because it was Pennsylvania, there was a mandatory twenty-four-hour waiting period before he could do the procedure. My appointment was set for one o'clock the next day.

Carla and I got back in her car and drove south toward Adams Mills. About ten miles outside of town, she jerked the car off the road, jounced across a potholed parking lot, and pulled up in front of a peeling concrete building with Budweiser and Yuengling signs blinking in the windows. "What's up?" I said. "Why'd you stop?"

She pushed her door open. "We're not going home and spending the next twenty-four hours sitting around in a dry town."

"Are you crazy? I'm not going into this place. Look at all those motorcycles."

"Don't worry about it. My cousin Marge's softball team comes here after all their games, and she says it's an okay place. Come on, we both need a drink."

We stumbled into Carla's house around two in the morning, completely wasted. God only knows how we made it back to town without getting pulled over and arrested or wrecking the car in a ditch. Her mother's bedroom was downstairs in the back of the house, and she was half-deaf besides, so we managed to get ourselves up the stairs without waking her. I was glad I'd had the presence of mind to call home while I was still fairly sober and tell my mother I was sleeping over. "You girls have a good time," she'd said. "Give Carla my love."

I woke the next day with the nagging feeling that I'd forgotten something. I grabbed the alarm clock from the nightstand and held it up to my face. Twelve forty-five. I came wide awake with a jolt. *My appointment.* I calculated in my head: we could get dressed fast and be on the road in maybe ten or fifteen minutes, but we'd still be over an hour late getting to Erie. My stomach started to heave. I kicked the blankets off, ran down the hall to the bathroom, and threw up in the toilet.

Carla was sitting up in bed when I came back in. Her blond hair was a mess, and her eyelids were rimmed with smeared mascara. "Frick, Jeanie. We way overslept."

"Yeah." I stood there in the clothes I'd had on since yesterday.

My throat hurt from screaming the lyrics to every Def Leppard song we could find on that skeevy bar's jukebox. "I guess I'd better go call and see if they can reschedule me."

The clinic set me up for the following day, same time. Carla and I went down to the kitchen to find some breakfast. There was a quart of milk and a greasy stick of margarine in the fridge, half a loaf of whole wheat in the breadbox. "Don't you guys *eat*?" I said.

"No." Carla was searching through the corner cabinet. "There's no Advil, no Tylenol, no nothing here. My head's killing me and I'm dying of thirst. Let's walk over to the Shurfine."

At the grocery store, we shuffled through the linoleumed aisles and filled a shopping basket with Cokes, frozen burritos, and a bottle of generic aspirin. I carried our things to the checkout and unloaded them onto the balding conveyor belt while Carla ran back to the Health and Beauty section for shampoo.

Someone got in line behind me. I turned around, expecting it to be Carla, but there was a baby staring at me. A tiny sweet girl in a soft yellow onesie, peeping at me from the crook of her mother's arm. Her feathery hair was light brown, just like mine, and her eyes were big and round and curious. We gazed at each other until the cashier interrupted us: "Paper or plastic?"

As Carla and I were leaving the store, my sister Debra and her big pregnant stomach came bustling through the automatic door. She had eighteen-month-old Travis strapped into the grocery cart, but Kyle, her three-year-old, was a free man. He hurled himself at my knees, almost knocking me into the seasonal charcoal briquette display. He showed me his sticky Airheads bar and matching blue tongue. Travis squealed and squawked at us, displaying a new tooth. Deb gave me a hug and kiss and tugged at the front of her maternity smock that used to be Marian's. Her hair was pulled into a cockeyed ponytail, and she wasn't wearing any makeup. "Gotta grab a few things before Kyle's swimming lesson," she said. "Stop by the house later so we can catch up. Trisha started gymnastics last week. She's got some new moves she wants to show you."

"Okay," I answered automatically. "Sure."

Back at the house, we microwaved the burritos into a pasty mess and watched *Pretty Woman* on VHS. "What a ridiculous story," Carla said when the movie ended. "As if a hooker would ever be able to fit into the world of a major businessman like that. It's lipstick on a pig."

"It's 'a modern-day Cinderella story,'" I said, quoting from the back of the tape box. "It's supposed to be a fantasy."

Carla stretched and yawned. "I feel like death warmed over. I think I'll go up and take a nap. You can hang out here as long as you want to though. *Dances with Wolves* is on HBO this month." She wrapped a ratty afghan around herself and slouched out.

I stayed there on the couch with the television turned off so I could have some quiet to think. The image of that little brown-haired baby was stuck in my head. I thought about my sisters' kids and how much I had always looked forward to seeing them on my school breaks. I was the fun aunt. I played Barbies with my nieces and Transformers with my nephews; we built blanket forts together in their bedrooms and raced around their backyards in rowdy games of Red Light, Green Light and Capture the Flag. I cheered for them at their T-ball and soccer games, and went to their school plays and music recitals whenever I could. They belonged to my sisters, but in a way, they belonged to me too. And so did this child I was carrying.

It was late in the day when I went upstairs and woke Carla. The sun had disappeared behind an overcast sky and the light in her bedroom was fading. "What?" she said sleepily. "What is it?"

I knelt beside the bed. "I can't go back there tomorrow. I can't go through with it."

"You can't?"

"I've made up my mind. I'm not going to do it."

She sat up, drawing her afghan with her. "You're not going to do it? You're sure?"

"Yes." We stared at each other in the dusky light.

"Can I stay here again tonight?" I asked. "I'll go home first thing in the morning and tell my parents everything. I just need a good night's sleep first."

"Absolutely." She moved over to make room for me in the bed, and I got underneath the covers. She dozed off right away, but I stayed awake for quite a while longer. A feeling of calm had come over me. I was going to face this, and my best friend would be right here to help me. My parents would help me too, once they got over the shock, and so would my sisters, I was sure of it. I closed my eyes and fell into a peaceful sleep.

Later that night, the bleeding started.

"You've got to put this behind you, Jeanie," Carla said as we pulled the blood-stained sheets from her bed the next morning. "You're lucky it ended this way. A miscarriage is better than an abortion."

I turned on her. "Lucky? You think I'm lucky? I probably brought it on by drinking all night in that crappy bar and breathing all that secondhand smoke."

"You did not. You know that couldn't have caused it."

I stuffed the bundle of sheets into her laundry hamper, to wash after her mother left for work. "I didn't eat a thing all day either. I feel like I poisoned the baby with alcohol."

"Are you kidding me, Jeanie? You did nothing of the sort. You're misplacing your guilt." Carla was a psychology major; she loved applying theory to me.

"Of course I feel guilty!" I snapped back at her. "I let my professor take advantage of me, I wasted my parents' money by failing out of school, and I had every intention of having an abortion when I knew it was wrong. I can hardly believe I was actually going to do it."

Carla was waving her hands frantically at me. "Be quiet! My mother'll hear us."

I pounded my thigh with my fist. "And on top of it all, I've been keeping every bit of this a secret from my family, when they all think I'm this sweet, innocent girl." A big lump lodged itself in my throat. "I don't know how I can face my mom and dad after this."

"I understand how you must be feeling, but you've got to get a grip."

"How? I can't let anyone find out about this, Carla. Not ever. I was kidding myself." My parents might have gotten past the scandal in time, but they'd never have gotten over the hurt I would have inflicted on them. I thought of my mother's lifetime of self-less homemaking and quiet faith, and my father driving off to work day after day in his rust-mangled pickup. They'd made a lot of sacrifices so I could go to college. They believed in me. They believed in my goodness.

"It's bad enough that I'm going to have to lie to them about failing out of school," I said. "But being pregnant? I can't ever tell them about that." I sat down on the hamper. "I've never felt so ashamed of myself in my life. I feel like absolute shit."

Several seconds passed, and then Carla spoke. "Let's go, then."

"Go where?" I said without looking up.

"Let's ditch this town. There's nothing here for us. We could go south, where the economy's better. We could go to Atlanta."

I lifted my head. "Atlanta?" I liked the sound of it—crisp and clean.

"Yeah, I read this article. There're tons of jobs down there, and the cost of living is pretty reasonable. And the winters are way warmer than here."

I rolled the idea around in my head. Move to Atlanta. I could find a job in a bookstore or something and save up money to finish my degree. I'd find a college that would accept my transfer credits, and I'd go part-time until I was done. The possibility of starting over again, someplace where nobody knew me or expected anything of me, was a spark of light in my miserable darkness.

Carla was hopping up and down in front of me. "We can go to the library as soon as it opens and start looking at the classifieds on the World Wide Web."

I jumped up and hopped with her. "We'll become city girls!"

"We'll get our own apartment and learn how to use public transportation!" Carla quit hopping and looked intently at me. "Do you mean it, Jeanie? Do you really want to do it?"

I was suddenly desperate to be rid of the anxiety and guilt that I'd been dragging around with me for weeks. I'd be running away from my family and my mistakes, but so what? Leaving Adams Mills just might be the best thing for me.

I clasped Carla's hands. "Yes," I said. "Let's do it." We grinned crazily at each other and danced around the bedroom. *"Atlanta, Atlanta,"* we sang. *"We're outta here, we're moving south!"*

I was relieved and rejuvenated, and ready for an adventure. I had no idea I was setting myself up for the biggest mistake of my life.

Chapter 3

We ditched the fields and forests of rural PA for the sunny urban sprawl of Atlanta. We found a cheap one-bedroom apartment in Little Five Points, a dingy neighborhood filled with vintage clothing shops, ethnic eateries, and black-clad teenagers whose earlobes bristled with safety pins. Carla registered with a temp agency and got a data entry job at a downtown insurance company, and I was hired as a sales associate at a Barnes & Noble in a ritzy Buckhead shopping center called The Peach.

Once we'd settled into our apartment and gotten over our fear of the MARTA trains, Carla signed us up to volunteer at the Peachtree Road Race, a big 10K run that the Atlanta Journal-Constitution sponsored every Fourth of July. "It'll be a good way for us to meet people," she said. "Maybe some hot single guys. You can't stay inside reading books every weekend, Jeanie. You've got to get yourself back out there."

On race day, we reported to our volunteer station in the big white tent at the finish line. We were handing out water and the browned halves of bananas when I noticed a guy standing a few feet away from us. He had his hands braced on his knees, and his brow was dripping sweat onto the trampled grass. He rubbed his arm across his face, straightened up, and reached for one of the Dixie cups I'd been setting out in neat rows on our table. Carla sidled over to me, alert as a cat. "Him," she whispered, pointing with her chin. "Go for it."

I dug a Gatorade out of the cooler we'd brought with us, walked over and offered him the icy bottle. He accepted it with a polite southern "Thank you, ma'am." The red fraternity letters on his shirt would normally have put me off, but he seemed friendly and he had a quick smile. Carla jabbed her elbow into my side, urging me forward. We both watched as he took a drink, and a lock of damp hair fell over his brow. He wiped his mouth, keeping his eyes on me. "Why are you volunteering instead of running?"

I tried to think of a quick fib. "I'm going to run next year," I said. "I'll be in better shape by then."

He grinned. "You're not from around here, are you?"

"No," I said. "We moved down from Pennsylvania about a month ago."

"Pennsylvania, that's cool," he said, as if I'd named an exciting foreign country. "So, where do you like to run?"

Uh oh. I looked around me at the crowds spilling out of the tent and into Piedmont Park. I knew it was a big place with a lake and picnic shelters and all kinds of playing fields and jogging paths. "Here, mostly," I said.

"There're lots of good trails along the Chattahoochee River. Have you ever run there?"

I shook my head. I hadn't even known there was a river in Atlanta.

"I could take you running sometime if you'd like. Show you around." His eyes were a warm brown, and he was tall and broad shouldered. I wasn't the least bit athletic, but if this cute guy wanted to run with me, I'd darn well run. Carla pressed her warm bare arm against mine and returned to her place behind the table.

I swallowed my shyness, abandoned my volunteer post, and walked across the park with him, away from the noise of the post-race party. He told me his name was Greg Mercer, and he was enrolled in the Executive MBA program at Emory University.

He found us a grassy spot to sit beneath the boughs of a big oak tree, and we shared a paper plate of bagels and fruit. He was from Augusta, Georgia, and he had one older brother who was married. He loved to play golf, and his family belonged to a country club—details that, to be perfectly honest with you here, weren't exactly plusses in my book—but he was also a fan of Garth Brooks and Travis Tritt, just like me and pretty much everybody else back in Adams Mills, so that kind of evened things out. And he was so well-mannered, so smart and handsome! I couldn't believe my good luck.

The following weekend, he took me to the river. The Hooch, he called it. As we jogged along the wooded trails, I told him I'd majored in English in college but hadn't finished my degree because I'd run out of money—which technically was God's honest truth. He didn't make a single crack about me being a book nerd like most people did. He thought it was *interesting*. He was a numbers guy himself, he said. I impressed him by naming every classic novel I could think of that had been made into a movie and didn't say another word about college.

We climbed a rocky stretch of trail and paused to rest in a shady grove of mountain laurel. Greg placed his hands on my waist, turned me toward him, and kissed me softly. He hesitated a moment, then kissed me again. I got the tingles in my arms and legs, and my head went dizzy. I was in heaven.

Saturdays became a regular thing for us—morning runs along the river, lazy afternoons wading in the stony shallows and eating picnic lunches on the riverbank. We talked and laughed and fell in love. On Sunday evenings I returned to Carla and our tiny apartment, gushing the praises of my awesome new boyfriend. "Go easy, Jeanie," she said one night as she heated up a package of buy-one-get-one-free ramen noodles from Kroger. "You haven't been going out with him that long."

I told her to stop worrying about it. Greg was kind and considerate, he treated me like a lady, and he seemed to think that I was pretty awesome too. I didn't tell her I was already picturing us getting married and having lots of babies. I had a plan: I would devote myself to marriage and motherhood, just as my own mother had, and that would somehow absolve me from my sins. The pregnancy, the near abortion, the miscarriage—all would be swept away and forgiven.

Greg proposed to me six weeks later. I said yes.

"You're crazy!" Carla shrieked when I came home and announced that I was engaged. "You hardly know him, Jeanie. How long has it been, a few weeks, maybe?"

I thought it was unseemly for a person with a bachelor's in psychology to call her best friend crazy. And I'd been dating Greg for exactly seven and a half weeks now, which was nearly two whole months. I huffed into the bedroom and shut the door in Carla's face, which was kind of pointless since it was her bedroom too. She came in a while later, after I'd undressed and gotten into bed, and clicked the overhead light on. "Come on, Jeanie," she said. "We've got to talk about this. I'm not saying you shouldn't marry Greg. It's just that it's happening so fast."

I wasn't going to debate it with her. Carla had always been sure of herself—she was the one with the self-confidence, the high grades, the good looks. Despite our similar upbringings, she didn't subscribe to the culture of Catholic guilt the way I did, possibly because her father had died when she was fifteen, and her mother had been too worn out with grief to enforce the old rules for long. There were times when I envied Carla's freedom.

I could sense her hovering over my bed, so I stayed facing the wall with my eyes shut. "Leave me alone."

"I just want to know one thing. Have you told him what happened with Professor Asner and how you got pregnant?"

I flipped over in my bed. "No, I haven't. And I don't plan to."

"Jeanie. You should tell him."

"Why? Why would I do that?"

"I don't think you should keep something like that a secret from the person you're going to marry. He should know what you've been through."

"He doesn't need to know. Now would you please leave me alone? You're not going to talk me out of this."

Holy matrimony would be my refuge. I intended to be the perfect wife to Greg, faultless and faithful. I would bear him many children and purge myself of the guilt that still gnawed at me for the one I'd lost. What had happened to me back in Pennsylvania would forever remain a secret.

"This is your chance to make friends with Mom," Greg said in the car on the way to the engagement dinner that his family had arranged for us. He looked great in his pressed khakis and short-sleeved polo, a touch of gel smoothing his unruly hair. He gave my knee a squeeze. "It's not that she doesn't like you. She just doesn't know you very well yet."

My nerves hummed as we turned into the parking lot of a trendy restaurant in Midtown. Up till now, my interactions with Greg's parents had been few—Florence and Howard Mercer were very busy people. His father was an executive at a company that sold specialty medical equipment, and he was frequently out of town at sales meetings; his mother was a high-end real estate broker, and she chaired a fundraising committee for the Augusta Junior League in her spare time.

We entered the restaurant and were shown to the private room in the back, where the Mercer party was already assembled. Howard, a heavyset man with a thick pouf of silvered hair, came right over to give me a welcoming hug. Greg's brother, Gordon, a darker-haired copy of his father, half rose from his chair and reached his bulky body across the table to shake my hand. Florence, sedate and elegant in her Ralph Lauren ensemble, remained seated at the head of the table. She tilted her auburn wedge, presented her cheek for me to kiss, and greeted me in a genteel drawl: "Ah'm so pleased to have you jawn us for dinnuh."

Greg introduced me to his Aunt Lillian, a gaunt woman with penciled eyebrows. He pulled out a chair for me. "Why don't you sit next to Mom so you girls can chat?" He kissed my temple and moved toward the other end of the table, where the waiter was serving a tray of drinks to the men.

I said hello to Ricki, Gordon's wife, and admired their one-year-old son, Preston, in the high chair next to her. Ricki squished her body against mine in a sideways girl hug. "I'm so excited for you and Greg," she said. "I'm sure you'll be as happy as Gordon and me." She reached behind her son's high chair and ran her lacquered nails across her husband's flabby back. Gordon, engrossed in conversation with his father, didn't appear to notice.

The waiter handed me a wine list that had no prices on it. I scanned it in a panic, afraid of ordering something that cost too much. "I'll have the same as her," I said quietly, gesturing toward Florence's white wine.

Florence turned to give me the up-and-down. I'd chosen a sleeveless navy sundress tonight—simple but flattering to my fuller figure. I was no Kate Moss by any stretch, but I was pretty enough I guess, when I kept my weight under control. I had moussed my bangs and pulled my permed hair back with a big banana clip, and in my nervousness, I'd forgotten to put on my earrings. As Florence looked me over, my sunburned nose began to itch.

"Darlin' dress," she said.

"Thank you . . . Florence."

I wondered when I'd get used to calling her Mom, like Ricki did. I watched as Ricki leaned into the conversation that was passing between Florence and Lillian. "Exactly, Mom," she said, flipping her platinum hair over her shoulder. "I couldn't agree more."

How would I ever fit into this family's gracious southern lifestyle? In Adams Mills, the popular pastimes were hunting, fishing, and all-you-can-eat spaghetti dinners at the Elks Club. My parents were solidly blue-collar, and it was only a year ago that my father had applied for his first credit card, a Discover Card with a whopping $500 limit. No one in my family except for Eileen's husband, the Agway rep, had ever traveled farther south than Virginia Beach.

Greg had taken me down to Augusta to visit his parents only once in the short time we'd dated. The Mercers lived in a gated community, and their plantation-style home overlooked a picturesque lagoon that was ringed by stately palmettos and trees that dripped moss. Greg and his father had played golf that Saturday while Florence and I sat in her Laura Ashley parlor, sipping sweet tea and making awkward small talk. I'd accidentally splashed some tea on her settee, and she'd pretended it was no big deal—*The maid will have that stain out in a jiffy*—but still, I was mortified. The next morning, Gordon and Ricki had joined us for mimosas and brunch at the country club. I'd sat there feeling underdressed and tongue-tied as Florence introduced me to her numerous lady friends and their impeccably coiffed daughters. On the drive back to Atlanta that evening, Greg had been in high spirits, having finally beaten his father at golf; I had sat forlornly in the passenger's seat, certain I'd flubbed the entire visit.

Aunt Lillian tick-tocked her glass at the waiter, and he returned minutes later with another tray of drinks. She hoisted her fresh martini. "Here's to the mother of the groom." She clinked glasses with Florence, then held her hand out to me. "Let's have a look at the ring." I obediently extended my left arm. "It's gorgeous," she said, simpering at her sister. "Flor, you have such good taste."

"Greg picked it out, actually," I said. "He—"

Lillian's attention skipped to the server, who was about to set her salad plate dangerously close to her martini. She whisked the drink out of harm's way and turned her focus to her food. The ring was forgotten.

Conversation was minimal throughout the salad course and entree. Gordon, who worked for the same company as his father, bragged about his latest accounts between mouthfuls of braised ribs. Ricki sliced a piece of chicken into slivers and fed them by hand to Preston, but hardly touched her own meal. "Still trying to lose those pregnancy pounds!" she said to me. At the far end of the table, Lillian's husband—to whom I hadn't been introduced—ordered another round of scotch for the men. I stole glances at Greg, hoping he'd look my way, and at last he looked up. He mouthed *I love you,* and I mouthed the words back.

A busboy began to collect the plates. Florence folded her napkin and gazed around the table until she had everyone's attention. "This reminds me of my own engagement," she said. "To Howard," she added, in case anyone was confused. "He was in graduate school at Emory. I used to ride the bus up to see him on the weekends, and I'd stay over with a girlfriend. I never spent the night at his apartment. It wasn't proper back in those days, even for us enlightened mainline Protestants." She flicked her eyes at me, and I felt my face redden. I'd moved in with Greg a few days after we'd gotten engaged. My parents thought I was still living with Carla, who had agreed to cover for me whenever they called.

"I suppose there is some logic to livin' together," Florence went on. "Sort of a trial period, before you tie that knot." She made a twisting motion with her fists. Ricki's knee bumped mine beneath the table.

"When Howard brought me home after the weddin'," Florence continued, "I was positively *horrified* to discover how much laundry he'd piled up. I had a mind to turn around and walk right back out when I saw it. Dirty clothes were crammed into every nook and cranny of that apartment. Laundry was all I did, for days on end!"

I tried to look amused, as a future daughter-in-law should.

"Oh, Mom, you poor thing. I can relate," Ricki said and cast a dark look at Gordon.

Florence paid no attention to Ricki's remark. "He had this great big hairy dog that he let climb all over everything. There was dog hair *everywhere*." I caught Greg's eye, and he winked at me. He had a dog too—a Lab mix named Ginger that he'd adopted from a pet rescue. He never allowed her onto the furniture, and he gave the apartment a diligent vacuuming every week.

"Then I saw the kitchen." Florence's voice rose into an unnaturally high key. "A *disaster*. The glassware was chipped, green things were growin' in the fridge, and there was no food in the pantry. I said to Howard, 'We're goin' to starve.'" Her eyes bugged out and her jewelry flashed. A polite chuckle rippled around the table. Howard's brow furrowed and he took a pull from his scotch. I looked over at Greg, who gave me an encouraging nod.

"What a funny story," I said, touching Florence's sleeve.

She moved her arm away. "And then the *bathroom*. Mold and mildew had taken over the shower. And the toilet! It—"

"Okay, Flor, they don't want to hear about that." Howard's double chin quivered. "We get it, the place was a dump and I was a poor slob, ha ha ha." He waved his hands as if to erase the images, looked around the table at his dinner guests, and clapped his hands together. "How about some dessert?"

At the end of the evening, Florence and Lillian air-kissed me goodbye, and Ricki squeezed me into another girl hug. The day's heat radiated from the asphalt as Greg and I walked across the twilit parking lot to his car. He unlocked the driver's door and was about to open it, then remembered himself and came around to help me in first.

"Did you have a good time tonight?" he asked as we drove off.

"Oh yes," I said. "It was so kind of your parents to treat us to dinner."

"I know my mom likes to be the center of attention some-times. Don't take it personally. It's just the way she is."

"I didn't. She was very pleasant."

"Don't worry about her Protestant remarks either. I explained to her how important it is for you to get married in a Catholic church. She says she's okay with it now." His expression turned playfully lascivious, and he ran his hand up my leg. "When we get back to the apartment, I'm gonna be all over you like white on rice."

A flutter of anticipation rippled through my body. I loved the novelty of going home with Greg at the end of the night, even though I knew my parents would disapprove of our premarital cohabitation. To tell the truth, I was getting kind of a thrill from my subterfuge. To rationalize my guilty feelings away, I reminded myself that we'd be married before too much longer. Greg was due to finish his MBA in early December, and he already had a job lined up with one of those new internet startups in Seattle. The wedding was scheduled for the weekend after his graduation, and we'd be on our way to the West Coast well before Christmas.

Greg made fabulous love to me that night. I lay awake for a long time afterward, mentally replaying the day's events as he snored softly beside me in the dark. I felt for the ring around my finger and brushed my fingertip over the blunt points of the diamond in its gold setting. I tugged at the sheet bunched at the foot of the bed, pulled it over us, and slipped my arm around Greg, gently, so I wouldn't disturb his sleep.

The dinner with the Mercers had reminded me of how much I missed my own family, and a wave of remorse sloshed over me. I pictured their sad faces again, as I broke the news that I was leaving Adams Mills. My mother and my sisters had teared up, and even my sisters' husbands had been dismayed to hear that Auntie Jeanie was going away. *Georgia?* they said. *So far from home!* My nieces sniffled and draped themselves over my shoulders, and my tough-boy nephews went out back to whip footballs at one another.

I wished I could have explained myself better, but I had to keep my failings to myself. My family would carry on with their rituals in my absence: They'd sign their children up for faith formation and CYO basketball, and bake their pies and cakes for the Palm Sunday Bake Sale. They'd go to Confession on Saturdays, get their foreheads smudged with ashes on Ash Wednesday, and try not to forget to go to church on the Holy Days of Obligation.

That was the world I'd been brought up in. The path was defined and the stakes were clear: act right or else! The consequences were a fiery eternity in Hell, or an uncomfortable interlude in the crowded waiting room of purgatory, possibly for decades, depending on how depraved you'd been in your earthly life. *I am sorry for these sins and all the sins of my past life.*

I missed my family every single day, but even so, I was glad I'd left. I never would have met Greg if I hadn't made the move to Atlanta. And how could I ever do without him now? He had become my world.

Now that we were getting married, we'd surely be seeing more of his family. Maybe we'd go down to Augusta for another weekend visit, or Florence and Howard would come to see us in

Atlanta. It would feel good to be part of a family circle again.

A faint doubt was tugging at the edge of my thoughts, but I whisked it aside. The Mercers did seem kind of standoffish, and they were maybe a little bit full of themselves, but I was sure they'd turn out to be perfectly nice people once I got to know them better. Ricki especially seemed to want to be my ally. I was looking forward to having her for a sister-in-law.

Greg was different from the rest of his family anyway. He was considerate and genuine, and I loved his good nature and easy sense of humor. I snuggled my head against his shoulder and floated off to sleep, thankful I'd found him.

Chapter 4

Seattle, one year later

I climbed onto the examination table and the paper crackled beneath me as I settled myself against the backrest. I lifted my shirt and the matronly ultrasound technician squirted a cool blob of gel onto my abdomen. She held the probe poised in her hand. "Ready, Mrs. Mercer?" I nodded. I was twenty weeks pregnant and today was the day of revelation—a boy or a girl? I should have been excited.

The tech poked the probe into the gel and adjusted the controls on the monitor, and an image appeared on the screen in grainy black and white. My heart jumped when I saw the curve of the baby's head and its tiny eyes and nose. I looked up at the tech and smiled.

"Would you look at that," she said and pointed out the delicate arm raised toward the mouth—the baby was sucking its thumb. My eyes welled up. "I'm going to check the uterus and placenta first," she said. "Then I'll have a look at your baby's anatomy to make sure everything's developing normally." I nodded again, not really hearing her. My thoughts were slipping backward, into memories that I didn't want to revisit. My palms prickled with sweat, and anxiety began to bubble inside me. *Chill out*, I told myself. *This time is different.*

A knock sounded at the door, and a second later my husband was at my side, reaching for my hand. "Greg!" I said and swiftly wiped my eyes dry. I stretched up to him for a kiss, and his newly grown goatee tickled my cheek. "How did you get away from work?"

Greg was the director of finance at a fledgling internet sporting goods retailer called eMarket. The company's website had gone live that morning, so I hadn't expected him to make it to my appointment. "My team's monitoring the website traffic," he said. "They'll give me a report when I get back." He peered at the monitor. "Did y'all get to the good part yet?"

"Not yet," the tech said. "I'm going to take some measurements first." She maneuvered the probe across my belly, leaving shiny splotches on my skin, and paused now and then to enter data into her computer. After a few minutes she turned back to us. "All right, you two, are you ready to see what you're having?"

"We sure are," Greg said. He squeezed my hand, and I squeezed back.

The tech wiggled the probe around some more, then held it still. "Okay, there we are."

I could tell what it was right away, having read so many pregnancy books. I looked at Greg for his reaction, but he continued to study the screen. "I can't really tell what I'm looking at," he said after a moment. "What is it?"

"It's a girl."

"A girl! That's great!" He kissed me again. He was beaming.

The tech clicked at her keyboard. "Based on today's measurements, I'm going to adjust your due date slightly, from December thirtieth to January first."

Another memory tried to push its way in. I shoved it back and forced a smile.

"A New Year's baby," Greg said. "That is so cool—" A beeping sound interrupted him, and he reached for his belt. He had a brand-new Motorola e-mail pager, courtesy of eMarket. "Hold on a sec." He read the message and stroked my arm in apology. "Sorry, Jeanie, it's Ken. He says a reporter from the Seattle Times is coming for an interview, and he wants me back at the office ASAP."

Darn. I was hoping we could go out to lunch together after this. I noticed the tech was watching me, so I gave her a little shrug to show that I wasn't bothered by my husband running off so quickly—this sort of thing happened all the time in the heady world of e-commerce. Greg had warned me that this job would require his all-out effort. The company wanted to "get big fast" in a growth-over-profits strategy that was designed to expand their market share ahead of the competition. I needed to be patient and supportive of his long and sometimes unpredictable work hours. A team player, as he liked to put it.

"Wow," I said. "The Seattle Times. You can't miss that."

Greg kissed me goodbye and went out, but he poked his head back into the room a second later. "I'll bring us something from Ivar's tonight, so you don't have to cook." He waved at me and was gone.

The tech pressed a button, and her machine printed out a shiny four-by-four-inch picture. "Here you go, Mrs. Mercer. Your first baby." The bubble of anxiety expanded inside my chest. I gazed at the picture for a moment, then slipped it into my purse.

I drove toward home around the south end of Lake Union, past the converted warehouse where eMarket was located, and up the slope of Queen Anne Hill. We lived on the second floor of a 1920s Craftsman with wide eaves and cedar beams that jutted over a broad front porch. The house had originally been a single-family residence but was now divided into two flats. The downstairs tenant had the use of the front door, while we accessed our apartment by way of a staircase tacked on to the back of the house. The rent was insane, but Greg said the view of the Seattle skyline was worth it.

I let myself into the apartment, hugged Ginger, and held the door open so she could run down to the fenced backyard. I passed through the kitchen and went down the hall to the spare bedroom that Greg used as an office. His desk was neat with only a phone and a desktop computer on it, but a hardcover notebook was lying face down on his swivel chair. I put the notebook away in the top desk drawer, took the ultrasound picture from my purse and propped it on the keyboard, where Greg would be sure to see it when he came home from work.

Back in the kitchen, the package of frozen chicken breasts I'd taken out early that morning was sweating on the counter. I'd meant to put it in the fridge to defrost before I left for the doctor's office, but I'd been distracted by Ginger, who hadn't felt like coming in from the yard when I called her. I touched a finger to the plastic wrap, and the meat felt close to room temperature. Probably not safe to eat anymore. What a waste. On the counter next to the fridge, the light on the answering machine was glowing red—once again, I'd forgotten to reset it. My mother had probably called earlier, disregarding the time zones as usual, and been unable to leave a message. What was the matter with my head anyway? I didn't seem able to keep track of the simplest things lately. I'd have to look up "memory issues" in *What to Expect When You're Expecting* and see if the authors had anything to say about it.

I picked up the cordless phone and dialed my parents' number. "Jeanie dear!" my mother sang out. "I tried you a while ago, but there was no answer. How was your doctor's visit? Did he tell you if it's a boy or a girl?"

My mother was a total June Cleaver who was stuck in the Fabulous Fifties of her youth. She couldn't bring herself to utter such a coarse word as "sex," and doctors were always assumed to be male.

"We're having a girl, Mom. I'm so excited."

"Oh my, how many girls will that make now? I can hardly keep count of all my grandchildren anymore."

"Seven," I said. "Seven girls, six boys."

"Seven, that's wonderful. Such a blessing."

Everything was a blessing in my mother's world, even injury and illness, which provided the opportunity to offer one's sufferings up to the Sacred Heart of Jesus. Mom rambled off on a trail of platitudes, and I leaned on the counter, half listening. Rain spattered the kitchen window. Oops, Ginger was still outside. I covered the phone and whistled to her from the top of the staircase. Yesterday, I'd left her out in a drizzle for nearly an hour while I was engrossed in assembling a pan of lasagna, Greg's favorite. I was going to get reported if I wasn't more careful.

"I'd let you speak to your father," Mom was saying, "but he just left for work. He's covering for someone on the swing shift this week. You'd better get off the phone anyway so you don't run up Greg's long-distance bill."

"We have an unlimited calling plan, Mom. It's not an issue. Besides, it's not Greg's—oh, never mind." There was no point in arguing with a woman who'd dropped out of secretarial school for her MRS degree. "All right," I said, "I'll talk to you next week, Mom. Love you."

I rubbed Ginger dry with a kitchen towel and gave her a Milk-Bone, and then I looked up a salad recipe in the copy of Good Housekeeping that I'd swiped from the obstetrician's office. I chewed my way through a few healthy bites of spinach and dried cranberries, then pushed the bowl away. I was craving something high-calorie and innutritious, like peanut butter and jelly on plain old white bread, not the weird fibery stuff that they sold at the bakery down the block. I fixed myself a fat sandwich, poured a glass of 2 percent, and went back down the hall to the office.

This was going to be the baby's room. Greg had said he would move his desk out to make room for nursery furniture, but work was keeping him so busy he hadn't gotten around to it yet. I stood in the doorway, picturing how everything would look: a white crib and matching dresser, a rocking chair by the window, one of Mom's pretty watercolors on the wall. Curtains, a rug, and fresh paint—sage green or yellow were popular shades for baby's rooms these days. I could walk over to Five Corners Hardware this afternoon, pick up some paint chips, and show them to Greg after dinner. It was hardly raining at all anymore, and I could certainly use the exercise.

I pulled my windbreaker on and folded some cash into my pocket as Ginger stood wagging by the kitchen door. I was about to take her leash from the hook, but instead I pulled a chair out from the table and sat down. Just like that, my energy was gone. Last night had been a muddle of restless dreams, and I'd gotten up this morning feeling as if I hadn't slept at all. I went into the living room, dropped onto the couch, and curled up on my left side—the correct position for a pregnant woman, according to *What to Expect*—and closed my eyes.

I woke up in the midafternoon, perspiring and nauseated. I pushed myself upright and looked out the window. On clear days we could see the rounded shoulders of Mount Rainier glowing on the horizon, but the mountain wasn't out today. The Space Needle drifted through the swatches of fog that had crept in from the bay. I reached for the open box of Ritz crackers on the coffee table and sat there for a few minutes, chewing and staring at the wall of gray.

The crackers settled my stomach, but a vague sense of dread was still hanging over me. I got up from the couch and went over to our built-in bookcase—my bookcase really, since Greg wasn't much of a reader. I reached up to the top shelf where I kept my Hemingway and Steinbeck collections, and the Norton Anthology of English Literature that had been my Bible back in college. The thick Norton was soft and curling at the corners, and it splayed open at page two hundred and fifty, revealing a slip of paper tucked within. I removed it, held it up to the grayish light, and gazed at the eight-week ultrasound image of my real first baby.

I tucked the book under my arm, went to Greg's desk, and laid the picture next to the one from this morning. Today's image was recognizable as an actual baby: there were the arms and legs, the head, the ghost of a spinal cord. Last year's image showed only a tiny white blob floating at the perimeter of a black sphere. The estimated delivery dates were printed in the lower left corner of each picture, and they were eerily similar: January first on today's, January third on the other.

For the second time that day, tears filled my eyes. I was overwhelmed by the worry that I'd done something irretrievably foolish by deciding not to tell Greg I'd been pregnant before. Carla had been right—he was a good guy, and I should have trusted him to understand what had happened to me, and to sympathize with my circumstances back in college. Now I was living in fear that he'd someday find out my secret and feel betrayed because I'd hidden the truth from him.

A tear splatted onto the picture of the eight-week-old fetus, and I brushed it away with my sleeve. I knew it was risky to keep holding on to this piece of paper. Safer to tear it into pieces or crumple it up and flush it down the toilet. But this fuzzy image was all I had. It was a memento of the wrongs I needed to atone for.

A car door slammed outside, and I jumped. I heard Ginger scrambling across the kitchen floor, a sure sign that Greg was home. I snatched up the damning picture, stuck it back into its hiding place between the pages of the Norton, and ran to the living room as Greg's step grew louder on the staircase. I shoved the book back into its slot, straightened my blouse, and turned to greet my husband.

He burst into the kitchen clutching two takeout bags and a six-pack. He dangled the beer for me to see. "It's nonalcoholic," he said with a grin, "so we can both have some." He plunked his things onto the table and came at me for a hug. His facial hair was damp against my cheek. "Hello, baby girl," he said, bending to pat my tummy. He took his wet jacket off and draped it over the back of a chair. "Ken felt bad about calling me away from your appointment. He told me to take the rest of the afternoon off, since I've been putting in so many extra hours lately. You look sleepy. Were you taking a nap?"

I nodded, afraid my voice would give away my flustered state. I enjoyed the luxury of afternoon naps because I worked only three days a week as a children's library assistant. Greg said there was no point in me pursuing a full-time position when I'd be going on maternity leave in a few months. We could get by on his salary for the time being.

I set out plates and silverware while Greg unpacked the food. "Looks like the website launch went off without a hitch," he said. "Customer orders are starting to trickle in. A few bugs have cropped up, but the IT guys are gonna work around the clock to fix them. They've got Kozmo delivering them Starbucks and Jolt by the case."

The company was staffed by a bunch of twenty-something techies who were only a few years younger than Greg. Ken Clayton, the CEO, was considered an old dude at age thirty. Greg's goatee and Nirvana T-shirts were an attempt to mirror his team's grunge rock aesthetic.

I slid our fish 'n chips out of their cardboard boats and onto plates, and got out a bottle of ketchup. "Marketing's got a radio advertising campaign in the works," Greg said, "and Ken's leveraging some connections to get us a spot on *The Oprah Winfrey Show*. Oprah, man! Is that cool or what?"

"Yes," I said. "Very cool." I was proud of him for landing this job and helping eMarket get off to a good start. I'd even started perusing the Marketplace section of The Wall Street Journal at the library so I'd know what people were talking about when we attended Greg's work functions.

I globbed a packet of tartar sauce onto my fish and scarfed down the whole piece, plus all my fries. I felt very full. I really needed to get control of my eating. I was halfway through my pregnancy, and I'd already gained fifteen pounds, which my book said was too much. I slipped a pinch of my crab cake under the table to Ginger and pushed the rest across to Greg. "You can have mine if you want."

"Thanks." He pushed his chair back, chugged the remainder of his beer, and held up the empty bottle. "They say this stuff does have a small amount of alcohol in it. I guess if I guzzle about five of 'em right quick, I might actually catch a buzz."

His goofy jokes ordinarily made me laugh, but the gloominess of my dream was still with me. I reached for his plate and stacked it on top of mine, and he got up to rinse his bottle in the sink. "You feeling okay, babe?"

"Yeah, I'm just a little sleepy still." I rose and started to clear the table.

"My e-mail's backed up, so I'm gonna go try and clear out my inbox." He took another beer from the fridge and left the kitchen.

I scraped the remains of his coleslaw into the trash can, washed and rinsed the plates and silverware, and placed them in the drainer. I thought of my mother and wondered how long

I should stay out of work after the baby came. I was wiping the table when Greg called out to me. "Jeanie, could you come in here, please?"

His voice sounded funny, and I froze with the dish cloth in my hands. *Oh, no. No. I did not mix those pictures up.* I dropped the cloth and hurried down the hall.

Chapter 5

entered the room with my heart thudding. Greg swiveled his chair around and raised his hands at me, palms up. "Have you seen my diary?"

"Your what?"

"You know, my executive diary. The one I write all my work notes in. I couldn't find it at the office today, and now it isn't here either. Did you do something with it?"

I shot a glance over his shoulder and saw the ultrasound picture still propped on the keyboard, but I couldn't tell if it was the right one or not. I stepped closer, pulled the top drawer of the desk open, and reached my other arm behind Greg to cover the picture with my hand. I lifted the notebook out of the drawer. "Do you mean this?"

"Yeah, that's it." He took it from me and thumbed the pages. I slid the picture off the desk and hid it behind my back.

Greg marked a page with his finger. "I thought I'd left this right here on my desk."

"You did, but I came in earlier and tidied up."

He swiveled away from me. "I wish you'd leave my stuff where I put it so I know where it is."

It was just a notebook, for goodness' sake, and I'd only moved it a few inches. "All right, Greg," I said to his back. My stretchy maternity leggings didn't have any pockets in them, so I tucked the slip of paper into the back of my waistband and tugged the tail of my shirt down over it.

In the kitchen, my hands trembled as I checked the picture. Yes, I had screwed up royally and left the wrong one out on the desk. Oh my God, was that a close call. I was a frigging idiot. I really, really needed to be more careful. I went down the hall until I could see that Greg was still sitting at his desk absorbed in his notes, then dashed to the bookcase and switched the pictures.

I went back in to Greg. "Look what they gave me at the doctor's this morning," I said and set the correct picture in front of him. I rubbed my hands over his shoulders, trying to smooth away his irritation. "The rain's stopped, and the forecast is calling for sun breaks this afternoon. Pike Place Market will be open for another hour. Do you want to go?"

He set his diary aside. He looked like his normal, good-natured self once again. "Sure, why not? It'll be nice down by the water."

"Great. I'll go get ready." I kissed his cheek and made it all better. Just like my mother used to do.

We strolled past the bronze pig at the entrance to the market and joined a crowd of people who were clustered around a seafood counter. Spiky orange crabs and shiny gray shrimp were heaped on beds of ice. A bearded fisherman in rubber overalls came over to us, and Greg began to ask him about the various types of shellfish.

"I thought you didn't like seafood," I whispered.

"I want to embrace the Seattle life. I've heard the Dungeness crab is really good. How 'bout we try some?"

"Sure," I said, delighted by his enthusiasm. The man behind the counter wrapped up parcels of crab, clams, and king salmon for us. I asked for a cookbook as well so we could figure out what to do with it all.

We meandered down the aisle and stopped at a flower stall,

where Greg had me pick out a bouquet of pink and violet dahlias. We paused again at a bakery stand, where he bought a cinnamon bun and a bottle of water for us to share. I took a small bite of the rich bun and passed it back to Greg. I finished off the water and tossed the plastic bottle into a trash can. Two women in dreadlocks and knitted hats turned to stare at me, aghast. "That's recyclable," the first one said, revealing a glimpse of her pierced tongue. The second woman fished the bottle from the trash and lovingly deposited it in the bin marked *Plastic*.

"We're new here," Greg said. "We didn't know." The couple regarded us gravely for a moment, then moved off, leaving behind the strong scent of incense. Greg and I looked at each other and rolled our eyes.

The produce stands were beginning to close up, so we exited the building and walked down the street to a park that overlooked the waterfront. A white-and-green state ferry was heading across the windswept bay toward Bainbridge Island. A streak of sunshine sliced through a gap in the clouds and lit up a section of the harbor, and the Olympic mountains were a dark silhouette on the horizon. We stood hand in hand for a few minutes, absorbing the stunning scene.

"Let's sit down," Greg said at last and looked around. All the benches were occupied by huddled figures. A man with matted hair sat on a patch of grass, muttering to himself as he sorted through a garbage bag filled with empty cans. The sun disappeared, and the breeze blew a cold sprinkle of rain into our faces.

"Maybe not," said Greg. "Let's go to Starbucks instead."

The coffee shop was crowded with a Saturday afternoon mix of locals and tourists. Greg ordered two tall decafs, and we found seats at a table in the back. He nodded a greeting to a pixie-haired young woman who was seated in an armchair by the fake fireplace. "Girl from merchandising," he said in a low voice.

He pried the lid off his coffee and tasted it. He liked it black. "Ken called a meeting with the department heads yesterday afternoon. He wanted to talk about the company's timeline for the IPO."

Greg had explained to me how an initial public offering worked: eMarket was currently privately owned, but the company planned to eventually offer shares for sale to the public on the New York Stock Exchange. The IPO would occur two to three years from now, which would give the company plenty of time to grow and establish itself in the online retail sector.

"It's gonna be awesome," Greg said. "They gave me a ton of stock options as part of my compensation package. As soon as the lock-up period ends after the IPO, I can flip my shares. We could wind up sitting pretty on a mighty big hunk of cash." He waggled his eyebrows at me. "We ought to start thinking about buying a house."

"Really, Greg?" I said. "Already?" I'd recently read a newspaper article about a twenty-five-year-old programming whiz whose company had given him so many stock options that he was now a millionaire—on paper anyway. He'd bought a pricey condo on Lake Washington and leased a Porsche on the strength of his virtual worth. This dot-com boom was making people crazy.

"Maybe we should wait till after the baby comes," I said. "When we've got more money saved up."

"Forget waiting. The economy's on a roll, baby, and I'm gonna riiide the wave." He swooped his arm back and forth, almost knocking over his coffee. He caught it in time, looked at me, and laughed. "Don't worry, Jeanie, I've got this."

Over by the fireplace, the girl from merchandising got up from her chair and stuffed the novel she'd been reading into her knapsack. She waved at Greg, and he raised his hand in return.

"One of Ken's little kiss-asses," he said when she'd left.

"Everyone at the office is trying to brownnose him because he's best buds with Paul Allen or something." He pressed the lid back onto his cup and ran his fingers around the rim to secure it. "He's apparently a fitness freak too. He asked me if I'd do the Elliott Bay Triathlon with him in October."

"A triathlon? You don't like to swim."

"Yeah, but I thought I'd better do it to stay on his good side. We're going to start running together on our lunch hour, and I'm gonna swim laps at the Queen Anne Pool in the evenings and bike as much as I can on the weekends. I've got only a few weeks to train, so I need to step it up right quick."

His training plans made me feel lazy. I hadn't been jogging since the start of my second trimester, when it had become too uncomfortable. I couldn't stand the feel of all that jiggling around. I tried to walk Ginger every day to keep my weight gain in check, but it had rained every day this week, so I hadn't walked at all. "That sounds great, Greg," I said. "Maybe I should start swimming too."

Greg walked into the kitchen early one Saturday morning, wearing his spandex bicycling shorts and jersey. I set the newspaper down and watched as he filled his water bottle at the sink. "Where are you biking today?"

"Discovery Park. Ken mapped out a route for me."

"Could I go with you? The weather's supposed to be good today. I'll bring a chair and a book, and pack some sandwiches. We could have a picnic when you're done."

He answered without looking at me. "Nah, I'm gonna run first, then bike about thirty miles. You'd get bored waiting for me." He tucked PowerBars into his fanny pack, poked his Oakleys into his bed head, and headed for the door. "See ya later."

I banged my coffee mug onto the table. He'd been brushing

me off like this for weeks now, ever since he'd started his training regimen with Ken. I was trying not to let it upset me—it was a triathlon, after all, and last weekend his swim-bike-run workout had been pretty intense. It would be over in a few more weeks anyway. I could bear with it till then.

I leaned back in my chair and stretched my arms over my head, wondering what I'd do with myself all day. I still didn't have any friends to hang out with. My coworkers at the library were middle-aged and dull, and our neighbors were mostly older professionals or dot-commers who seemed to work as much overtime as Greg did.

I clipped Ginger's leash on and headed down the hill to Kerry Park, my favorite spot on Queen Anne. It was a breezy morning of alternating sprinkles and flashes of sunshine. I sat on a bench and Ginger lay at my feet. Seagulls dipped and twirled over the bay, and a loaded container ship with a tugboat at its bow moved slowly toward the orange cranes at the freight terminal in West Seattle.

A young couple leaned against the stone wall, taking in the view. The woman was carrying a baby in a woven cotton sling that looked quite cozy, but I couldn't figure out how she got the baby in and out of it. I watched as she stroked her child's head, and the man circled his arms around the both of them. It made me feel like a loser, sitting there all by myself. The dog didn't count.

This wasn't what I'd expected at this point in my marriage. Our Saturdays should have been filled with shopping at Babies R Us and pasting up wallpaper borders in the nursery. We hadn't bought any baby gear yet—no crib, no high chair, no stroller— and the desk and computer were still sitting in the spare bedroom. Greg said he was too busy with his training regimen to make time for rearranging the furniture.

A guy and girl in fleece jackets cruised past me and stopped to take a look at the rusty circles-and-squares sculpture. I bent to pet Ginger so I could spy on them without looking like a creeper. He pulled her in for a smoochy kiss; she giggled and smooched him back, and I felt a twinge of longing for my husband.

Greg got back later that afternoon, dripping wet from his ride. He came into the bedroom, clunked his Sony Discman and headphones onto the dresser, and began to peel off his soaked cycling outfit. I sat on the bed and watched him get naked. I rubbed the satin edge of the blanket between my fingers. "Greg, honey?"

His chest hair clung to his skin in damp curls, and red welts from his bike shorts circled his waist and thighs. He didn't look terribly appealing at the moment, but it was more of Greg than I'd seen in a while. I breathed through my mouth to avoid the BO. "I was just wondering. Is there a rule or something in triathlon training, that guys aren't supposed to have sex?"

He stopped in the doorway and jerked his head around. "Huh?"

I tried to smile and look coy, but I wasn't very good at playing sexy. I'd shaken my hair loose from its clip and put on a low-cut T-shirt that showed off my big pregnant boobs. I tugged my top down a little, to reveal more cleavage. "I'm serious. I just wondered if you were supposed to conserve your testosterone for your workouts or something." Greg's mouth opened, and a bit of dried saliva clung to his bottom lip. I tried not to look. "I wouldn't mind if you used some of it on me. It's been a while, ya know?" I was trying for playful, but I was afraid I looked dumb. "Maybe after your shower . . . ?"

"Ah," he said. "No, no rules against it." He took a step backward into the hall. "Let me get cleaned up first." He ducked into the bathroom and shut the door.

I sighed. At least he hadn't flat-out turned me down like he had last Saturday, when he said his lumbar something-or-other was hurting him after doing such a hard workout at the pool. I leaned back on the pillows and reached for *What to Expect* on my bedside table.

The shower ran for a long time, then shut off. I heard the shuffling sounds of Greg toweling himself dry, and then the blow-dryer buzzed for a minute or two. I pictured him tugging a comb through his thick hair, trying to make it cooperate.

I stretched my legs out and gazed up at the ceiling, one hand resting on the mound of my abdomen. Something bumped my fingers, and I held very still. There it was again; I'd definitely felt something. "Greg, the baby's moving!" I called out. I sat back and waited, hoping for another flutter of movement.

Greg's cell phone clamored from the dresser. The bathroom door flew open, and he appeared amidst a cloud of steam. He crossed the room in his plaid boxer shorts, grabbed the phone, and flipped it open. "Gregory Mercer."

I stared up at him, willing him to look at me. He turned away and spoke smoothly to his caller: "I'm doing just fine, Ken, thanks. Had a great bike ride today. How can I help you?" I reached out and tickled his leg, but he jabbed his hand at me, warning me off. He left the bedroom and talked his way down the hall to the office.

This was just temporary, I told myself. Between his training and all the stuff he had going on at work, he didn't have a minute to relax. When the triathlon was over, he'd be back to his old self. I rolled onto my left side and closed my eyes.

Chapter 6

By December, the triathlon was long past, and the baby's room was finally painted and furnished. I sat down at the computer in the living room, intending to reply to an e-mail from Debra, and noticed a small cream-colored envelope lying in Greg's inbox. I opened it and found a note written in curlicued blue ink. *Dear Greg and Jeanie, Please join us for dinner at our home next Saturday evening.* An address and directions followed, and the note was signed *Ken & Paige*, with a little circle dotting the *i*.

Greg was watching *Friends* with his feet propped on the coffee table. I waved the invitation at him during the commercial break. "We're going to the Claytons' for dinner this weekend?"

"Yeah, I meant to tell you. His wife wants to meet you. They would've liked to have us over months ago, but with them building their new house and all, there wasn't any opportunity. Their place in Cedar Heights is supposed to be amazing. They've got a golf membership too."

A golf membership. Big whoop. I was annoyed that he hadn't checked with me before accepting the invitation, but there was no point in complaining. When Ken called, Greg jumped.

I studied the notecard, which had *Mrs. F. Kendrick Clayton Jr.* embossed on the front in gold cursive. "I wonder what the F stands for?" The TV commercial ended, and the bouncy *Friends* music came back on. Greg apparently didn't hear my question.

On Saturday afternoon, I dithered on my side of the bedroom

closet, trying to decide which of my shapeless maternity dresses was suitable for dinner at the boss's house. "We don't want to be late," Greg said as he buttoned the oxford shirt I'd ironed for him. "Don't take too long getting ready."

Like I ever took too long. I wasn't into elaborate outfits like his mother, or big hair and makeup like Ricki. I slipped my corduroy jumper off its hanger and tugged it over my head. The fabric was snug across my breasts and belly. I needed to go a size larger with all my maternity clothes, but it didn't seem right to spend the money when I had only four more weeks to go.

Greg stuffed his wallet into the back pocket of his khakis and picked up his keys. "I'll go warm up the car for you. Come down as soon as you're ready."

I checked myself in the mirror. The gold crucifix necklace my parents had given me for my high school graduation was too snug around my turtleneck and made me look like a nun. I took it off and put it back in my jewelry box. I sat on the bed and worked a pair of tights up my legs and over my huge waist, then squeezed my swollen feet into my least-uncomfortable pair of flats. The phone rang, and I scooted along the edge of the bed to the nightstand. The caller ID showed my sister Eileen's number.

"I have bad news, Jeanie. Dad's in the hospital. He had a stroke this morning."

I clutched the handset. "Is he okay?"

"He's stable now. The doctor said he has moderate weakness in his right arm and leg, and his speech is affected. They're sending him by ambulance to the VA in Erie first thing tomorrow. They say there's a good rehab program there and his chances of recovery will be better."

I opened my jewelry box and retrieved the crucifix. "What can I do? Should I come home?"

"No, Jeanie, you can't travel in your condition," she said,

sounding exactly like our mother. "We'll be all right. Mom's handing out the rosary beads."

The kitchen door banged, and Greg's shout echoed down the hall: "You ready, Jeanie?"

"Coming," I shouted back. I pinched the phone between my ear and shoulder and looped the necklace around my neck. "I'll call Mom right now," I said to Eileen. I pulled the chain too tight, and the clasp broke off in my fingers.

"Better wait till tomorrow. She's tired out from being at the hospital all day. I've brought her to my house to get some rest. She's staying here tonight."

"Jeanie!" Greg called again.

"I have to go, Eileen. Greg's waiting for me." I left the broken necklace on the dresser. "Tell Mom I love her and I'll talk to her in the morning, okay?"

I hurried down to the alley behind the house, where Greg was waiting in the car. I got in on my side and hauled on the seatbelt until I could reach it around my big self.

"We're gonna be late," Greg said as he maneuvered out of our narrow parking space. He floored it down Queen Anne Avenue toward Mercer Street. "Our street," we'd called it when we'd first come to Seattle. He veered onto I-5, and I caught hold of the grab bar above my door. As we merged onto I-90, my thoughts were two thousand miles away as I prayed silently, *Please, please let Dad be okay.* Traffic was light on the bridge; Greg relaxed his hold on the steering wheel and looked over at me. "Why are you so quiet? You feeling okay?"

I told him about my father, and he reached over and patted my thigh. "Your dad's a tough guy. He'll be all right."

"Eileen's probably sugarcoating it, so I won't worry," I said, blinking back tears. I hated how I always cried so easily. I hated being so far from home.

"He'll be all right." Greg's hand was warm on my leg. It was the first time he'd touched me like this in weeks. I put my hand in his, and a minute passed before he spoke again.

"This dinner tonight is pretty important, Jeanie. I scored a lot of points with Ken by doing the triathlon with him, and I want to keep it that way." We exited the tunnel and sped across Mercer Island. Our island. "He's known for hiring and firing. That's how I got this job, you know. The original finance guy disagreed with him too much, so Ken canned him."

"So, what are you saying?"

"I'm saying we need to make a good impression tonight."

Great, I thought. *Of all nights.* "Okay, Greg," I said. "I'll do my best."

The Claytons' starter mansion was an extravagant assemblage of stacked stone, Palladian windows, and Greek columns. Paige greeted us at the front door in a tangerine minidress and high-heeled sandals, despite it being almost winter. She was shapely and very pretty with blond highlights in her stylish Rachel shag. I recognized the floral scent of Eternity radiating from her perfect skin—Greg had given me a gift set of the perfume and powder on our first anniversary. He kissed Paige hello, and I thought I saw his eyes wandering over her figure. Beside her, I felt like a cow in my tent dress.

Paige began to apologize for the shortcomings of their house. "The homes in Phase II are much more spacious, and they have fabulous views of the tenth fairway. We'll work up to that one day, won't we, Kenny?" Her gold bangles jingled as she slipped a tanning booth arm around her husband's waist.

Ken had the same all-American good looks as Greg, but he was clean-shaven and wore his hair in a neat Ivy League. He clapped Greg on the shoulder and waved us into the vaulted living room, where gas flames glimmered beneath an ornate mantelpiece. Our entrance stirred the fronds of a massive potted palm that stood as backdrop to a sectional sofa piled high with tasseled pillows.

Ken clicked a remote, and light jazz began to play. "My man Kenny G," he said. He poured a club soda for me and white wine for his wife, then cracked open two bottles of imported beer for himself and Greg. He motioned for Greg to follow him through the French doors that opened onto a covered patio. Through the glass, I saw an elaborate outdoor kitchen and the orange glow of restaurant-style heat lamps.

Paige slipped off her sandals, plunked herself kitty-corner from me on the sofa, and displayed her whitened teeth in a dazzling smile. Greg had told me she was from Georgia, just like him, but her family hailed from one of the poorer counties on the Alabama state line. She scooped her glossy hair up with one hand. "I've been wantin' to have y'all over for dinner forever, but with the boys doin' that tri-ath-a-lon thing, there just wasn't time till now." She paused to drink from the wine glass in her other hand. "You and I'll have to get to know each other now. We wives need to stick together, y'know—especially when our hubbies are away on business." She poked my knee with her sparkly big toe. "A bunch of us like to go out on the town for a good old girls' night every now and again."

I sipped my club soda and gave her a wan smile. I didn't expect to be going out for good old times any time soon.

"I expect you're goin' to quit your job soon. I don't blame you, now that your husband's on his way up in the world." I opened my mouth to correct her, but she talked right over me. "I don't work anymore either. I used to be in retail, but I left when Kenny got the CEO. He makes tons of money now, so why should I stress myself out with a job? Especially since we plan on gettin' pregnant real soon." She swallowed more chardonnay.

"It's okay if I indulge tonight," she said, waving her finger-nails at me. "We had intercourse fourteen days ago when I was ovulatin'. We have to do it right on schedule cause Kenny has low-motility sperm. I thought for sure I was pregnant this time, but then my monthly started this mornin'."

Too much information! I stared into my drink.

"I was tore up for a minute, but I'm sure we'll nail it next month. It's just a matter of time." She twirled the stem of her glass. "When's your baby due?"

"January first."

"Super! That's just a few more weeks. You must be so excited." She stretched her slender arm out for the wine bottle and topped off her glass.

"Yes," I said. "It's kind of scary though, since my mother's so far away." Mom had been planning to come out and help when the baby came, but that obviously wouldn't be happening now.

"I'm sure you'll handle it just fine." Paige switched the sub-ject to eMarket and began to rave about the new tennis store on the website. After a while, we ran out of things to talk about. She hopped off the sofa, pulled the French doors open, and hollered, "Ken, sweetie, are we fixin' to eat soon?" She pushed the doors shut without waiting for his response.

Two minutes later, I saw Ken crossing the patio with a smok-ing platter in his hands. Greg held the doors open for him, and the smell of burned food wafted into the room. Paige crinkled her nose. "Kenny! What'd you do to the meat?" Her husband whisked past us with the mound of charred kebabs, a fresh beer bottle dan-gling between his fingers.

We filed into the dining room and seated ourselves around a varnished table. The chairs were cloaked in heavy maroon slip-covers that matched the drapery on the floor-to-ceiling windows. Greg wobbled as he pulled his chair out from the table; I gave him a *Be careful* look, wondering how many beers he and Ken had pounded outside.

Over dinner, the men swapped college fraternity stories while Paige told me everything I didn't need to know about the expansion of the Bellevue Square mall. She ushered us back to the living room for dessert, and the conversation shifted to an online bookseller called Amazon that was trying to elbow its way into the e-commerce sector. By ten o'clock, I was struggling to keep my eyes open.

Greg noticed me stifling a yawn and clapped his hands onto his knees like an old grandpa. "Well, folks, we'd better be going now. You've been wonderful hosts." He and Ken exchanged handshakes and hearty back slaps as Paige and I embraced over my stomach. Greg kissed Paige's cheek, and I thought his hand lingered on the small of her back. She waved to us from the front steps, her curvaceous body backlit by the chandelier blazing in the foyer. "Bye-bye!" she called into the dark. "Sorry about the meat!"

As we headed back to the city, I began to worry about Dad again. Greg's mind was on other things. "This company's going to open doors for me, Jeanie," he said, practically bouncing in his seat. "Ken confirmed the company's on track for an IPO in about twenty-four months. I'm gonna make so much money Gordon'll be pissing himself jealous."

He slapped his hand against the steering wheel. "We can trade this piece of shit car in for a new one." We were passing through Issaquah on a lighted stretch of highway, and I could see the excitement in his face. "There's no need for us to wait on buying a house. Ken says my income will only go up over time, so I should buy as much house as I can afford now while interest rates are low. He knows a loan officer at Washington Mutual who'll massage the numbers for us, so we can qualify for a jumbo mortgage."

A jumbo mortgage? What even was that? He pulled my hand

into his lap and rubbed his thumb across my knuckles. My hands were swollen and the pressure on my ring finger hurt, but I didn't want him to let go.

"We'll have a house like Ken's before long, babe," he said. "I'll be wining and dining clients in the clubhouse and closing deals on the golf course."

I couldn't imagine myself living in a swanky neighborhood like the Claytons', getting weekly manicures and playing tennis in the Ladies League, and I was certain my wardrobe wouldn't cut it. "I'm not sure if Cedar Heights is exactly our style," I said.

Greg took his eyes off the road to look at me for a second. "Don't worry, we'll live someplace more down-to-earth than that. But just think—you won't have to go back to work after the baby comes. You can be a stay-at-home mom."

We hadn't yet discussed what I'd do about work after the baby came. In fact, we hadn't really talked about much of anything lately. There never seemed to be time. "But, Greg," I said, "I want to go back to work. My supervisor says I can take night classes at Seattle U, and the public library system will hire me on full-time once I finish my degree. Then I could start working on my master's—"

Greg shook his head. "With eMarket ramping up for the IPO, I'll need to be ready to travel on a moment's notice. It'll be better for me if you stay home so we don't have to juggle schedules and childcare and all that mess. This is my career, Jeanie. I need to do whatever it takes to make it a success."

I wanted to say, *What about my career? What about what I want?* But instead I just sat there, sifting through my thoughts. None of my sisters had gone to college. They'd all married straight out of high school and had sort of fallen into jobs as their children grew older. Eileen was an aide at the county nursing home, Marian was a part-time receptionist at a dentist's office, and

Debra occasionally substituted as a preschool assistant when she could get Mom to babysit. And there you had it—nurse, secretary, teacher. The Holy Trinity of acceptable career paths for women of my mother's generation.

I had been a surprise baby, born eight years after Debra, and I'd come of age in the 1980s, when the rules were beginning to change. I'd been determined to get a college education and become a modern working woman, and I would have done it if I hadn't let Professor A-hole screw everything up.

I knew I didn't want to turn into a Paige, lolling around the house swilling wine and doing nothing more intellectually strenuous than planning dinner every night. But the unknowns of new motherhood loomed before me like an unmapped wilderness. I could hardly think how I'd juggle a baby, night classes, and a traveling husband without anyone in my family nearby to help me. Maybe it *would* be smarter and less stressful if I didn't go back to work for a while, and put my college plans on hold. I needed to be there for my child, just as my mother had been there for my sisters and me.

Besides, it was what Greg wanted. I looked over at him, but we had passed into another darkened stretch of highway, and I couldn't read his expression. "I guess you're right, Greg," I said. "I probably should stay at home."

I caught the glint of his smile as he traced his thumb in a circle on the palm of my hand. His touch made me shiver.

Chapter 7

was convinced I was sliding off the end of the bed. I pressed my fists into the stiff hospital mattress and tried to push myself up, but my lower body wouldn't budge. "Can you help me?" I asked Greg. "I'm slipping down."

"You're not, Jeanie. You're fine." He patted my hand gingerly, afraid of the IV in my wrist.

"It's the epidural kicking in," the midwife said. "You haven't budged an inch."

"I can't feel anything," I said. "How will I know when to push?"

"You'll feel pressure in the perineum." The midwife checked the fetal monitor. "Look, there's a contraction building right now." I lay still, waiting to feel something as the squiggly line on the screen crested. She frowned. "You didn't feel that?"

"Nope," I said. A giddiness had overtaken me, as if I were a little bit drunk. "Didn't feel a thing."

The midwife threw a look at the anesthesiologist, who was busily packing up his cart. "All righty then, I'll tell you when to push. Get ready." She studied the monitor. "Okay, start pushing now. *Push push push push push.*" I squeezed my eyes shut and gave it everything I had. I felt Greg take hold of my hand, and our palms flattened together, hot and wet with sweat.

Our daughter, Rebecca, arrived at 6:55 that evening, pink and perfect. We were moved to a post-partum room, and my legs continued to feel as if they weren't attached to my body. A nurse had to help me get up to use the bathroom and then walk me back to bed. She swaddled the baby in a striped blanket and placed her in my arms, set the call button within reach, and left us alone. Greg stretched out on the recliner in the corner of the room and closed his eyes.

My stomach growled. The meal tray on my bedside table held a plastic-wrapped sandwich, a bowl of orangey soup, and a cup of vanilla pudding. Greg had promised to bring me a Deluxe Cheeseburger and chocolate milkshake from Dick's Drive-In so I wouldn't have to eat the hospital food. "Greg?" I said. His eyelids flickered. "Would you please go pick up my dinner now?"

The footrest released with a *thunk*, and he stood up. "Sure, I'm pretty hungry myself."

He was back in twenty minutes. I carefully transferred the sleeping baby to the bassinet beside my bed as Greg repositioned the bedside table. A plastic bag bearing a green-and-yellow logo rolled toward me, and I regarded it in puzzlement. "What about Dick's Drive-In?"

"Subway was closer."

I was surprised by how disappointed I felt. *It's only food*, I chided myself. *Not a big deal.* Greg resettled himself in the recliner and bit off a mouthful of his footlong meatball marinara. I unwrapped my sandwich, and the odor of tuna salad rose from the paper. Tuna was better for me than a cheeseburger anyway. Fewer calories.

"Wait a sec," Greg said, "I almost forgot." He reached into his pocket and drew out a small box with a ribbon around it. He climbed out of his chair and brought it over to me.

"What's this?"

"A little something for all the hard work you did today." I untied the bow, lifted the lid, and saw my crucifix necklace coiled on a pad of white cotton. "I noticed you broke it a while back," he said, "so I got it repaired for you. I know how much you like wearing it."

That was my Greg—he always made up for his lapses in the end. "That was so sweet of you," I said. I put the chain around my neck, being extra careful with the clasp this time, and centered the cross between my collarbones. "Thank you. I love it."

When I'd finished my sandwich, I leaned over the bedrail to gaze at our tiny daughter. We'd decided to call her Becky for short. She was absolutely beautiful, but so tiny and fragile too. I hadn't held an infant in years. I'd babysat my sisters' kids dozens of times but mostly when they were older. Babies were a bit of a mystery to me.

My body ached from pushing, and my stomach was a flabby mess. I was worried I wouldn't know what to do when the baby cried during the night, or be able to lift her out of the bassinet when my abdominal muscles were so weak and sore. I looked over at the recliner. "Greg?"

"Hmm?"

"Will you help me with her during the night?"

"Sure, just wake me up." He adjusted his pillow. A minute later he was snoring.

Three weeks later, I was a zombie from lack of sleep, my nipples were sore from breastfeeding, and my shoulders were kinked with worry. Greg was getting ready to leave on a two-week business trip to meet with prospective vendors for eMarket, and I was freaking out over the prospect of being alone that long.

"Maybe my mom could come give you a hand," he suggested as he placed a stack of undershirts in his suitcase. I stood beside him with Becky in my arms, swaying from side to side, doing the mommy rock. Florence coming to help me? That was funny. Greg and I had been married for over a year now, but his mother still hadn't warmed to me. I had the strong impression that I was too small-town for her refined tastes. Too *country*.

"I don't know," I said. "I wouldn't want to inconvenience her. She's always so busy."

"She's been itching to see the baby. If I call her tonight, she could be on a plane by tomorrow or the next day. It'd be perfect if she came to visit while I'm away."

"But don't you want to see her too?"

He opened a drawer and rummaged around in it. "Sure, I do." He tossed several pairs of dress socks on top of the undershirts. "I'll see her when I get back. So, what do you say?"

"Well, maybe." I knew I'd be yearning for company while he was away, and I could certainly benefit from Florence's parenting experience. It was only fair to invite her to come meet her new granddaughter. She'd been asking when she could visit, but Greg had put her off so many times, I'd begun to wonder if he felt as uncomfortable around her as I did.

"All right," I said at last. "Ask her if she can come."

Greg got up at four in the morning to shower and dress for his trip. Before he left for the airport, he peeked into the baby's room, where I was walking back and forth with Becky, rubbing her back and humming a lullaby. She'd woken up crying every hour since midnight, and I was desperate to get her to sleep. I put my finger to my lips, and Greg waved a silent goodbye to us.

I continued to pace, and Becky remained quiet. I tiptoed over to the crib and laid her down in slow motion, then held my breath and counted to one hundred. She didn't stir. I left her bedroom door ajar and trudged to the bathroom, peed, and got a drink of water without turning on the light. I leaned wearily on the sink. The apartment was dark and silent. My stomach was in a knot.

I tried to convince myself that I'd get used to this over time.

Greg had to travel, and I had to learn how to handle things on my own. Florence was coming tomorrow, so I wouldn't be alone for long. Everything would be all right.

"Here I am, ready to help!" Florence pushed a large suitcase over the threshold, followed by a wheeled carry-on, and a bulging tote bag swung from her shoulder. *Good God*, I thought, *how long does she plan to stay?*

I landed a quick kiss on her powdered cheek as she threw off her coat. She wore a smart ecru pantsuit with coordinated gold jewelry, and her hair was sprayed perfectly into place, despite the hours she'd spent on the plane. She strode past me into the living room, sat in the armchair with her ankles crossed in a picture of ladylike gentility, and held her arms out for the baby.

I lowered Becky to her grandmother's lap. She'd fallen asleep only minutes ago, and I prayed she wouldn't wake up and start squalling again. It had been a long, tiring morning of fussy crying and spit-ups.

"Bless her heart," Florence said. "She has her daddy's hair."

"Yes," I agreed.

"And her granddaddy's nose."

I pictured Howard's bulbous scotch-drinker's nose. "Mm," I said, not wanting to contradict. I perched on the edge of the sofa bed that I'd made up fresh that morning, trying not to wrinkle the sheets. I handed Florence a burp cloth to protect her beautiful suit. "She's had some trouble sleeping the past few nights," I said.

"All newborns have trouble sleepin'," Florence said with authority. "My boys cried like all get out when they were infants. It'll be months before you get a full night's sleep again."

I swallowed hard. "I've been reading this book—"

She flapped her hand at me. "All these new theories. We didn't have parentin' books back in my day. We had to—" She stopped short when she saw the baby's eyes open. Becky squinched up her face and yowled.

"You'd better take her." Florence handed her back to me and brushed off her slacks.

"She's due for a nap," I said. "I'll go try to put her down." I carried Becky to her room, fished a pacifier from the pocket of my sweatpants, plugged it into her mouth, and laid her in the crib. She sucked a few times and went back to sleep.

Back in the living room, Florence was standing with her hands on her hips, surveying our things. She stepped over to the sofa bed and pressed it with both hands. "This'll be cozy." She brushed a stray dog hair from the pillowcase and twitched it straight.

"Would you like some coffee?" I asked. "It's already made. It's Starbucks."

"I'd prefer tea if you don't mind." She circled the room, examined our framed wedding photo, and glanced at my books in the bookcase. I boiled water and prepared two cups of tea, listening all the while for sounds from Becky's room. I set placemats, milk, and the sugar bowl on the kitchen table and invited Florence to sit down.

She dunked her tea bag. "I understand Greg will be travelin' every week from now on."

"Every week?" I said. "Oh, no. He says after this trip is over, he'll have to go out of town only a few days a month."

"That's not what he told me." Florence reached for the sugar. "This internet startup is quite a résumé builder for him." She set her spoon down on her saucer. "I'm so proud of his accomplishments."

"Yes, I'm proud of him too," I said, a touch defensively. I wiped a spot of milk from the table. "It's just that—it gets so lonely sometimes when he's away."

"Well, he can't avoid travel in his profession. You knew that before you got married. You should appreciate how hard he works to keep you at home with your little one."

I looked down, embarrassed. Here I was, whining to my mother-in-law, whom I rarely even talked to. I heard my mother's voice in my head, giving the warning she'd often repeated to my sisters and me: "Keep your business to yourselves, girls."

Florence spooned more sugar into her cup, and her tone softened. "I know how hard it can be for a young mother. Howard traveled constantly when our boys were small." I nodded, grateful for the scrap of sympathy, but then the lines around her mouth hardened. "I reared those children on my own. I can't count how many sleepless nights I spent nursin' them through their childhood illnesses while their father was off gallivantin' in another city, eatin' at fine restaurants, sleepin' in luxury hotels—"

We both jumped at Becky's cry. The sound triggered my letdown reflex, and breast milk seeped into the cups of my giant bra. I made a show of looking at the clock. "Oh, my goodness, it's time for her next feeding already."

I shut Becky's bedroom door behind me and scooped her up, inhaling her sweet baby scent. I'd already fed her an hour ago, but I was discovering that a nipple in her mouth was about the only thing guaranteed to soothe her. I sat down in the rocking chair to nurse, and we rocked quietly for several minutes. I reminded myself that Florence was here to help me, and it was kind of her to come all this way to see us. I brushed my lips over Becky's soft forehead and closed my eyes. I was so tired. I'd just rest for a few minutes.

I awoke sometime later with a stiff neck and pins and needles in my arm. I laid Becky in her crib and snuck out of the room, working my arm back and forth to get the feeling back into it. Florence had *Headline News* on. Chuck Roberts was rehashing last year's O. J. Simpson murder trial, and he informed us that the

Brown and Goldman families were planning to file a civil suit for wrongful death. I sat down, and we watched as the broadcast cycled through the financial news, the sports highlights, and the local headline capsule, and arrived back at the top of the hour—six o'clock. Florence looked at me. "What are you doin' about suppuh?"

I was supposed to take a pan of baked ziti out of the freezer that morning, but it had slipped my mind. I apologized for my oversight. "We could order pizza instead," I said. "There's a place nearby that delivers pretty quick."

"Pizza?" She ran a critical eye over my body. I had on a pair of Greg's sweatpants because my own didn't fit me at the moment. "Well, if that's what you want," she said.

I called for a delivery and plugged *Forrest Gump* into the VCR. We ate in front of the television, hitting the pause button frequently so I could tend to Becky. Florence lounged on the sofa bed in her floral pajama set, massaging lavender-scented lotion into the backs of her hands. At eight o'clock she pronounced herself ready for bed. "It's eleven Eastern time, remember. I need to get my beauty rest."

I wished her a good night and brought Becky with me to my room. I was longing to hear Greg's voice, but he was in New York tonight, and he probably had an early morning meeting. I didn't want to disturb him if he'd already gone to bed.

I called my mother instead. "Jeanie dear! What a nice surprise. How are you and your precious baby doing?"

I described Becky's crankiness and fitful crying. I'd been wanting to ask Mom what I should do about it, but I hadn't wanted to trouble her when she had so much to worry about with Dad. "You poor dears," she said. "She'll settle down soon, don't worry. You need to get her on a schedule. Nurse her every two hours, and don't keep her up for too long afterward. Infants require a lot of sleep. That will do the trick."

I felt my tension easing. "I'll try that," I said. "Thanks, Mom. How's Dad doing?"

"He's making good progress. His physical therapist comes to the house three times a week, and I help him with his exercises in between. He's graduated from the walker to a quad cane, and his speech is improving. Now, how is Greg?"

I didn't want to tell her he was out of town—she wouldn't approve of him going away so soon after his daughter's birth. My father had never taken a business trip in his life. "Greg's working hard," I said. "He's very busy." I was tempted to gripe about Florence, but Mom didn't tolerate uncharitable talk. I didn't have anything nice to say, so I'd better not say anything at all.

When I came out of my room in the morning, Florence was already up and nosing around in the kitchen. I had just finished nursing Becky, so I sat down in the armchair to burp her. Florence poked her head around the doorway. "Do you have any cream cheese? Fat free, preferably."

"I don't know," I said. "Check the left-hand drawer in the fridge."

"You don't know?"

I clenched my teeth. "No, I don't. Greg did the shopping last week."

Florence's eyebrow popped up. "Greg did the shoppin'?"

My hand stopped patting Becky's back. "Florence, I gave birth three and a half weeks ago. My episiotomy hurts, I'm still bleeding some, and my breasts are leaking milk like crazy, so yes, Greg did the shopping."

Florence stared at me. She hadn't applied her costly cosmetics yet, and her eyelids looked pink and droopy. "Well, excuse me," she said. "I was just askin'."

Becky burped, and milk dribbled down the front of my nightgown. I got up and placed her in the battery-operated swing that

I'd purchased from Target. "I'm going to shower," I said. It was rude of me to hog the bathroom ahead of my guest, but I needed to compose myself. Arguing with my husband's mother was no way to start the day.

I let the hot water run over my head for a full fifteen minutes. I got dressed, clipped my hair up wet, and invited Florence to take her turn in the shower. When she emerged from the bathroom, she resembled a page from the Talbots catalogue. Becky had begun to fuss in the swing, so I was walking around the kitchen with her, trying to clean up the breakfast dishes with one hand.

"She ought to be sleepin'," Florence said. "Don't you want to put her down?"

Yes, I want to, you old bat. I can't. "I tried," I said. "But she cries every time."

"You're goin' to spoil her by holdin' her so much."

The phone rang and I jumped for it, glad for the distraction. "Hey, it's Ricki," my sister-in-law chirped. "How *are* you?"

I joggled Becky in my arms to try and quiet her. "Okay, I guess."

"Sounds like you've got your hands full, so I'll let you go. Can I talk to Mom? There's a hitch in the contract on the Montgomery property." Ricki was an agent in Florence's real estate office; she said "Montgomery property" like it was the Biltmore Estate. I handed the phone over to Florence and escaped to my bedroom. It was going to be a long week.

Chapter 8

Greg returned from his trip, and Florence was on her feet the moment she heard him at the door. She hip-bumped me out of the way so she could get her hug in ahead of me, and then we both stepped back to take a look at Greg. He'd gotten his hair cut shorter, and his goatee was gone. The resemblance to Ken was disconcerting.

He peeked in on Becky asleep in her crib, then joined us in the kitchen. His trip had been extended by a day, so he had only a few hours to spend with his mother before her flight back east that evening.

"You must be hungry, darling," Florence said, opening and closing kitchen cabinets.

"Not really. I had a meal on the plane."

"Airplane food," she said with distaste. She went to the refrigerator and took out a package of cold cuts and a jar of mayonnaise. "I'll fix you a sandwich."

Greg raised his eyebrows at me behind his mother's back. I intercepted her at the coffee maker as she was about to put on a fresh pot. "I can get it."

Florence set a full plate in front of Greg. "How was your trip? Did you make some good business contacts? What did you think of New York?" He gave short answers as he forced down bites of sandwich. His mother jumped up from the table to fish in her giant tote bag. "Did you see the latest issue of *Seattle Magazine,* Greg? There's an interview with your company's CEO." She pushed the magazine at him.

"I know," he said. "I heard."

"Look, here they are in their new home in Cedar Heights." She rolled the pages back to display a glossy photo of Ken and Paige standing in their marble foyer. "I did some research, and the houses there look spectacular. You should plan on buying there soon while there's plenty of inventory to choose from."

I glanced at Greg, but he was concentrating on his food. "We think Cedar Heights might be too upscale for us, Florence," I said. "We thought we'd look at some of the older neighborhoods in the city that aren't so expensive."

She eyed me over the rim of her glass of Crystal Light. "That would suit you better, wouldn't it? Considering where you come from."

I looked at Greg again, but his mouth was full of ham and cheese. "I just meant we'd prefer someplace more down-to-earth to raise our family in."

"Naturally." Florence blinked innocently at me. "I'm sure you'll be wanting to catch up with those sisters of yours. Having babies is what you Catholics are all about, isn't it?"

My cheeks went hot. Greg continued to chew his food, his face a blank.

"Tell me," Florence said, "do they really enjoy being housewives, hidden away up there in the backwoods?"

Greg scraped his chair back from the table. "That's enough, Mom."

I didn't know what to say. I got up and called to Ginger.

Greg glanced at his watch and wiped his mouth with his napkin. "I'll go print your boarding pass." He went into the living room, and his mother went with him. Ginger came trotting into the kitchen. I grabbed my windbreaker from the peg by the door and followed her down to the backyard.

The grass was cold and wet, and moisture seeped through the sides of my sneakers until my socks were soaked. I dug at my eyes with my knuckles. Why did I always cry when I was angry? It made me feel like such a wimp. I wished I had stood up to Florence and said something, *anything*, but I wasn't quick or clever like that. I hated to argue with people.

The door opened, and Greg and his mother appeared at the top of the stairs with her luggage. Greg carried the bags down to his car and loaded them into the trunk. Florence flounced past me and opened the passenger's door. For a second I thought she was going to get in without saying goodbye to me, but she stowed her tote up front and turned around. "It was lovely spending time with you and the baby." She gave me a limp hug and kissed the air near my cheek. "Be sure to send photos." Greg got in on the driver's side, neglecting his customary good manners. Florence climbed into the passenger's seat and shut her own door. In a moment they were gone.

I went inside and checked on Becky; she was still asleep. I stripped the sheets from the sofa bed and threw them into the washing machine with a load of towels, then turned my attention to the bathroom. Tackling the housework always helped me to calm down when I was upset about something. It was a trick I'd learned from my mother.

As I scoured the tub, I mulled over what Florence had said about my family and my hometown. It grated on me to admit it, but there was a kernel of truth in her words. We Flanagans weren't sophisticated people. Folks in Adams Mills drove around in trucks and spent their disposable income on four-wheelers, snow-mobiles, and the Pennsylvania Lottery. My sisters didn't give a flip about fashion, and none of their husbands made much money. It was no wonder Florence and I couldn't relate to each other.

Why on earth had I connected myself with a family like the Mercers and thought it would work out okay? I recalled the Pre-Cana classes Greg and I had been required to attend at the Catholic church back in Atlanta. For five weeks, we'd assembled in the basement along with a half-dozen other engaged couples. On the first night, the married couple who ran the class had handed out the syllabus, and Greg had nudged me and pointed— the topic for Week #4 was Intimacy and Family Planning. "We're skipping that one," he whispered. "We'll study at home." I smothered a giggle and shushed him as the wife began the presentation.

"When you get married to someone, you're also marrying their parents and siblings." She paused a moment to let that sink in. "You are marrying that other family's value system, their style of communication, and their ways of expressing emotions."

The husband continued: "The dynamics of emotional processing and conflict resolution are key elements of our world view, which is formed within our family of origin. We bring those dynamics with us when we enter into a marriage, and they have a significant impact upon the way a husband and wife interact with each other."

I stared at him. I'd never thought about it in quite that way. I heard a soft *pffft* from Greg, and his lips brushed my ear as he whispered, "Psychobabble."

I was folding the laundry in our bedroom when Greg returned from the airport. He dropped onto the bed alongside my pile of clean towels and sighed. "My mom raised a stink because she didn't get enough time with me. I told her she was welcome to stay longer, but she said she had too much to do at home." He folded his arms behind his head. "To tell the truth, I didn't really want her to stay." He looked up at me. "I'm sorry about what she said to you. I hope the whole week wasn't like that."

I chose my words carefully. "There were a few difficult moments. But I appreciated her company."

"Probably wasn't such a good idea to invite her to come after all. Every time I see her, I think it's going to be different. But it always turns out the same."

I smoothed a hand towel into a neat rectangle. "She can be kind of opinionated sometimes. Hard to please. I felt like I was doing everything wrong."

Greg sat up. "Ya think? That's how it was for me the whole time I was growing up." He shook his head. "She can be such a bitch."

The B-word startled me. I'd never heard him talk about his mother like that.

Greg inhaled deeply and let out a noisy breath. "I don't think I ever really told you what it was like for me growing up, did I?"

I shook my head.

"She was always comparing me with my brother. Gordon was the athlete, I was the brain. She'd brag about him for being the big football and track star, but then she'd tell me in private how disappointed she was in him for being such a dumb jock. She said I was her 'special child,' the one she could count on. It got kind of weird, like she was trying to pit us against each other to see which one of us loved her more. It wasn't normal."

My hands went still. Greg had shared some basic information about his family when we were dating, but nothing at all like this. I knew Florence ran the show at home and Howard was a well-meaning pushover, but I'd heard very few details about Greg's childhood.

"All through high school," he went on, "I had to deal with her manipulative shit. Everything was about her, no matter what it was. In high school, I made honor roll four years in a row and graduated third in my class, but you'd think she was the one who did all the work, with the way she complained about the cost of private school and how much time she spent chairing the Booster Club and all these other committees. I couldn't wait to go away to college. She wanted Gordon and me to go to big name schools, but he was too stupid to get accepted anywhere but the community college. He got a two-year technical certificate, and then my dad called in some favors and got him a job at his company. It was only an entry-level sales position, but Mom made a huge deal out of it because she needed to show off to her society friends."

He picked up a washcloth and wrung it into a tight cylinder. "I was busting my ass at Emory, meanwhile. I wanted to go into computer programming, but that wasn't glamorous enough for my mother. She threatened to quit paying my tuition unless I switched to a business major, and my dad went along with her. He knew it'd be easier than crossing her.

"Then Gordon and Ricki got engaged. I'd just been accepted into the MBA program, but all Mom could talk about was my brother's wonderful fiancée and their fancy wedding plans. She didn't even like Ricki at first because she worked at a hair salon and her dad was a plumber or something. Once the engagement was a done deal, though, Mom changed her tune right quick. I guess she figured she could mold Ricki into the kind of wife she really wanted for Gordon, if she spent enough money and effort on her. That's how Ricki ended up with a real estate license."

Greg tossed the twisted washcloth back onto the pile of unfolded towels. "Turns out, Ricki's the spitting image of my mother. She rides Gordon's back like you wouldn't believe. She's always demanding stuff from him and bitches if he doesn't deliver. I felt sorry for him at first, but then I saw how he always gives in to her to keep the peace, just like my dad does. They're both totally pussy-whipped."

"I'm sorry," I said. "I didn't know it was like that."

He swung his legs over the edge of the bed so that he was sitting sideways to me. "When I met you, the first thing I noticed was how you were the exact opposite of my mother. You were so gentle and caring. So real. I knew right away I wanted to marry you. When I told Mom, she just about had a fit. She couldn't stand it that you were from a farm town up north and hadn't finished college. But I held my ground." He turned his head, and his eyes met mine. "I thought that marrying a girl like you would somehow erase her power over me. I knew you'd be a good wife and mother. You were my chance for a normal, happy family."

He opened his arms to me, and I fell into them. Towels slithered to the floor. "I should have shared this with you a long time ago, Jeanie," he whispered. "I was so worried after we got engaged. I thought you'd change your mind about marrying me if you knew what my family was really like. I was sure my mom would scare you off, so I tried to steer us clear of her as much as I could." He let out a wry laugh. "God, she's a piece of work."

He tightened his arms around me. "I know I haven't been spending as much time with you and the baby as I should. I let myself get sidetracked by the triathlon, and then there was all that work and travel stuff. Things will be different from now on, I promise. We'll share everything. No more secrets."

No more secrets. I hid my face in his shirt.

Greg was wrong. I wasn't a good wife. I wasn't a good person at all. I was weak and deceitful, and I could never, ever let my husband find out the truth about me. I would keep my secrets hidden from him for the rest of my life. It would be my cross to bear.

Chapter 9

A year went by, and I was pregnant again. Greg and I stood on our recently purchased cul-de-sac lot in Cedar Heights, surrounded by sizable homes in varying stages of completion. The sound of power tools and generators filled the air, even though it was a Saturday. Houses in the Heights were selling as fast as the builder could put them up, and construction crews were working overtime to keep pace with the demand.

I hadn't wanted to buy here, but Greg had won that one. He had driven out to the development by himself a few weeks ago and toured the model home. He'd been taken in by the generous square footage, custom amenities, and sweeping views of the valley. This lot was the last one left on the street, and he'd made a full-price offer on the spot. I didn't think we could afford such an expensive property, but Greg wasn't worried. We'd have a ton of cash on hand after the eMarket IPO, he said. The mortgage payments wouldn't be an issue.

The foundation of our future home jutted from the muddy ground, and banded stacks of two-by-fours lay on the crushed stone of the temporary driveway. I was glad we'd left Becky asleep in her car seat. I stepped around a pile of broken cement blocks, holding on to Greg's arm for balance. I was almost four months along, and my pregnancy was beginning to show.

Greg kicked a chunk of wood out of my way. "The foreman

says they're on track to finish construction in the spring. We'll be moved in before the baby comes."

The wind caught my hair, and I pushed it behind my ears. I was afraid this was going to be a lot more house than we needed. The builder's agent had shown me the blueprints when we signed the closing documents. The house would have four bedrooms, formal living and dining rooms, a gourmet kitchen, a den, an office, and a "bonus room" over the three-car garage. Three thousand square feet in all. Our kids would get lost on their way to the bathroom.

Greg seemed to be reading my mind. "We'll grow into it," he said, taking my hand. "We're gonna love it here."

I looked across the cul-de-sac to a pretty house with cedar shingles and a front lawn of freshly laid sod. The garage was filled with packing cartons and colorful children's toys. I spotted a scooter with shiny streamers dangling from its handlebars, and a red rubber kickball had rolled down the gentle slope of the driveway and landed on the sidewalk. The neighborhood did have a pleasant family feel to it, I had to admit.

A windstorm blew down from the Cascades on our moving day, sending dead leaves and construction debris swirling between the building lots. The moving van rolled up in front of our house, and two rangy men climbed down from the cab. The wind immediately peeled their ball caps off their heads and sent them skipping down the street.

Greg had a meeting to get to and was leaving me in charge. "Keep your eye on these guys," he said under his breath. "They look like they just got out of detox." He tossed his briefcase into his car and drove off.

I set the Pack 'n Play up in the echoey bonus room and sat Becky in it with a few toys to keep her occupied. I walked from room to room with the moving men, pointing out where I wanted them to put our things. It didn't take long, since we'd gotten rid of most of our secondhand furniture when we cleared out the Queen Anne apartment. Greg wanted to buy all new.

It was half past noon when the movers left. I pushed the front door shut, muting the roar of the wind. Upstairs, Becky had begun to squawk. She was gumming the padded edge of the Pack 'n Play when I went up to her, and her little face burst into a smile when she saw me. I lifted her out and hugged her, then carried her over to the window so we could look down at the street.

A woman was out in the yard of the shingled house across the way. She bent to pick up a plastic bat and T-ball stand and put them away in the garage. A stroller was parked at the foot of the front steps, and I could see a pair of wiggly toddler's legs sticking out. As I watched her water her flower bushes, I envisioned backyard barbecues with neighbors, children riding bicycles, playmates for Becky. I'd make friends with this woman, and we'd bring our kids to play in the park and take turns carpooling to preschool. Maybe living here would turn out okay after all.

I carried Becky downstairs and stood in the middle of the spotless living room carpet, breathing in the clean scents of fresh paint and new wood, and I felt happy. We were home. I searched for my purse and found it beneath a drift of crumpled packing paper, took out the flip phone Greg had given me for my birthday, and called to tell him we were moved in.

Our son, Nathaniel Gregory, arrived in early June. The summer whirled past in a blurry cycle of naps, feedings, and diaper changes. By September, chubby Nate was smiling and holding his head up on his own, and Becky was toddling around the house and putting words together in short sentences.

I turned the TV on one morning so I could listen to the news while I gave Nate his bottle. A montage of Princess Diana photos was fading in and out on the screen, accompanied by the mournful melody of Elton John's *Candle in the Wind*. The newscaster repeated the details of the fatal Paris car crash and the tabloid speculation that Diana had been pregnant. I sat Nate up for a burp. I didn't usually pay much attention to celebrity news, but the princess's death had pierced me. That poor woman. What a sad way to go after throwing so many years away on stuffy old Charles, and leaving her two little boys behind.

Winter came. Greg began to travel more frequently, and the few days that he actually worked at the office often stretched late into the night. As Becky's second birthday approached, I realized I needed to get out of the house more and start making some friends.

The woman across the cul-de-sac was named Perla, and she was from Indonesia. Her husband worked for Microsoft, and she stayed at home with their two daughters, who were ages three and four. She said she was organizing a neighborhood playgroup, and she invited me to join it.

One week later, I hung Nate's baby carrier over my arm and took Becky by the hand, and we crossed the street and climbed the steps to Perla's front door. The din of children's voices reverberated inside the house. I pressed the bell, and the door flew open. Perla was a tiny lady with long black hair and dark eyes, and her flowy pink cardigan was a welcome spot of color in the gray morning. She hugged me, stooped to admire Nate, patted Becky's cheeks, and pulled me down the hallway toward the kitchen. "I will introduce you to the nice moms," she said in an adorable accent. "You so sweet you will make friends quick!"

Women and children came pouring into the house. Toddlers clutched at their mothers' legs as a gaggle of preschoolers barged into the kitchen in search of snacks and juice boxes. I watched the chaos unfold with Becky hanging on my arm, twisting this way and that as children careened around us.

"Don't worry!" Perla shouted to me over the clamor. "It calm down after a while!"

I escaped to the relative quiet of the den and found Perla's older daughter, Megan, hunkered behind the couch with her My Little Ponies, safely out of the fray. Her younger sister, Emily, squatted nearby, peacefully stacking a set of squishy building blocks. I sat Becky down to play beside Emily, unbuckled Nate from his carrier, and nestled him against my chest. He was due for his midmorning nap and had already dozed off, in spite of the noise. Becky appeared to be content with the blocks, so I wandered off to have a look around the house.

The living room had been ruled off-limits to children. I walked through it, admiring Perla's Asian decor, and peeked into an adjacent room that was furnished as an office. The desk held a framed photo of the family on a tropical beach, and on the opposite wall there was a large wedding picture showing a radiant Perla in her big American husband's arms, surrounded by a smiling multicultural mixture of family and friends.

I went back to the kitchen. A man about my age was sitting at the round table in the breakfast nook. His daughter, who looked to be a few months older than Becky, was leaning against his knee and sucking a juice box dry. They were ringed by four curious women who were hurling questions: How do you like being a stay-at-home dad? How does your wife feel about being the breadwinner? Do people think you're a pedophile when you go to the park? The man stroked his daughter's hair and answered with patient good humor.

Bedlam raged throughout the morning. As I went to check on Becky, I saw two girls kneeling at the head of the carpeted staircase, pushing Tonka toys off the top step. A bulldozer hurtled past me, crashed onto the tile in the foyer, and ricocheted off the front door. I retreated into the kitchen. The lone dad's interrogators had been replaced by a bunch of pint-sized boys. They surrounded the table, shrieking and flinging plastic army men at one another. The dad rose from his chair and herded them out of the kitchen.

"It's all fun and games till someone loses an eye," he remarked as he handed his daughter a cookie from the plate on the table. She grabbed it and ran from the room. Two women with infants strapped into BabyBjörns were standing by the stainless-steel refrigerator, talking simultaneously about their deliveries.

A complicated coffee maker sat on the countertop nearby, with mugs and spoons arranged next to it on the gleaming granite. I set a mug in place and poked at the buttons, trying to figure out how it worked. Perla materialized at my side, inserted a K-cup for me, and started it brewing. She winked at me and flew back out of the kitchen—Tonka trucks were crashing on tile again. I heard her raised voice: "No more throwing of trucks! You girls come down here and act civilize!"

The dad had noticed my difficulties with the Keurig machine. "I have a good old Mr. Coffee at my house," he said. "Same one I had in college. Still works, believe it or not. My name's Ed, by the way."

He held his hand out and I shook it. "I'm Jeanie."

The women with the infants had gone to investigate the ruckus in the front hall. I sat down at the table with Ed and searched for something else to say, wondering what you talked about with a man who didn't have a job.

"What sort of work does your wife do?" I asked. *Lame.*

"She's a detective."

"Ha ha. Funny." Ed just looked at me. "You're joking, right?" I said.

"No, I'm serious. She's with the Washington State Patrol."

I pictured a butchy female police officer, feet planted and arms raised in a sturdy isosceles stance, aiming her 9mm Glock at a dangerous criminal. I sized Ed up: he was about my height and on the skinny side. He had dirty-blond hair, wire-rimmed glasses, and a gawky air that made me think of Bill Gates. His wife could probably kick his ass.

"Do you live nearby?" I asked.

"We're down the hill in the townhomes. Where the regular people live." He grinned good-naturedly. His daughter zoomed back into the kitchen and collided with another child. The boy's mother rushed in behind him, scooped him up, and shot Ed a dirty look.

"Sorry," Ed called out to her. He caught hold of his daughter around her middle and she flailed her arms, trying to get away. He turned her around to face him and spoke firmly: "Ada. Go play with the girls in the den. Stay away from the boys." He gave me a sideways glance and curled his lip at the other mother's back. Ada wriggled free and ran off.

Perla darted back in and flung herself into the chair next to Ed. "My God, some of these kids! Like savages!" She dug her fingers into her glossy hair. Ed laughed, and Perla looked up with a rueful smile. "I guess I ask for it, by inviting everybody." She finger-combed her hair out of her face. "Next time, not so many of these *people*," she said, throwing a dark look in the direction of the front hall. "Maybe just us and our kids." She reached out for my arm and Ed's and gave us both a friendly squeeze.

Chapter 10

Greg was cleaning his golf clubs in his home office. Brushes, towels, and bottles of spray cleaner were spread across the mahogany desk he'd purchased from Pottery Barn, and his television was tuned to CNBC with the sound turned down.

He'd played eighteen holes on the Cedar Heights course that morning and had come home unimpressed. "It's too crowded," he complained. "Everyone and their brother plays there." He picked up his Big Bertha and began to buff it. "There's this other golf club in the Sammamish Valley that I've been hearing a lot of good things about." He paused to check the stock ticker rolling across the bottom of the TV screen. He changed the channel to Fox News, and there was President Clinton, wagging his finger at America and denying sex with "that woman."

"I know this guy from Boeing who's a member there," Greg went on. "He said he'll sponsor my membership application if I want to join."

I nearly choked when he told me the annual fee. "Holy crap, Greg, that's crazy."

He fitted a cover over the head of the driver. "It's my money, you know. You don't contribute financially to this household, so you don't have a say in how it gets spent."

My mouth dropped open. He inserted the Big Bertha into his golf bag and flashed a grin at me. "Just kidding, babe. Seriously, though, I can make a lot of good business contacts at that other club. I'll keep the social membership here at the Cedar Heights Club so you can go there for lunch sometimes with your friend what's-her-name, Paula?"

"Perla." I shook my head at his cluelessness. As if Perla or I would ever want to take our four fidgety little kids to eat in that stuffy place, where the waiters wore bow ties and the dress code forbade jeans.

Greg started spending money as though he'd already flipped his IPO stock. He wrote a hefty check to the golf club in the valley, signed a lease on an Audi A8 sedan, and replaced his grungewear with a much more expensive GQ-style wardrobe.

He began traveling Monday through Friday, meeting with fund managers and potential investors. A car service transported him to and from the airport, and the flashy Audi stayed parked in the garage. When I sat down to breakfast with Becky and Nate each morning, I would invent stories for them: "Daddy's in Florida today, where this orange juice was made" or "Daddy's on his way to New York City, where the Statue of Liberty is." Nate banged his sippy cup on his high chair tray, and Becky munched her Cheerios. They were getting used to their father's absences.

The year rolled over into the new millennium without the predicted Y2K meltdown. The Dow Jones Industrial Average hit a new high that January, and the Nasdaq peaked two months later. The financial pundits on the cable news shows resurrected Alan Greenspan's warning about irrational exuberance, but that didn't temper Greg's optimism about eMarket. His accounting team started working on the company's registration statement for the Securities and Exchange Commission, beginning the process for the IPO. I dropped a few hints to Greg about having another baby, thinking that another child might draw his attention back to home and family, but he didn't go for it. "Not now," he said. "I've got too much other stuff going on. Maybe next year."

I passed the wet spring days with Perla and Ed. We dressed our children in slickers and rain hats and walked to the neighborhood playground in the morning. We often met up again in the afternoons for story time at the library or went on outings to the Aquarium or the Children's Museum.

On one especially blustery day, Perla persuaded me to join her for lunch at the Cedar Heights Club, for something different to do with the kids. We had an uneventful meal in the "family dining area," a windowless cubbyhole adjacent to the main dining room, where rambunctious children couldn't do too much damage. Afterward, we went down to the lower level of the clubhouse to take a look at the fitness center, which I had yet to set foot in.

I almost bumped right into Paige as she was coming from the ladies' locker room. I hadn't seen her in quite a while, but I'd heard she spent a lot of time working out on the machines and attended the morning Pilates classes. Her hair looked freshly blown out, and she'd applied a bit too much perfume after her shower; when we hugged, I had to stifle a sneeze. "How have you and Ken been?" I asked.

"Just super," she said with a bright smile. "Kenny's busy as a bee, travelin' all the time."

"Yeah, same with Greg."

She gave an exaggerated shiver that made her boobs jiggle beneath her tight sweater. "This rain sure has me missin' my Georgia sunshine." Her lipsticked mouth sagged. "Kenny's in Memphis this week for some sorta convention. I wanted to go with him, but we're havin' the bonus room remodeled into a home thee-ay-ter, so I had to stay behind and supervise the work."

Her smile reappeared as she squatted in front of Nate, who was squirming in his stroller. "What a little darlin' you are!" She tickled his leg and he laughed. She gazed at him for a moment, then stood up and smoothed her size-zero capris. "I'm headin' to the lounge for a salad and a glass of wine," she said. "Care to join me?"

Still not pregnant, I guessed. I felt sorry for her. "Thanks, but we've just had lunch," I said. Paige gave Nate a last wistful look and went on her solitary way.

It was Ed's idea to take the kids on a picnic. We were planning to go in two cars, but then Perla had to cancel at the last minute, so Ed came to pick me and my kids up in his Subaru Outback. He squeezed Becky's and Nate's car seats into the back with Ada, and I got in the front with him. We drove down the hill and headed east on the interstate, toward Snoqualmie Pass and the state park that was our destination.

It felt funny to be sitting next to Ed with our children in the backseat. As if we were a family. He had wisely placed Ada in the middle seat, to prevent sibling trouble between Becky and Nate. He laid down the rules: no screaming, no touching each other, no looking at someone who didn't want to be looked at. I smiled, reminded of the car rides of my childhood when my parents took me and my sisters to visit our relatives in Pittsburgh.

Ed proved to be quite entertaining. He turned the radio to an oldies station and belted one out with Martha and the Vandellas. He had a truly awful singing voice. Ada shouted over him until he agreed to play the Wiggles CD she wanted, which was even more awful. He finally turned the music off altogether and taught us the words to a song he'd learned in the Boy Scouts, a never-ending ditty about a little red wagon that no one was allowed to ride in. I watched in wonder as he led the children through verse after verse, bobbing his head and conducting with his free hand.

The Outback was a manual transmission, and he downshifted as the highway climbed up to the pass. A passing rain shower slicked the pavement, and he kept both hands on the wheel now. Far below us, a riverbed churned with spring meltoff from the higher elevations. I opened packets of Fruit Roll-Ups and handed them to the girls in the backseat. Nate was fast asleep.

Ed put a Hootie and the Blowfish CD in and lowered the volume so we could talk more easily. "What's Greg been up to lately?" he said. "Busy traveling?"

"Oh, yes, he's real busy," I said, being deliberately vague. I was actually on my own for the whole week. Once again. It was getting embarrassing.

The interstate skirted a long body of water. "That's Keechelus Lake," Ed said. "The source of the Yakima River." I wanted to ask him about his wife, Lindsay, but I didn't want to seem nosy. I hardly ever saw her around the neighborhood, and I'd only met her once. We drove without talking for a few more miles, until the highway straightened out and our exit was coming up.

We carried our coolers down to a picnic table on the lakeshore. The sun came out again. A reflection of the forest rippled on the dark water, and the mountains stood tall in the distance, patches of white dotting their summits. I took off my fleece vest, shook out the old plaid blanket I'd brought, and smoothed it out over the stones. The mild breeze held the scent of pine. Ada and Becky skipped off to explore the beach, and Nate trotted after them.

I unpacked hot dogs, buns, and potato chips from my cooler. Ed went over to the grill, and I watched as he stuffed crumpled newspaper into a blackened coffee can, filled it with charcoal, and stuck a lit match through the holes punched in the bottom. "That's neat," I said. "My dad used to do it the same way."

Ed tapped the wooden handle that was screwed onto the can. "Made it myself. Another Boy Scout trick." When the coals had ashed over, he spread them out across the bottom of the grill and removed a plastic container from his cooler. "I brought barbecue chicken for the grown-ups. Since Perla couldn't come, there'll be extra for us." He seared the chicken, then moved it over to the cooler part of the grate to slow cook. He produced a bag of wood chips and laid a handful on top of the fire.

I sniffed the smoke. "Is that hickory?"

"Yup."

The smell brought back family camping trips in the Alleghany National Forest. My parents didn't do hotels. I gazed at the glowing coals, lost in pleasant memories.

The kids came running back and sat cross-legged on the blanket to eat their lunch. Ada dropped her hot dog and smeared mustard all over her pants. Ed wiped distractedly at it with a paper napkin and pointed out a spotted sandpiper scurrying along the water's edge. I helped myself to a second piece of chicken.

After lunch, we went for a walk along the lakeside trail. Ed led the way in his long-sleeved shirt and baggy hiking pants, a bright film of perspiration on his forehead in the warm afternoon. Nate got tired and asked to be carried. "I've got him," Ed said and swung him up. Ada and Becky followed behind them, pausing here and there to pick the wildflowers blooming at the edges of the path. I brought up the rear, enjoying the sunshine and the girls' chatter and the sight of little Nate riding high on Ed's shoulders.

We returned to our picnic spot, and Becky and Nate ran off with Ada again, collecting rocks and odd-shaped pieces of driftwood. I removed my sneakers and socks, rolled my jeans up to my knees, and sat on the blanket with Ed. I gathered a handful of smooth pebbles and dropped them one by one into a small mound between my bare legs. I fanned the stones into an arc, scooped them up, and fanned them out again. "How does Lindsay like her job with the State Patrol? It must be really interesting."

Ed perked right up at my question—I needn't have worried about being nosy. "She loves it. There's always something different happening. She's on a drug investigation in the city right now. Directing undercover officers, doing a lot of surveillance. Pretty cool stuff." He gave me a crooked smile. "But that's all I can tell you. Confidential law enforcement business. She can't even tell me that much."

I smiled back at him. "Sure, I understand." I rearranged my pebbles. "Do you worry about her when she's working?"

"Oh yeah, all the time. But she's doing what she loves, you know? She joined the army right out of high school. Said she always knew she wanted to serve. She went into the police academy after that. She doesn't make a ton of money at it, but she's done very well. She got an award for outstanding service last year. I was really proud of her."

I gathered the stones in my fist. I wished I felt that way about Greg. "What did you used to do, before you had Ada?"

"I was an emergency medical technician. Rode on an ambulance. The hours were too erratic, and the pay wasn't high enough for me to stay with it after she was born. Most of my salary would've gone to cover daycare, so we decided that Lindsay would work and I'd stay home with the baby." He leaned back on his elbows. "When Ada starts kindergarten, I'll go back to work for the county and get licensed as a paramedic. We've got it all planned out." The sun glinted off his glasses, and he raised a hand to shade his eyes. "How about you?"

"I used to be a children's library assistant. Not much money in that either. I didn't finish college." I needed to change the subject before he asked me why. "Are you glad you did it? Stayed home, I mean."

"Yeah, for sure." His eyes followed the kids as they zigzagged along the beach. They stopped and their heads bent close together as they stooped to dig at something in the sand.

"Me too," I said. "I love being home with my kids, but I didn't really have a choice. I kind of had to agree to it because Greg travels so much. He's never around, and sometimes—" A finger of guilt poked me. I was being disloyal to my husband. I heard my mother's voice, reprimanding me: *Keep your business to yourself.* "Never mind," I said with a wave of my hand. "It's all good."

Ed opened his cooler, pulled out two bottles of water, and handed one to me. I unscrewed the cap and took a drink. My unfinished sentence floated away on the breeze.

Ada came running toward us with Becky and Nate on her heels. She tripped and went face-first onto the stones. Ed jumped up, ran over, and lifted her to her feet. He brushed the sand from her knees and kissed the top of her head, and I felt a tightening in my chest. *That's what I want,* I thought. *That's what I'm missing.* Nate came over and dropped into my lap. I ducked my head and hugged him to me so Ed wouldn't see my face.

The children fell asleep on the drive home. I reached for my water bottle in the cupholder at the same moment that Ed reached for the gearshift, and our hands touched. Electricity zinged up my arm, startling me. I turned away and looked out the window.

Ed spoke after a few minutes: "We could go to this place called Rattlesnake Lake next time. It's a lot closer."

I wondered if he'd invite Perla to come too, or if it would be just us again. "I'm afraid of snakes," I said.

He laughed. "There aren't really any rattlers there." He explained how the lake had been formed decades ago, when the water behind a Seattle City Light dam had seeped through the glacial sediment it was built upon and flooded the railroad town that lay downstream. "The houses are gone now. All you can see are these spooky tree stumps glimmering beneath the lake's surface."

I liked the way he described things, and how he took an interest in the world around him. A guy like him wouldn't last a week in a job like Greg's, crunching numbers and chasing wealthy investors. Ed probably wouldn't be caught dead on a country club golf course.

"Thanks for driving," I said as we pulled into my driveway. "It was a fun day."

Ed got out to help me. I unlocked the front door, and his arm brushed mine as he reached past me to set Nate's car seat inside the house. When he straightened up, we were standing very close. There was that zinging sensation again, but it went all through me this time—up my arms, down my legs, roiling around my insides. We gazed at each other for a second or two, then he touched my shoulder, turned, and went down the steps to his car.

"See ya, Jeanie," he called through the open driver's window. I stood in the doorway, Nate tugging on my hand and Becky clamoring to watch Dora the Explorer, and wondered what was happening.

Chapter 11

I spent the Labor Day weekend at home with my children while Greg courted venture capitalists on the golf course at Pebble Beach. The following Tuesday brought the horror of the September 11 terrorist attacks.

Greg was stuck in California until the ground stop was lifted. I sat up every night with the cable news, the newspaper, and a numbing glass of wine, waiting for him to call and check in. He finally made it home around midnight on Thursday. He went straight upstairs to look in on Becky and Nate, and then he came into our room, shucked off his shirt and slacks, and got into bed in his underwear. "I'm not going to work tomorrow," he said. "I need to get some sleep."

I awoke in the morning to Nate tugging at my elbow. The clock showed six thirty. I lifted the covers and helped him scoot up into the bed. He snuggled with me for a minute, then clambered over me to his preferred spot in the middle of the bed and patted his dad's head.

Greg stirred and opened his eyes. Nate smiled big, showing off his cockeyed baby teeth. His father looked at him blankly for a moment, rolled away, and pulled the comforter over his head. Down the hall, I heard Becky begin her merry morning singsong. I picked up Nate and got out of bed.

I put Becky onto the school bus at eight fifteen, and there was still no sign of Greg at nine o'clock, which was unusual for him. I turned the TV to Nick Jr., went upstairs, and eased the bedroom door open. Greg was propped up on the pillows with his Blackberry at his ear and his laptop open on his thighs. He signaled me to be quiet. I sat at the foot of the bed and waited as he listened to a long, droning voice mail. His face was drawn and there were dark smudges beneath his eyes.

He set the phone down. "Did you have a good rest?" I asked.

"No, I couldn't sleep anymore after you woke me up, so I've been working." His sour morning breath wafted across to me. I could see he wasn't in a listening mood, so I didn't say anything back. He pushed his laptop aside, and the front of his boxers gaped as he swung his feet to the floor. He adjusted himself and rubbed his stubbled cheeks. "I've got a lot of administrative bull-shit to catch up on today. I think I'll go over to the clubhouse. They've got a workspace there that I can use."

"But you just got home." I didn't think I could bear another day as a single parent, not after everything that had happened this week. "I thought you weren't going to work today. I was going to make you a big breakfast and then let Nate watch a movie so we could have some alone time to talk."

He picked up his Blackberry and started scrolling through his messages. I clenched my hands in my lap. "Please, Greg, can't you work from home today? I'll make sure the kids don't disturb you. Just please don't leave me alone again." I started to choke up and I turned my head away, ashamed. I was begging my husband for attention.

Greg stared at me for a moment and sighed deeply. "I suppose I could."

"Thank you," I whispered. "I'll make it a good day."

I realized how frumpy I must look—still in my pajamas, my hair twisted into a messy bun. I showered fast while Greg finished checking his voice mail. He came into the bathroom as I was flicking on a quick coat of mascara. "Don't bother with breakfast, okay? I'm gonna shave and shower real quick, and then I just want coffee."

I went downstairs to brew some fresh and start a load of laundry. I hadn't seen Greg's suitcase in the bedroom, so I went down the hall to check his office. He'd tossed his sport coat onto his desk and as I reached for it, I whisked a stack of papers to the floor. I stooped to gather them and an airline ticket slid out of the pile. I picked it up and examined it: United Airlines, Seattle to Chicago/O'Hare. Friday, September 28. Samantha M. Romano.

Who was Samantha Romano? I searched my memory, trying to place the name. Could she be Sam, the new administrative assistant that Greg had mentioned a while back? The one he said was so organized and efficient, and who I'd assumed was male?

Questions piled up in my head. Was this Samantha person working with Greg in Chicago? Was she married? How old was she anyway? I straightened the papers and set the ticket on top of the stack. Greg's rolling suitcase was standing next to the desk. I laid it on its side and unzipped it, and his dirty clothes tumbled onto the rug.

He was suddenly beside me. He was shirtless and had a bath towel wrapped around his waist. His face was clean-shaven, and I caught the sharp lime scent of his shaving cream.

"I was just getting your things out to wash," I said.

"Thank you."

Greg never thanked me for doing his laundry. His eyes shifted to the desk, and my gaze followed his. The plane ticket was sitting there in full view. He stepped over to the desk and tapped the ticket with his fingertips. "That's for my assistant, Sam. I cashed in some frequent flyer miles for her so she can visit her family in Illinois. She can't afford the airfare, so I thought I'd help her out." He dropped the ticket into his briefcase, clicked it shut, and thumbed the dial.

"That was nice of you."

"Yeah, well, she's been a big help to me. Was the least I could do."

"She's not afraid to fly so soon after the terrorist attacks?"

His shoulder twitched. "Guess not." He tightened the towel around his waist. "I'd better get in the shower now, babe." He pursed his lips and gave me a moist peck on the cheek. I waited for him to leave the room, then wiped the spot with my sleeve.

I had my head in the freezer when he came downstairs after his shower. He was saying something to me, but I couldn't hear him over the whir of the fan. I closed my hand around the pork roast I'd been digging for and pulled it out. "Sorry, what did you say, Greg?"

"I said don't count on me for dinner."

"No dinner? Why not? What are you doing?"

"Some people I need to meet with. Business contacts. We're gonna get together for a drink at the Cedar Heights Club. I'll grab some dinner there."

The frozen roast was burning my hands. I'd been saving this damned thing for a month, waiting for an opportunity for us to sit down to a nice meal together. I thunked it onto the counter. "No, Greg, not tonight. You need to stay home and eat dinner with your family. Becky and Nate need some time with you."

He raised his palm at me—*Talk to the hand.* "Just deal with it this once, Jeanette. I've been running full steam for weeks, and I need a night out. The kids'll be fine." He opened the refrigerator. "Do we have any Coke?"

"Only Diet."

He took out a can and popped it open with a grimace. "I hate Diet. Why didn't you buy regular?"

"Because you're never around to drink it."

He narrowed his eyes at me. "You don't seem to realize how

hard I've been working. Ken missed the meeting in San Francisco this week because he was doing some useless bullshit on the East Coast and he couldn't get a flight out. I had to handle the negotiations on my own. Now he's stuck in New York till Monday. Serves him right, the fucking idiot."

Nate was kneeling on a chair at the kitchen table, mashing his fist into a mound of purple Play-Doh. He looked up at his father, surprised by the bad word. "Ken's stuck in New York?" I said. "That's too bad. I saw Paige at the club not too long ago, and she said—"

Greg cut in with a snort. "That figures. I hear she hangs out at the bar all the time. If I were Ken, I wouldn't be leaving a wife who looks like *that* home alone."

The jab went deep. I stared at him in astonishment, and he seemed to realize the insult in his words. "You're different though," he said. "I trust you." He took a long drink from his soda and covered a belch. "I'm just saying, there are rumors going around about Paige Clayton."

I woke with a start that night and squinted at the clock—it was after midnight and Greg wasn't home yet. I checked the phone on my nightstand to make sure I hadn't left the ringer turned off, as I sometimes did when I went to bed early. I pulled on my bathrobe and went downstairs. The house was dark, and the Audi wasn't in the garage. I dialed Greg's number and it went to voice mail. *You have reached the cell phone of Gregory Mercer. I am unable to take your call at this time . . .*

I went back upstairs and checked on Becky and Nate, closed their bedroom doors, and sat down in the dark at the head of the stairs. My pulse was racing. Ginger padded up the steps and lay down with her head in my lap. I leaned against the wall and waited.

Headlights flickered across the front windows. I heard the garage door go up and down, and then Greg's dark silhouette appeared in the front hall. Ginger scampered down to greet him, and he deflected her with his foot.

"Hello," I said. Greg tipped his chin up at the sound of my voice. I realized how odd I must look, sitting there in the shadows.

"What are you doing up so late?" His tone was overly courteous. Sugary. "I hope I didn't wake you."

I started down the stairs. "Where were you?"

"Didn't you get my message?"

"What message? I didn't get any message from you."

"I called to tell you things were running late."

I stopped at the foot of the stairs. I could smell alcohol on him, but he didn't seem to be that drunk. I clenched my fists. "No, you didn't. You did not call me."

"Take it easy." He felt along the wall for the light switch, and the chandelier glared down at us. He shielded his eyes and regarded me with calm disdain. "I called your cell phone, Jeanie, so I wouldn't wake the kids."

I tried to remember where my cell phone was—probably in the bottom of my purse, which was hanging on the hook in the laundry room, underneath my Columbia jacket. No wonder I hadn't heard it ring. "Oh," I said. "Well, you should have called earlier so I wouldn't worry. I've been sitting here waiting."

"Just stop, okay?" He threw his coat onto the upholstered bench by the front door. "I can't deal with this right now." He spoke to me in a monotone, like I was a kindergartner: "I was out with some colleagues. Now I'm home. End of story." He kicked his shoes off and started for the stairs. I didn't move. "If you'll get out of my way, please," he said, "I'd like to go up to bed." I stepped aside and let him pass.

He took a quick shower and climbed into bed with me. We

were both silent for a minute or two, and then he said in a whisper, "There's some stuff going down at work. It's got me all riled up."

I turned over to face him. "What is it?"

"Ah, just a bunch of bullshit. We'll talk about it later."

I tried to sleep but it was no use. Greg breathed easily while my mind ticked the minutes away. Something was off. Something wasn't right.

The shower. That was it. Greg had showered before going to bed, when he'd already taken one this morning. I slipped out of bed and tiptoed downstairs.

His loafers were by the front door, one of them tipped on its side. I placed them under the bench, picked up his Brooks Brothers coat, and went to hang it up in the closet. It smelled of rain-dampened wool, but there was another scent mingled with it. I held the lapels to my nose and sniffed, and caught a hint of perfume.

I went back up to the bedroom. Greg was lying on his stomach now, snoring into his pillow. I went through the bathroom to our walk-in closet, shut the door, and turned on the light. His dirty clothes were draped over the edge of the hamper. I picked up his blue button-down, took a whiff, sniffed it again. *Eternity.* My thoughts jumped to the day I'd had lunch at the club with Perla and we'd run into Paige. Paige wore Eternity too.

I ran downstairs and felt inside Greg's coat pockets until I found his wallet. I took it into the powder room, opened it, and saw a receipt tucked in behind his cash. It was from the restaurant at the Cedar Heights Club, time-stamped 9:35 p.m. I went to the laundry room and dug my cell phone out of my purse. Sure enough, there was a missed call from Greg at 9:50. My hands were shaking. So where was he the rest of the night? With Paige? Maybe he'd actually gone home with her, since her husband was stuck in New York.

It couldn't be. It just couldn't. Greg didn't like ditzy women like Paige, and she clearly loved her husband. They were trying for a baby, for heaven's sake! It had to be my perfume that I'd smelled. It had rubbed off onto Greg's coat the last time we'd gone out together, and his shirt had gotten mixed up with my clothing in the hamper. I was imagining things.

I replaced the receipt in his wallet, returned the wallet to his coat pocket, and put his coat back on the bench where I'd found it. I went upstairs, got back into bed, and lay awake for the rest of the night.

Chapter 12

Perla and I decided to form a Daisy Scout troop for our daughters and their first-grade friends. We went to the bank together, to open a troop account. A young man in a tie showed us into his office and asked for our driver's licenses so he could fill out the paperwork. "I see you just had a birthday," he said to me with a smile.

"What?" Perla slid my license across the desk and looked at it. "Your birthday was last Saturday! Why didn't you tell me?"

"I don't know. I forgot, I guess."

"You forgot?" She swatted my arm. "Bah! What did you do? Did Greg take you for a delicious dinner?"

"He wasn't home, actually."

"No!" Perla frowned. "He was not home on a Saturday?"

I shrugged. "He's very busy at work right now. He has to travel a lot."

The banker kept his eyes on his keyboard, pretending not to listen. "That Greg," Perla muttered and tossed her dark hair over her shoulder. "He is home now?"

I shook my head. "He's out of town seeing clients. He'll be back Friday."

She sniffed in disapproval, but then her face brightened. "I know what—we will have a party!"

"No, Perla. No party."

"Yes." She slapped spastically at my hand. "Tomorrow afternoon, after the Daisies meeting. I will take care of everything."

Strollers were parked haphazardly in my driveway, and my kitchen was filled with people. The neighborhood women had brought whatever food items they'd had on hand at home—boxes of crackers, veggie sticks and dip, mixed six-packs of beer, and the inevitable juice boxes covered my kitchen island. One of the men had turned on the stereo, and U2's "Beautiful Day" was blasting through the house. Small feet pounded the stairs, and children's voices rang out in the bonus room above.

Ed was there, in jeans and a Phish T-shirt. He pulled a stool out for me at the island and handed me a glass of white wine. I surveyed the smorgasbord of leftovers. To make up for the wine calories, I filled a plate with carrots and celery and skipped the dip.

The doorbell rang. "Who is that?" Perla said as she glugged the remains of a two-liter bottle of soda into a glass. "They can let themself in."

Lindsay entered the kitchen a moment later, tall and smooth and dressed all in black. Ed jumped up, and I watched as he hugged and kissed her hello. The other wives stole sidewise glances at them and exchanged looks with each other: *This woman is way cool.* Ed kept his arm around his wife's waist as though someone might try to steal her. Ada came barreling through the grown-ups, and her mother caught her up in a bear hug. The three of them made a sweet family picture.

I turned away and tried to tune into the conversations buzzing around me—soccer sign-ups, the new school principal, the Thai restaurant that was supposed to be opening soon. I drank my wine and searched through the clutter on the island for a matching bottle of white to refill my glass with.

It was Perla who noticed first. "Oooh," she said, pointing down the hall toward the front door.

"What?" I said, without looking. The wine was spreading warm fuzzies through me. I took another sip and crunched a celery stick.

She reached over the veggie tray and whacked my arm. "Greg is home," she hissed. "He looks mad."

"What?" I said again. "He's not supposed to be back until tomorrow." I turned and looked down the hallway. Sure enough, Greg was standing in the foyer with his overcoat over his arm. My heart did an unexpected flip-flop at the sight of him—he was a handsome figure in his starched shirt and slacks. He looked past me to the people in the kitchen. His face was tight.

Uh oh, I thought. *He really is mad.*

I hopped off my stool and called out to him. "Hi, Greg." My neighbors turned around in surprise, and the conversation died down. I took a step toward him. "We're having a party."

He started down the hall, his dress shoes clicking the hardwood floor. "I can see that," he said with a thin smile. The men greeted him with "Hey, buddy's" and quick handshakes. The women began to look around for their children. Perla's husband stole into the den and turned the music off.

"It's for my birthday," I said. "A belated birthday party." I felt like a foolish child, busted red-handed. "I wasn't expecting you home yet."

He nodded but didn't say a word. The other husbands slipped quietly from the room as their wives gathered up diaper bags and coats. They herded their children out the front door and toward the waiting strollers, calling out "Thank you" and "Goodbye" as they left. Within minutes, everyone was gone. Greg disappeared, and a moment later I heard his office door bang shut.

I began to clean up. I dumped the plates of cheese and

crackers straight into the garbage, and the leftover soda and beer went down the sink. I wiped the counters, and my irritation rose with each swipe of the dish cloth. I'd been having fun with my friends until Greg came and ran them off. *My* friends. He probably didn't even know half their names.

I made sandwiches for Becky and Nate to eat. I wasn't hungry anymore, and I didn't care if Greg was or not. I finished my wine, washed and dried the glass, and put it away. I took the kids upstairs and ran their baths, got them into their pajamas, and helped them brush their teeth. I went into the master bedroom and spoke to the closed bathroom door: "Greg, the kids are ready for you to say goodnight."

As I tucked Nate into bed, he pulled his shiny thumb out of his mouth. "I want Daddy," he said and plugged it back in.

"Daddy will come in a minute, honey." I nuzzled his soft cheek and smoothed the covers over him, left his bedside lamp on, and went to look in on Becky. She was sitting on her bed looking at a picture book. I went back to my room and cracked the bathroom door. Greg was standing in front of the mirror in his shorts, looking at his Blackberry. "They're waiting for you," I said.

"Mm hm. Be right there."

I waited till he'd left the room before I changed into my nightgown. For some reason, I felt funny about him seeing me undress. We hadn't made love in God only knew how long. Greg came back in, settled himself in bed with his hands folded on his chest, and closed his eyes. He looked as if someone had laid him out in his coffin. "Whooo, I'm tired," he said. The covers lay flat between us.

"How come you're home early?"

"Same old shit at work. I don't feel like talking about it."

"Do you realize what you did tonight? You blew off my friends. We were having a good time until you walked in, and they all felt like they had to leave right away."

He kept his eyes shut. "Jeanette, I'm extremely tired. That was not what I wanted to come home to."

"But I didn't know you were coming home! You could have called and told me. I wouldn't have had people over if I'd known."

"We'll talk about it later." He pulled the sheet up to his chin. "Would you please turn the light off? I have a ton of work to do tomorrow. I've got to get some sleep."

He rolled onto his side, away from me. I could picture his body under the covers: fetal position with his arms clamped between his thighs, guarding his privates. He did that to ward me off these days, even when he was in a good mood.

I turned off the lamp and lay very still. Greg was quiet, but I could tell he wasn't asleep yet. He was probably making a mental to-do list for tomorrow, and I was pretty sure his wife and children weren't on it.

I tried to turn my thoughts to happier things. I pictured Nate snug in his big-boy bed, and Becky dreaming away with her fluffy white unicorn tucked under her arm. I replayed that bright June day with Ed at the lake, when he'd carried my son on his shoulders and his touch had sent electricity dancing up my arm.

Tears trickled from my closed eyes as I finally admitted to myself how much my marriage sucked. My husband was gone for days on end, and when he came home, he didn't touch me, didn't even want to talk to me. He ignored his children and barely spoke to his neighbors. My breath caught in a sob, but Greg didn't stir. I could have been having a heart attack right there next to him, and he wouldn't have even noticed.

Greg was preparing to leave on another business trip. "Could you e-mail me your itinerary?" I asked him as he carried his bags down to the front door. "In case something happens, I'll want to know what flights you're on and what hotel you're at."

He glanced out through the sidelights, checking to see if the car service had arrived yet. He didn't like to drive himself to the airport anymore. "If there's an emergency, you can always call Sam," he said. "She books all my travel, so she'll know where I am."

"But what if it's late? I can't very well call her up in the middle of the night."

A Lincoln Town Car swung into the driveway. "Bye-bye, kid-dos," Greg called to Becky and Nate, who were eating cereal in the kitchen. "Daddy's leaving now. Be good for Mommy." He picked up his briefcase and gave me a light kiss. "Quit fussing, Jeanie. Everything will be fine."

There was no school that day because of a teacher's workshop, so the kids and I met Ed and Ada at the park later that morning. A chilly rain had fallen during the night, and Ed, the always-prepared Boy Scout, had brought a towel to wipe off the swings. I fitted Nate's chubby legs into the molded plastic kiddie swing, and Ed and I stood side by side, pushing our children's backs in tandem. He was brooding over something, and he kept his gaze on the tall evergreens surrounding the play area, not saying much. I stuck one hand in the pocket of my hooded jacket to warm it up and alternated pushing Becky and Nate with the other. Several minutes passed before Ed shook himself from his thoughts. "Greg out of town again?"

Why was this always the first thing anyone ever asked me? "Yeah."

He gave Ada another couple of pushes, still gazing off at the trees. "It must be hard on you with him away so much."

"Yes," I said. "It is."

We continued pushing our kids in a steady rhythm. "Lindsay hasn't been home much lately either," Ed said. "She's been working mandatory overtime since September eleventh."

So that's what was on his mind—he was missing his wife.

"The State Patrol is working with the FBI," he went on, "tracking down leads on suspected terrorist activity. She's not allowed to tell me anything about it."

I nodded in sympathy. His spouse couldn't talk about work, and mine simply wouldn't. The clouds darkened and it started to sprinkle. Ed pointed at the sky. "Do you want to go in?"

"No. I'd rather stay out a while longer. Why don't we go for a walk so we can keep warm?" I lifted Nate out of the swing and plopped him into his stroller, and we set off down the street. At the corner, we turned right and began to climb the hill to the gated section where the Claytons lived. We paused at the top to watch a dark bank of clouds churning in from the northwest. The gate clanked open and Paige's giant white Escalade rolled through. I twitched my hood down over my face when I realized who it was. Ed noticed but didn't say anything.

Paige roared past without acknowledging us. The wind was fierce up here, so after a minute or two we turned to go back down the hill, and Ada and Becky ran ahead of us. Ed kept looking at me funny. "When does Greg get back?" he asked.

I was tired of answering these questions. "I don't know, Ed, okay? I never know. He goes when he goes, and he comes back when he feels like it." It was the first time I had voiced my marital frustrations to anyone, and it felt good to let it out. "I think half the time he's lying to me about where he goes and what he's doing."

I stopped in the middle of the sidewalk, gripping the curved handles of the stroller. "Your wife comes home at night. You have dinner together, you do things as a family. You don't know how lucky you are to have that. All I have is shit. My husband worked nonstop this entire weekend, and on Saturday night he went out without me, and I think—"

"You think what?" Ed reached for my arm, but I shook his

hand off. My eyes welled up, and I felt like an idiot for crying in front of him. "It's all right, Jeanie," he said quietly. "It's not all perfect at my house either." He stuck his hands in his pockets and looked up the hill toward the Claytons' house, then back at me. He seemed as if he was about to say something else, but I didn't want to hear it.

"Let's go," I said. "I'm getting cold." I gave the stroller a hard push. Nate kicked his legs and squealed.

"Look what we got at the library." Perla waved a DVD case at me. "The Sounds of Music." Her girls came running into my kitchen, followed by Ed and Ada. Perla's husband was going to the Sonics game tonight, Lindsay was working the night shift, and Greg, as usual, was out of town, so we were having a movie night at my house.

We ate the pizza that Ed had brought, then went up to the bonus room. The kids sprawled on the floor with blankets and pillows, and the adults took the couch. "I love this Julia Andrew," Perla said at the opening scene. "She is so cute and perky." I tried to focus on Fräulein Maria as she twirled in her Austrian meadow, but my mind wouldn't stop wandering. Greg was in Chicago for the weekend, and today was September 28, which meant his assistant Sam was there now as well, on her free plane ticket. I'd been trying not to think about it all day.

Megan and Emily were fast asleep when we got to the intermission. "I am forgetting how long this movie is," Perla said with a yawn. "I better take the girls home. You guys keep watching. I will come get the DVD tomorrow." She woke her daughters and they went home.

That left a blank spot in the middle of the couch. I hesitated for a moment, then moved closer to Ed so there wouldn't be an obvious awkward space between us. I dozed off as the von Trapps were pushing their pretend-broken car out of their courtyard, straight into the hands of the waiting Nazis. I woke some time later to the glow of the film's title screen; chirpy birds and a tolling church bell sounded over and over on a loop.

Ed was asleep. His legs were propped on the ottoman alongside mine, his head was tilted back, and his glasses had slid down his nose. He had an arm draped across the couch cushion behind me, and I could feel the warmth of his skin on the back of my neck. My head had fallen onto his shoulder, and my hand was resting on his thigh. On the floor, Becky, Nate, and Ada were a sleepy jumble of arms and legs.

I sat there absorbing the feel of Ed's body close to mine, breathed in his smell. I hadn't felt this secure and comfortable in such a long time, and an intense longing filled me. I closed my eyes, trying to will myself back to sleep. I wanted to stay like this all night.

But this was wrong, *so* wrong. What would Greg think if he could see me now? And what would Ed do when he woke up and found me draped over him with my hand practically in his crotch? I swiftly disengaged myself. Ed woke and looked around, groggy-eyed. "Guess I fell asleep." He pushed his glasses up and scratched his stubbled chin. "How long was I out for?"

"Not long." I stooped to shake Becky and Nate awake. "I'm going to get them into bed."

Ed lifted Ada into his arms. "I'll go put her in the car. Be right back." His Subaru was parked in my driveway for all the world to see, at eleven o'clock on a night when my husband was out of town. Great.

I laid Nate in his bed fully dressed, but Becky insisted on getting changed. As I pulled her nightgown over her head, I heard a car door shut, and then the front door opened and closed, and Ed's footsteps came back up the stairs. I went into the hall and saw him hunched over in the bonus room, pressing buttons on the DVD player in the TV cabinet. "I'll take the movie with me," he said. "I can drop it in Perla's mailbox on my way home."

I could barely make out his face in the dark. The sweet feeling of waking up next to him was still with me. I didn't want him to go yet. I followed him down the stairs, opened the front door partway, and stood there twisting the knob. "Thanks for bringing the pizza."

"No problem."

"We should do this again."

"Yeah, definitely."

"Maybe a shorter movie next time."

He laughed. "For sure." He took a step closer, and then his arms were around me. We'd never hugged before and it felt strange. Strange but good. I hugged him back.

Slowly, slowly, he leaned back until we were eye to eye. His face was shadowed, but his balding forehead was illuminated by a slice of light coming in from the street. He pressed his lips gently to mine, and my whole body went rigid—*we shouldn't be doing this!*—but I let him go on kissing me. My legs turned to water, and my hands came up and clutched the back of his shirt. I felt as if I'd fall over if I didn't keep hold of him.

The kiss went on and on, and my mind started to disintegrate. We paused for air. *What are you doing?* my brain screamed at me. *This isn't right. But oh God, it feels so good!*

"Mommy."

We sprang apart. Nate was standing at the head of the stairs with his blankie pressed to his cheek. He pulled his thumb out of his mouth. "Mommy."

Did he see us? My voice came out in a squeak. "Coming, Nate." I ran up to him. He was only four; he wouldn't get what was going on. It was just Mommy hugging her friend, that's all. A friendly hug, like I gave Perla all the time. Except that Perla and I didn't kiss. Or moan. I thought I might have moaned. I hustled Nate back to bed.

Ed was still standing by the door when I went back down. I hoped to heaven that none of my neighbors had been out for a late-night dog walk and seen what had transpired in my foyer. I stopped a few feet away from him, afraid of getting any closer.

"I'm sorry, Jeanie," he whispered. "I shouldn't have done that."

"It's okay." I didn't know what else to say. I was quivering, and a strange heat burned deep inside me. He needed to leave. Now. I pushed the door open wider, keeping my distance. "Go," I said. "Just go."

Chapter 13

I pawed through the dresser until I found Greg's old Emory sweatshirt, folded myself up on the couch with the sweatshirt pulled over my knees, and stared at a cutesy movie on the Hallmark Channel.

Why, oh why, had I let Ed kiss me? What had made me do something so reckless? We were both married and we both loved our spouses. There was no reason, no good reason at all, for allowing myself to act this way.

I woke the next morning with a shiver of pleasure and the feel of Ed's kiss on my lips. I poured juice and made peanut butter toast and let the kids eat their breakfast with the cartoons on. I set Nate's Hot Wheels track up in the den to keep him out of my way and launched myself into a frenzy of housecleaning. I had to figure out what to do about this thing with Ed. I had to get him out of my head before Greg came home tomorrow night.

I needed someone to talk to, but who? Not Perla, that was too close to home. I didn't really have any other girlfriends in the neighborhood, aside from the few acquaintances I chit-chatted with at the park. My sisters were definitely out—they'd only pile on the judgment and the Catholic guilt. Eileen and Marian were so pious they never even swore or watched R-rated movies. Debra might be willing to listen, but she had her own problems, with her boys cutting up at school and getting detentions all the time. And my mother wouldn't want to hear about any of this. She'd say

I had committed a grievous sin and needed to get myself to Confession before the Almighty Lord struck me down with a bolt of lightning.

I passed the morning scouring the inside of the oven—my mother's go-to cleaning project when she was distressed. The phone rang as I was rinsing my scrub brush in the sink, and Greg's cell number flashed on the handset. I let it ring four times before I picked it up.

"Hello there," he said. "How are you? I wanted to let you know that I won't be coming home tomorrow. The client wants to wrap up some loose ends here."

Good. That gave me more time to get my head straight. "All right," I said. "Do whatever you need to do."

"Okay then." He sounded surprised by my indifference. "I'll be home Friday night," he said. "Gotta run now."

After lunch, I sat down to take care of a pile of paperwork. I opened a bill from the cable company and was about to write out a check, then remembered that our bank had introduced an online bill-paying service that I hadn't set up yet. I switched on the funky "Bondi Blue" iMac that Greg had purchased down in Portland, to avoid the Washington State sales tax. As I waited for the computer to boot up, I gazed at the high school photo of me and Carla that I'd thumbtacked to my corkboard. We were dressed *Desperately Seeking Susan*-style with strings of rosary beads around our necks, fingerless gloves, and bright red lipstick. She'd sent the photo to me in a birthday card with a sticky note on it saying *Remember this??* She was married with children now and worked as a guidance counselor at our old high school.

I pushed the bills aside, got out my address book, and looked up her work number. She answered with a professional-sounding "Guidance Office, Mrs. Borland" but switched to her real voice when I told her it was me. "Jee-nay! How are you, girlfriend?"

I hadn't talked to her in ages, but once I got started, I couldn't stop. She was a good listener, and she waited till I'd finished blabbing. "Stop beating yourself up," she said. "You were feeling lonely because your husband was away, and you momentarily gave in to a mutual attraction. It was just a *kiss*, Jeanie. It's not like you're plunging head-on into an affair with this guy." She paused. "Or are you?"

"No! I would never do anything like that. You know that, Carla. It's just—"

"Take your time. I'm listening."

I took a breath to steady myself. "Things aren't so good between Greg and me. He travels all the time, and he pays hardly any attention to me or the kids when he's home. He shuts himself in his office and works, or goes out and plays golf all weekend. I have hardly any friends here, besides Ed and Perla. Some other couples in the neighborhood have invited us for dinner a few times, but Greg either isn't home or he doesn't want to go, so I always end up making excuses." I had to stop for a second to clear my throat. "Sometimes I'm so lonely I can't stand it."

"I understand." Carla's voice was soothing. "You need to sit down with Greg and talk about how you feel. Tell him how much you love him and miss him, and that you want him to spend more time with you. You've got to ask for what you need."

I wished I knew how to ask. I realized I had turned into my mother. Mom had dutifully kept house, raised the children, and taken care of my father's needs, and I'd never once heard her utter a single word of dissent or complaint. The difference between us was that her husband reciprocated her love and devotion, while mine couldn't be bothered with me.

"It's got to be my fault, Carla. Ever since we moved here, he's been wanting to live large and spend lots of money, and I've been resisting because that wasn't the way I was brought up. His mother made fun of me one time for being a hick, and sometimes I think she's right. I'm a stay-at-home mother with no job skills, and I haven't done a damn thing about finishing college. I feel like I'm not good enough."

"What a load of crap! You need to stop this negative self-talk." Carla went on, telling me to "silence my inner critic" and "reframe my maladaptive thoughts," and then a loud *bang* came from upstairs.

I said a hasty goodbye and ran up to Becky's room. She and Nate had pulled the bottom drawer out of her dresser and were filling it with stuffed animals. "It's a ferry boat," she said, immensely proud of herself.

I sat on the rug to watch them play and lost myself in thought. I'd just have to put my head down and push through this. My mother was a throwback to another era, no doubt about that, but there was a quiet dignity in her commitment to her husband. I needed to be more appreciative of Greg. He had a high-profile job with a lot of stress, and he deserved my loving support. I resolved to be a better wife to him from now on, and I'd start right now, by avoiding the temptation of Ed.

I called the car service the next day and canceled Greg's ride home from the airport. I freed my hair from its drab ponytail, put on some makeup, loaded Becky and Nate into the minivan, and off we went to Sea-Tac to surprise Daddy.

Greg stowed his bag in the back, kissed the kids, and got in beside me. I leaned over and hugged him, keeping an eye on the King County Sheriff's car that was creeping up behind me. "I thought we'd come pick you up for a change," I said. I gestured toward the grande Caffè Americano sitting in the center console. "We got this for you on the way."

We crawled along the 405 with the rush hour traffic. Greg sat with his hands flat on his thighs and sipped occasionally from his cup. Clouds hovered over Lake Washington. "Look, Daddy, Batman," Nate said, zooming his action figure back and forth.

Greg cranked his head around to the backseat. "Oh, Batman's flying. Very cool."

"Look what I'm reading, Daddy." Becky held a Junie B. Jones book up for him to see. Greg acted impressed and told her how smart she was. *This is perfect*, I thought. *He's engaging with his children. We're off to a good start, turning over that new leaf.*

"You must be tired," I said. "How did everything go in Chicago?"

He slid his hands down to his knees and tapped them once, twice. "Not good, actually."

"Why, what's wrong?"

"The venture capital firm we met with declined to offer us any financing. There's no way eMarket can stay on track for the IPO if we don't get an infusion of fresh capital soon."

I checked my mirrors, signaled, and changed lanes. "What does that mean?"

"It means the company's running out of operating cash. If we don't find more funding or get acquired by another company, Ken says we'll have to fold. I'll be out of a job."

"Oh, Greg." I looked over at him. "I didn't know."

"A lot of dot-coms around here are starting to go belly-up."

I knew that. I'd been reading about it in the paper. "But I thought eMarket was doing great and orders were pouring in."

"We're doing okay, not great. Ken talked it up real good to the analysts and the business journals, but the numbers don't lie." He rubbed his face. "The sad fact is, we burned through too much money by trying to expand so fast. It's been a good ride, but I'm afraid the IPO ain't gonna happen after all. We'll probably go under first."

I felt bad for him, but I saw a possibility here as well. To hell with all this dot-com mania. If eMarket went out of business, I might be able to persuade Greg to look for a normal job with normal hours and no travel. Maybe he could find something on the East Coast, where we'd be closer to our families. I wanted us to live like a real family again. The trouble was, we didn't seem to know how to do that anymore.

Later that night, I sneaked out to the garage after Greg was asleep and called Carla. "Go away together for a weekend," she advised me. "You and Greg need to have some fun and reconnect. Bruce and I like to drive up to Niagara Falls once in a while and do a little gambling at the casino. His mother watches the kids for us."

"We obviously don't have that option."

"Ask your friend Perla. I bet she'd keep them for you. Then get yourself some sexy lingerie from Victoria's Secret. Something really raunchy, like those panties with no crotch? That'll turn him on. One time, Bruce asked me if I would—"

"Stop it. I don't need to hear the details."

"Jeanie, you are such a priss. You've been married for what, eight years now? And you still can't talk about sex?"

"I don't *want* to talk about sex, okay?"

"Fine, we won't talk about it. But you should definitely book a romantic getaway, and make sure you get a room with a Jacuzzi. I'll bet Greg would love it if you poured some bubble bath in, then got down and—"

"La, la, la," I sang. "I can't hear you. I'm hanging up now. But thanks for the suggestion."

Another Monday morning on my own. Greg had caught a flight to Minneapolis last night, and he said he'd be there for a full week of meetings. I lay in bed with my eyes shut, trying to organize the day in my head: grocery shopping, laundry, cleaning, bills. The typical tedious round of household tasks.

"Hi, Mommy." Becky appeared at my side in her Ariel night-gown. She held a can of Libby's peaches in one hand and the can opener in the other. "Let's eat."

When I reached over to hug her, I noticed blobs of goo in the corners of her eyes. I took a closer look and saw that the whites of her eyes were tinged a spidery red. Pink eye. *Crap.*

I heard Nate coughing. Becky trailed me into his room, chattering about the yummy peaches. Her brother's eyes were glassy and crusty snot streaked his reddened cheeks. I got out the thermometer and his temperature registered one hundred and three. If we hurried, we could make it to walk-in hours at the pediatrician's office.

I dressed without showering, hustled the kids into the minivan, then remembered I hadn't let Ginger out yet and ran back inside. I pushed her out the back door, and she dawdled around the yard, sniffing and poking her nose into the bushes instead of getting down to business. She finally started to circle around and around on one spot, but then she paused and started to turn more circles in the opposite direction. "Come *on*," I hissed at her through my teeth. She stopped and looked at me. "Forget you," I said and shut the door on her. She could stay outside until we got back. Hopefully it wouldn't rain.

Dr. Stewart wrote a prescription for eye drops for Becky, then examined Nate. "It's only a cold virus," he said. "Make sure he drinks his fluids and gets plenty of rest."

I hoisted Nate into my arms and carried him out to the car with Becky hanging on to my sleeve. I buckled them both in and stood there a moment, debating. They hadn't eaten anything yet, so the smartest thing would be for me to fill the prescription at the Bartell Drugs drive-thru window, then go straight home for breakfast. But I was low on everything at home, and I needed soup and juice for Nate, so I decided to drive to the Safeway in

Issaquah. I could drop off the prescription at their pharmacy counter and pick up my groceries while I waited for it to be filled. We'd be in and out of there in just a few minutes.

I freed a cart from the tangle in the Safeway parking lot and bent to lift Nate. He kicked and screamed as I attempted to cram him into the kiddie seat. Becky took her cue from him and danced away from me, just out of my reach. I had to grab her by the arm and practically drag her inside. Nate screamed all the way to the pharmacy at the back of the store, and then Becky sneezed, spraying a gooey mess down the front of her jacket.

I'm that mother, I thought. *The one who brings her sick children out in public, spreading germs all over the place.* I stared straight ahead as I wove through the aisles, avoiding eye contact with the other shoppers.

As we were leaving the store fifteen minutes later, I spotted Ed crossing the parking lot with Ada in her bright yellow raincoat. We were almost to the minivan, so there wasn't time for me to maneuver my loaded cart in another direction. Nate was so happy to see them that he stopped whimpering and almost pitched himself headfirst from the cart.

We hadn't seen each other in the three weeks since the night we'd kissed. I hadn't responded to his phone messages or gone over to Perla's when I knew he was there. I tried to act like I was busy with my groceries and didn't see him, but he came right up to me. "How are you, Jeanie?"

"We've just been to the doctor." I picked up two of the plastic grocery bags and went to put them in the back of the van. "They're both sick, so don't let Ada get too close." One of the bags slipped from my fingers, and three cans of Campbell's Chicken & Stars tumbled to the ground.

"Let me give you a hand." Ed stooped to pick them up. I pulled the side door of the minivan open, told Becky to climb in, and helped her with her seatbelt. Ed pushed the cart around to the back of the van and loaded the rest of the groceries, then handed Nate in to me. He could see I didn't want to talk. He took Ada by the hand. "See you later," he said with a brief wave and walked away.

I started the engine, but then I sat there for another minute or two as reality hit me: I had lost a friend.

At home, I noticed poor Ginger waiting at the back door. I also noticed it was raining. I let her in and stroked her bedraggled head in apology. I found a soup bone in the freezer and set it on the floor in the laundry room for her, to make up for my neglect. She cocked her head at me. "It's okay," I said. "You can have it. Good dog."

I found Becky rifling through my closet when I brought my cleaning supplies upstairs that afternoon, after I'd put Nate down for a nap. "I'm playing mall, Mommy." She grabbed the hem of one of my dresses, pulled it off its hanger, and dropped it onto a pile of clothing on the floor.

"That sounds fun, honey, but not with my nice dress." I held it up and looked at it—it was a totally nineties pleated dress with a big lacy collar and a full skirt. I'd bought it shortly before I became pregnant with Becky, and I hadn't been able to fit into it since.

I handed it back to her. "Never mind, it's okay." I spotted a couple of Greg's dress shirts in the pile, picked them up, and shook out the wrinkles. "You can't play with these. They're Daddy's good shirts. Why don't you play mall with your own clothes?"

I shooed her out of my room, but she popped back in a while later as I was scrubbing my bathtub. "Come to the mall, Mommy."

"In a few minutes."

I rinsed out the tub and started on the toilet, and there she was at my side again. "Here's your Veeza. Let's shop." She showed me the credit card she'd filched from my purse and tugged on my arm. I dropped the toilet brush into the bowl, removed my rubber gloves, and brushed my hair from my face. I pried my Visa card from my daughter's hot little hand and allowed her to lead me down the hall.

I stopped short at the top of the stairs. Becky had somehow managed to slip out of my bathroom with my economy-sized box of Stayfree maxi pads. She'd pulled the paper backing off every one of the one hundred and twenty pads and stuck them to the steps. Maxis flowed down the staircase like a whitewater river, interspersed here and there with Barbie and her anatomically incorrect girlfriends in varying stages of undress, riding the rapids in brazen commando style.

I smothered a laugh. "Becky, those are Mommy's . . . things. I want you to pick them up, right now." Down below in the foyer, a line of shoes snaked down the hall toward the kitchen. I leaned over the banister for a better look and saw that she had unearthed several of my old purses to supplement her mall merchandise, and some of my toiletries were tastefully displayed on the bench by the front door.

She reluctantly worked her way down the stairs, sending Barbies tumbling over waterfalls and spinning into whirlpools. A coating of carpet fibers adhered to the pads as she peeled them free. I supposed I could still use them; it would be such a waste to throw them away. We collected a bunch of the pads into a sticky mass that I squished back into the box, and I stuck the remaining pads to the outside of it. I could peel one off whenever I needed it. "It's a pillow," Becky said, patting the puffy box.

I laughed. "Yes, it's a funny pillow." I regarded the bloated box. If Greg saw it, he'd think I was a very strange person. I hid it in the back of the bathroom cabinet where he wasn't likely to find it. "Go play in your room now," I told Becky, and went to finish my housework.

I was carrying my cleaning things downstairs later that afternoon when a horrible smell hit me. The laundry room door was open and there was no sign of Ginger. I followed my nose into the living room and discovered the source: a dark plop of dog poop in the middle of the creamy carpet. A heavy stain that looked and smelled like blood had leached out around it. Becky came running into the room, caught a whiff, and gagged.

I stepped closer and discerned a sliver of bone in the mess. My dog was bleeding internally. This was my doing—I had given her that bone. I dropped my cleaning bucket and swore. Becky pointed at the nasty pile and pinched her nose. "It's poopie, Mommy. Nate made poopie on the rug." I fell to my knees and hugged her tight. *I've killed my dog.* I tried to think what I should do. Where was Ginger, anyway? For all I knew, she was already lying dead and stiff in a corner somewhere.

"Here, Ginger," I called. I searched the house with Becky close behind me. We went into the den, and Ginger slunk from behind the couch and scuttled over to me with her tail down. I scratched her behind the ears. "Are you okay, girl?" She brightened some at my touch and started licking at a corn flake that had dried onto the front of Becky's shirt. She didn't seem to be in distress, so I decided to wait things out before calling the vet. In the meantime, I'd get to work cleaning up this mess.

The stain turned pink as I worked at it with a sponge. Greg would be pissed if he came home and found his pristine carpet ruined. I made a solution of bleach and water, but after twenty minutes of alternately dabbing and blotting the spot, the outline of it was still visible. If it was still showing after it dried overnight, I'd have to rearrange the furniture.

The day wore on, windy and pouring rain. I parked the kids in front of the TV and prepared them an early supper. It was only five o'clock, but I had hit the wall. I closed the blinds in their bedrooms to hide the fact that it was still daylight outside and started to get them ready for bed. I gave Becky her eye drops, read them the shortest bedtime story I could find, and kissed them goodnight. This day was over.

After I'd cleaned up the kitchen, I looked around for Ginger and found her—still breathing, thank goodness—in her corner of the den. I let her out to the backyard, and this time I waited for her. I made myself a cup of tea and sat at the table with the phone in my hand. I needed to talk to an adult or I'd go crazy. My thoughts automatically went to Ed. He'd been kind to me this morning, despite the fact that I'd been giving him the brushoff for weeks. I started to dial his number but stopped myself—that was over now. Done with.

I dialed Greg instead. "I'm glad you called," he said. Traffic roared in the background. "I'm on my way to meet some people for dinner, but I've got a couple minutes to chat. How are things at home?"

"The kids are both sick. I had to take them to the doctor this morning."

"Aw, I'm sorry." He sounded like he really meant it. "Anything serious?"

"No, just pink eye and a cold."

"How about you? You're not getting sick too, are you?"

"I'm fine. Just tired."

A siren blared on his end, and he waited for it to pass. "That's good. I'm glad you're okay. Listen, I'm almost to the restaurant so I've got to go. Kiss the kids for me."

I tapped the phone against my palm, wondering who else I could call. Perla's parents were visiting from Jakarta, so I didn't want to intrude, and there wasn't really anyone else around here who I was inclined to call up just to chat. It wasn't that late yet on the East Coast though. I dialed my parents' number, but the line just rang and rang; I guessed that they'd gone over to one of my sisters' houses for dinner. Dad got around with his cane pretty well now, and they liked to get out of the house whenever they could.

I set the phone down. I had run out of people to call. The refrigerator hummed and the furnace kicked on. I missed my husband like a piece of something was missing inside my body. I got up and started turning out the lights.

Sunlight flooded Becky's room when I raised the blinds in the morning. Her eyes looked much better. I boosted Nate onto her bed, and we all leaned on the windowsill and squinted at the bright blue sky. The wind was quiet and the clouds had retreated into the mountains. The wet trees sparkled in the sun and a pair of hawks circled low over the valley.

I made pancakes, and Nate giggled as Becky made funny faces at him over her plate. Ginger romped around the backyard, restored to her chipper dog-self.

I decided to keep Becky home from school for one more day. While she and her brother were playing in her room that afternoon, I did a Google search and made a reservation for two nights at a four-star hotel and spa in the Cascades. The deluxe room featured a mountain view, a wood-burning fireplace, and a king-sized feather bed.

And a Jacuzzi.

Chapter 14

Perla agreed to have Becky and Nate stay overnight at her house. "A romantic weekend in the mountains!" she said. "That is just what the doctor orders."

I went to a chic Italian deli near Pike Place Market on the day before our trip. A Sophia Loren look-alike waited on me, and she nearly swooned when I told her my idea. "A picnic supper?" she burbled. "Fabulous." She swooped through the shop in her long, filmy dress, plucking imported products from the shelves.

"You will *love* these." She showed me a jar of stuffed olives and hugged it to her breasts before thrusting it into my basket. "Taste this," she said and waved a pungent chunk of Fontina under my nose. She selected a stick of salami from the deli case and sighed orgasmically as she wrapped it up in thick white paper. Last, she chose a "seductive" Chianti to go with the food and sent me happily on my way.

I dropped the kids off at Perla's on Saturday morning, then walked aimlessly around my house, resisting the impulse to call upstairs to Greg and tell him to hurry up. This weekend had to go off perfectly, without any friction. I turned on the news and watched a spokesperson from the Bush administration field questions about the "shock and awe" bombing campaign that had begun in Iraq.

Greg appeared, freshly showered and dressed, and carried our overnight bags out to the car. We drove north and then east on a highway that wound through the Wenatchee National Forest. I told him about the champagne and chocolates that would be waiting for us upon our arrival, and the spa appointments that I'd scheduled for later that afternoon. We were both getting hot stone massages that were supposed to magically reduce our stress. I was leery of getting undressed for a complete stranger, so I'd been sure to request a female masseuse. Or was it masseur? I had no idea. After our massages were done, I planned to surprise Greg with the picnic supper, and I had requested a dessert platter and coffee to be delivered to the room in the evening. Maybe I'd even ask him again about us having another baby.

The pressures of home slid away as we drove deeper into the woods. I turned to Greg and smiled. "I can't wait to sleep in tomorrow morning, in that big feather bed." He responded with only a nod. The highway had begun to climb in switchbacks, and his attention was on the road. I was talking too much. I thought I'd better shut up for a while so I didn't distract him.

We emerged from the shadows of the forest, and the elegant stone-and-timber lodge appeared around a bend. A valet welcomed us on the circular driveway and whirred the Audi away. We walked into a high-ceilinged lobby with huge windows framing a vista of misty mountainside.

"Beautiful place," Greg said, and I congratulated myself for my good choice. He chatted with the desk clerk and politely declined the bellman's offer of assistance with our small amount of luggage. He picked up both our bags, I put the picnic basket over my arm, and we ascended the carpeted staircase to the second floor.

Our room was done up in placid northwestern greens and grays. A bottle of champagne was buried in a bucket of ice on a small table by the fireplace, and rose petals were strewn around two sparkling flutes.

"Isn't this lovely?" I let myself fall backward onto the huge bed, and my head sank into the cloud of pillows. My pulse quickened as I thought of the lacy Victoria's Secret bra and panties that I'd bought specially for the weekend. Greg was going to be amazed.

From the bed, I could see him in the full-length mirror opposite the bathroom door, lining his toiletries up on the counter. "Our spa appointments aren't until four," I said. "Do you want to just relax for a while?"

"Yes, let's." He came over to the bed and kicked his loafers off, pulled the duvet back, and got under it, fully dressed. I lifted the duvet on the opposite side and scooted in beside him until our hips touched. The seams of my jeans scraped the silky sheets.

Greg cleared his throat. "We should talk."

"Mm." I nestled into the billowy pillows. I would have preferred that we started tearing each other's clothes off this second, but if Greg felt like talking for once, I guess we'd talk.

He rubbed a hand through his hair. "I've been pretty stressed out lately."

"I know. This weekend's going to be so good for you. You can unwind and forget about work for a while." I stretched my arms over my head and turned my face toward the window. The glass was wet, but the clouds were glowing white around their edges, as though the sun was trying to break through.

Greg stared up at the ceiling. "All this traveling I've been doing has given me a lot of time to think about things."

"I guess we'll have to figure out what's next for us, if eMarket shuts down. What do you think you want to do?"

"That's what I want to talk about." He shifted his body so that we were no longer touching. "I know you planned this special weekend so we could reconnect with each other."

"That's right." I touched the back of my hand to his cheek.

It was cool and smooth. He didn't say anything, and a chill came over me. "Right?"

"That's just it."

I froze. "*What* is it?"

He blurted the words, sharp and quick: "I don't love you anymore."

I was dumbstruck for a second, then I recoiled in horror. I sprang from the bed and stood over him, trembling. "Are you kidding me? You leave me alone with your children week after week, then you come home and ignore me, you won't even touch me or talk to me, and now you're saying *you* don't love *me* anymore?"

He sat up on the side of the bed. "I knew it would be like this," he mumbled to the floor.

I was shaking uncontrollably. I grasped my elbows, trying to make it stop. This wasn't happening. It couldn't be real.

"This marriage isn't working," Greg said. "It hasn't been working for a long time."

"I know it isn't working! How could it, when we're never together? Don't you realize that I did all this—" I flung my arm out, taking in the whole room "—to try to make things better?"

"Be quiet." His voice was hard. "We don't need the entire hotel hearing us."

"*I don't care who hears us.*" I was near hysteria. "You don't mean what you're saying, Greg. You can't mean it—" A sob choked me and I sank onto the bed. I felt sick to my stomach. Greg got up and stood with his arms folded, staring out the window as the room darkened and a gray drizzle obscured the view of the mountains. I covered my face with my hands and tried to regain control of myself.

The shaking subsided after a minute, and I drew a ragged breath. "I can't stay here. I want to go home." I pictured myself on the shoulder of the wooded roadway, running away from this hotel, away from Greg. I'd hitchhike if I had to. I got up and seized my overnight bag. The picnic basket that I'd so lovingly packed was sitting on top of the dresser, and I knocked it to the floor as I passed. The obscene stick of salami rolled out across the carpet and disappeared beneath the bed.

"What about the room?" Greg said. "We can't just leave."

"I don't give a shit about the room. You can figure it out. Tell them we have an emergency at home or something. Maybe you can get your precious money back."

I went down to the lobby and asked for the car to be brought around while Greg argued over the room charges at the reception desk. The Audi pulled up, and the valet expressed his regrets that Mr. and Mrs. Mercer were unable to stay the weekend.

We drove home in stony silence, and I agonized the whole time. Greg was stressed out and exhausted; that's all this was. He still loved me, and I loved him. We would talk this through until we were clear again. I was sure I could make things right again, if he'd only listen to me.

We sped past Perla's house, and Greg pulled the car into our garage and immediately lowered the door. I went inside and fell into a chair, thankful the children weren't there. Greg sat down opposite me, pale and grim.

We talked in circles for hours, trying to make sense of what was happening to us. By nightfall I was drained. The anger that had been bubbling beneath my skin for so long had bled out of me. I let my head fall onto my arms. "I feel so empty."

Greg rubbed his temples. "Me too." He looked completely deflated.

Maybe he really was depressed. That would explain so much—his irritability, his detachment from me and the kids, his disinterest in sex.

Sex. Fear stabbed me. Was he having an affair?

Greg went into the den and turned the TV on. I sat on the coffee table, right in front of him. He tried to look around me, but I moved over and blocked his view.

"I have to ask you something, Greg. Please understand that I have to ask, just to be sure." I took a deep breath. "Is there someone else?"

His eyes flicked to mine, then darted away. He slammed the remote down. "I knew you'd accuse me of something like that. You have a lot of nerve, you know that? I'm out there working my tail off every day while you're sitting around here at home taking it easy. More likely it's you who's got someone else, not me."

I backed right off. He kind of had a point there.

He stood up. "I need to take a break from all this talking. There's just one thing though." He fixed me with a threatening look. "Don't go telling the whole neighborhood about this. It's none of anyone else's business."

"I wasn't—"

He held up his hand. "I'm gonna go shower and then try to get some rest. I'll sleep here on the couch tonight."

Perla brought Becky and Nate back the next day around noon. I met her on the front steps before she could walk into the house in her usual friendly way. "How was your weekend?" she asked with an expectant smile.

Her carefree manner grated on my raw nerves. "Great," I said. "It was a great place." I bent to hug the kids, and I hid my face in Becky's soft hair. "I feel like I'm coming down with a cold though, so you'd better not come in."

"Oh, too bad. I hope it didn't spoil your times."

"No." I kept my face averted. "We'd better get inside." I picked up the children's backpacks and half turned toward Perla. "Thanks for watching them."

She cocked her head. "You're welcome. I hope you feel better."

I closed the door and led Becky and Nate into the den. Dear Perla. If she only knew how much shit had hit the fan yesterday at that overpriced lodge. She'd be glad Greg didn't get his money back.

I let Becky turn on the television, and I went up to the bedroom. Greg was talking on the phone, something to do with his flights. His travel case was open on the bed, partially packed for his trip to Dallas tomorrow. I sat in the armchair, waiting. I was afraid of him leaving with nothing resolved between us.

He concluded his call and resumed packing. "We've got to do something, Greg," I said. "Couldn't we try marriage counseling?"

"I will not discuss my personal business with a stranger."

"But we can't give up without trying. Talking to someone might help."

He glared at me. "Who have you been talking to? You've told Perla, haven't you? Which means the whole neighborhood will know our business by tomorrow."

"I haven't talked to anyone! When did I even have a chance to?"

He threw a handful of socks into the case, shut it, and yanked the zipper. "Just keep quiet, all right? I'm warning you—telling everyone what's going on with us will only drive me further away. I've got enough to contend with as it is. I'm meeting with a potential buyer for the company on Tuesday, and if we don't strike a deal, eMarket's fucked." He hefted his bag and strode out of the room.

"Wait, Greg. Please." I trailed him down the stairs. I glanced into the den and saw Becky and Nate immersed in a Little Bear cartoon. Greg opened the front door, and there was a silver town car parked in the driveway. The sight of it stopped me cold. He wasn't supposed to leave until tomorrow.

My voice wobbled. "I didn't know you changed your flight."

He took his overcoat from the closet and pulled it on. "I think we need some time apart." He concentrated on his coat buttons and didn't look at me.

"But that's the problem," I said. "We're always apart. We need to be together so we can work this out."

He wound a cashmere scarf that I'd never seen before around his neck. "It might be better if I got my own place."

My mouth fell open. "You mean you want to move out?"

When he finally looked at me, my heart almost stopped. His eyes were cold. "Yes. I think we should separate."

He couldn't possibly be serious. Separation meant divorce, and divorce was unthinkable. My stomach clenched and my vision blurred. I put a hand on the wall to steady myself. Greg picked up his briefcase and waved to the waiting driver.

Chapter 15

The meeting in Dallas was a bust. Greg came home in a foul mood, and his plans to move out got lost in a frantic effort to keep eMarket alive. The company's board of directors voted to withdraw the IPO filing, and the announcement came a day later: eMarket would cease operations at the end of February. Greg's dream of instant wealth disappeared into the Seattle fog.

An article about the company's demise appeared in *Businessweek*, and Ken Clayton was quoted extensively. "Screw him," Greg said and flung the magazine across the den. "He should never have been hired as CEO. He didn't have the balls for it. I could've done a better job than him." He clicked the television from Nick Jr. to the Golf Channel, disregarding Becky and Nate's wails of protest. He unzipped his laptop case. "I'm gonna get rich one way or another. I can demand a six-figure salary now that I've got these years of e-commerce experience under my belt. Ken can go to hell."

"Come on, kids," I said, "let's go play upstairs so Daddy can work." Best to leave him alone until his fury blew over.

Greg threw himself into a manic job hunt over the next several weeks, and I was relieved by the distraction. Searching for a new job meant he didn't have time to look for his own apartment. The reprieve might be only temporary, but I was thankful for it nonetheless.

In April, a few days after Nate's fifth birthday, Greg was offered a partner-track position with a private equity firm in Boston. He flew there to sign the paperwork, then went down to Augusta to play golf with his father. I was a mess of jangling nerves at home, waiting and wondering what he'd have to say when he returned. Would he want to take me and the children with him to Boston, or would he rather go on his own and leave us behind?

He arrived home in an exultant mood. He strutted back and forth across our bedroom, relating the details of his trip. "I met all the top players at Carbide Equity, and they love me already. There's a shitload of opportunity in the northeast. I'm gonna rake in millions. I don't know why I bothered coming to Seattle in the first place." He bragged a while longer about his golf game—the incredible drives he'd crushed, the amazing putts he'd sunk—while I sat there wishing I had the guts to cut him off and say, *What about us?*

He finally stopped his restless roaming and sat down. "I had a long talk with my dad on the golf course. Told him we've been having some troubles."

I tensed up, afraid of what was coming next, and a huge knot grew hard in my stomach.

"Dad says no one understands the stresses of work and family better than him. It turns out, he and my mom split up for a while when Gordon and I were kids. I was too young to know what was going on, but I do vaguely remember us staying at my gram's house for a long time one summer. I was used to my dad being on the road a lot, so I didn't think anything of it, but now I get it. He didn't tell me any of the details, just said they eventually worked things out. He did give me some advice though. He says this job change is a great opportunity for us, and we need to be united as a family."

Greg paused and pressed his palms together. "That stuff I said before—you know, about us separating? I didn't mean it. I was stressed out because of what was happening to eMarket. But that's all over now. We can forget about it. I want us to move on, Jeanie. I want us to make this move to Boston together." He brushed my hair behind my ear and cupped my cheek in his hand. "Okay?"

The knot of fear inside me loosened. "Okay, Greg," I said.

Perla looked stricken when I told her we were moving. "It'll be better for us in Boston," I explained. "It's a major financial center, so Greg won't have to travel hardly at all anymore. He says he might need to go to New York City now and then, but it'll be an easy day trip."

She started to cry, and that made me start too. I fished linty Kleenex from my coat pocket. "I'll be so much closer to my family too," I said, after we'd each given our nose a good blast. "I already MapQuested the driving route." After all these years of living two thousand miles from home, an eight-hour drive from Boston to Adams Mills was nothing.

The house sold quickly, and the Mayflower moving crew came and packed up our belongings. Greg and the kids went to pick up some snacks for our red-eye to Boston that night, and I walked through the empty rooms one last time, remembering how happy and hopeful I'd been on that windy spring day when we'd moved in.

"Hello?" a man's voice called from below. "Jeanie?"

Ed! I flew down the stairs and practically threw myself at him. He caught me up in his arms and hugged me for what felt like a full minute. His lips were warm in my hair. "I would've come by sooner but Lindsay's father died and we've been away." He gently pushed me to arm's length. "I'm sorry you're leaving. I hope you'll be okay."

Did he know something was wrong? I hadn't said a word to anyone, not even Perla. Greg's warning had kept me quiet. All I could do was hug Ed back and try not to lose it. I wanted badly to kiss him, but I didn't dare when my husband might be back at any moment. Ed seemed to sense my longing. He pulled me close and held me as I sniffled into his shirt. I was going to miss him so much.

I heard a car pull into the driveway. I disentangled myself from Ed's arms, looked outside, and saw the rental car we'd been using since our vehicles had been packed onto the moving truck. "It's Greg," I said. I felt guilty for Ed being there, even though it was all completely innocent.

"I'll go then," he said. "Take care, Jeanie." He gave me one last squeeze and went out the door. He passed Greg in the driveway, but they didn't shake hands or appear to even speak.

Greg entered the house and regarded me coolly. "All done here?"

"Yes."

"Then let's go." He locked the door behind us and we got into the rental. Ed was ambling along the sidewalk, and he nodded at us as we passed. I kept my hands in my lap and looked the other way.

Chapter 16

Welcome to Boston Logan International Airport. Local time is 7:49 a.m. The weather this morning is seventy-five degrees and sunny."

The Fasten Seatbelt sign went off with a *bing*, followed by the metallic clicking sounds of hundreds of seatbelts being released. Passengers spilled into the aisle, eager to stretch their legs after the red-eye from Seattle. In the window seat next to me, Becky yawned and stretched; on my other side, Nate was still asleep with his cheek stuck to my arm. Across the aisle, Greg adjusted his stiff Red Sox ballcap and checked his Blackberry.

Wayfield was a quaint colonial town on the northern outskirts of Boston. It was known for its excellent schools and had one of the highest median household incomes in the state. The housing stock ranged from modest Cape Cod cottages to ivy-covered mansions. Towering sycamores and beeches lined the orderly avenues, and front yards overflowed with hydrangeas and rambling roses in the first blooms of summer.

The price of real estate was inflated and the market was tight. Greg said he didn't want to jump into buying anything right away, so we signed a lease on a three-bedroom, one-bath Cape on a shady street near the elementary school. The house was so small that half our furniture had to go into storage, but it had a cozy feel that I loved. The children's bedrooms were tucked under the eaves upstairs, and there was a grassy backyard with a sagging rock wall that separated our yard from our neighbor's. At the end of the street, a path wound through the woods to the schoolyard.

It took me only a few days to get our new home in order. I walked Greg around the house, showing him how I'd made efficient use of our limited space. The closet in our first-floor bedroom was jammed full of my limited wardrobe and Greg's numerous dress shirts and slacks. His suits had to go in the living room closet, alongside the vacuum and a couple of packing boxes that had been designated for storage but had been delivered to the house by mistake.

I drove through the town with my MapQuest printouts on the seat beside me, learning my way around as I attended to the myriad tasks involved in getting established in a new place. I transferred our auto registrations and insurance, got the Audi and the minivan inspected, and purchased E-ZPasses for the Massachusetts Turnpike. I brought the children's academic records to the elementary school and registered them for the fall; contacted a new pediatrician, eye doctor, and dentist; and found a vet for the dog. I figured out how to get "dump stickers" for the town landfill—you took care of your own trash and recycling here in Wayfield—and signed a contract for a winter snowplowing service, a necessity I might have overlooked if our landlord hadn't reminded me.

The summer streets were quiet and we didn't see any children around. The only person outside one morning was old Mrs. Koppelman from next door, who was diligently weeding the perennial border between our yards. She leaned on her spade and pushed a lock of gray hair from her face with a dirt-crusted gardening glove. "Not many people at home right now. A lot of folks go to the shah this time of year."

"The shah?"

"Or down the Cape. The Cape is very populah in July and Ahgust."

It took me a second or two to decipher her New England accent. She smiled down at Becky and Nate. "When school stahts, you'll have plenty of friends to play with."

We fell into a routine as the summer days went by. The four of us ate breakfast together every morning before Greg left for work, and then I'd turn to my endless to-do list and check off a few more items. If there was time before lunch, I'd walk Becky and Nate over to the schoolyard to play on the slide and the monkey bars, or we'd hang over the railing of the footbridge in the woods and drop twigs into the trickling creek. Afternoons were for swimming lessons at the municipal beach on Chase's Lake or a trip to the town library. At suppertime the kids would set the table while I cooked, and when Greg came home, we'd all sit down to a family meal.

There was no further discussion of what had transpired back in Seattle, no mention of the rift between us. We weren't lovey-dovey by any stretch, but we weren't actively at odds either. The status quo was good enough for me for the time being, and I was determined to tread lightly to maintain it.

Greg worked mainly out of the firm's satellite office in Wayfield, and toward the end of the summer, the office manager gave the entire staff a Friday afternoon off to go to a Red Sox game. A motor coach was chartered to transport everyone to a private pre-game party at Jillian's, a sports bar near Fenway Park, and game tickets were provided for everyone at no charge.

It was Greg's and my first time going out alone together since the move. I'd never been to a major league baseball game before and I was ready to have some fun. I found a neighborhood girl to babysit and waited excitedly for Greg to pick me up that afternoon.

He called at a quarter after four. "I'm still in the city and don't have time to come get you. I ordered a taxi to take you over to the office so you can ride the bus with everyone. I'll meet you at Jillian's."

A crowd was milling around a Yankee Line bus when the taxi pulled into the office park. I took my time getting out of the car. Surely Greg had asked one of his coworkers to keep an eye out for me, since I didn't know a single person there? People in red-and-navy Red Sox jerseys and baseball hats were standing in the sunshine, laughing and bantering with one another. I waited to see if someone would step forward with a friendly greeting, but no one took any notice of me.

The bus door whapped open. I moved with the flow of the crowd, boarded the bus, and took a window seat halfway back. A stream of people filed past me, calling to their friends. A woman with frizzy hair paused and pointed at the empty seat next to me, and I smiled and gave her a welcoming gesture. She sat down, swiveled her legs into the aisle, and continued her conversation with the person across from her. The driver cranked the door shut and the bus rumbled out of the parking lot with me sitting by myself like a middle school dweeb.

The bus smelled of peanuts and diesel fumes. I pretended to check messages on my cell phone for a while, then gave up the pretense and stared out the window. Greg had better be waiting for me at the bar.

We rolled up to Jillian's. The other passengers poured out onto the street and mobbed the entrance, impatient for the free buffet and open bar. I lingered at the door for a minute to allow my eyes to adjust to the dark interior, then looked around for my husband.

The bar area was packed with young people grooving to the Black Eyed Peas and taking enthusiastic advantage of the free drinks. I scanned the crowd for Greg but didn't see him. I made a circuit of the place, which turned out to be quite large. In a room at the back, a family of five was grouped around a pool table. The three boys were wearing gray jerseys with BOSTON stitched in red across the front, and the father was hamming it up for his sons, chalking his stick and taking exaggerated care in lining up his shot. There was a *crack*, and the eight ball disappeared into a corner pocket. The boys hooted, and the dad grinned as his pretty wife snapped photos.

I returned to the front of the bar and perched on a tall chair at a high top near the door so I'd be sure to see Greg as soon as he came in. Every person in the place seemed to be part of a couple or attached to a lively group, all laughing and having a good time. I checked my phone again, but there was no message. Greg must have gotten held up by his client.

A cute waitress stopped to offer me a Corona Light from a frosty bucket. "I'm waiting for my husband," I said.

"I'll leave one for him too." She set two lime-wedged bottles on the table and glided away. I set the lime aside and took a big gulp from my beer. At least the two bottles on the table made it look like I wasn't a total loser, sitting there all alone.

I peered around the flashing Sam Adams signs in the window. Traffic was at a standstill in the street, and baseball fans swarmed the sidewalk. I scanned the room again, and at last I spotted Greg over by the bar. He had a beer in his hand, and he was talking to a tall, tanned man who had an equally tall, tanned woman at his side. I slid off my chair and went over to them.

"Well, hello there," Greg said, kissing my cheek. He was still wearing the sport coat and slacks he'd had on that morning, but he'd removed his tie and folded it into his pocket.

Before I could say anything, he started making introductions. "Royce, I'd like you to meet my wife, Jeanette. Jeanette, this is Royce Benedict, director of strategic initiatives." Royce activated a politician's smile and shook my hand. "This is Royce's wife, Daniella," Greg said, indicating the glowing blond woman. Daniella was clearly a good thirty years younger than Royce's sixty. The unnatural jut of her breasts threatened to pop the buttons off her shirt. She was struggling to contain a pudgy three-year-old who was trying to squirm out of her arms.

"This is their son Aspen. Isn't he a cutie?" Greg made wiggly fingers at the boy.

"Say hello, Aspen," Daniella wheedled. Little Aspen glared. He opened his fist, and a glob of gummy worms slithered into his mother's cleavage. He giggled and grabbed her platinum hair in his sticky hands.

"It's so nice to meet you, Jeanette," Daniella said but didn't offer her hand—she needed both of hers to keep her grip on her son. She canted her head sideways in an attempt to free her hair from his grasp. "Greg has told us so much about you."

"It's nice to meet you too," I said and stepped out of Aspen's reach.

"Still up for yoga Monday evening?" Royce asked Greg.

I looked at my husband. Yoga? Seriously? "Sure thing," Greg said. "Wouldn't miss it."

They chatted for a few more minutes, and then Greg clapped Royce on the shoulder. "We'll let you folks get back to your other guests now. Great party, Royce."

"That guy's a real dick," he said under his breath when we were safely out of earshot. "I can't stand him but he's very powerful. I have to kiss his ass a little."

"What was that about yoga?"

He flapped a hand. "Royce is ex-military. He's really into physical fitness. He says yoga improves your mindfulness, whatever that means. He keeps bugging me to join him, so I thought I might as well go with him and act like I'm into it too. Can't hurt."

He snagged another beer from a passing waitress and waved to someone across the room. "There are some people over there that I need to say hello to."

He placed his hand in the center of my back and steered me over to an attractive couple standing by the buffet. The man had on a dark shirt and black jeans, and the woman wore a tank dress that looked so good on her it had to be designer.

"Kirin. Marla. Good to see you." Greg shook hands with Kirin and kissed Marla's pale cheek. "These two are wine collectors," Greg said to me. "They've acquired some of the finest vintages in the country."

I searched my brain for something informed or clever to say. "That's so interesting" was the best I could do. I knew next to nothing about wine, but I did know that western New York State was grape-growing country. "I visited a winery in the Finger Lakes region when I was up in New York one time," I said. "What do you think of their wines?"

"I don't," Kirin said. Marla smirked.

Greg frowned at me and turned to Marla. "How's that project you're managing in Minneapolis?" This prompted a detailed discussion of workstreams and deliverables. I pretended to follow the conversation and nodded along with them. I began to feel invisible.

After fifteen minutes of this, Greg detached us from the snooty wine connoisseurs and propelled me through the room, introducing me to colleagues and their spouses, until we noticed that Royce had raised his hands in the air in a silent request for attention. Heads turned and talk ceased. Royce took his time gazing around the room. When he felt his minions had waited long enough, he bellowed "Game time!" and conducted us out the door.

We walked the three blocks to the stadium, Greg flanked by two junior financial analysts who were hanging on his every word.

I looked around for the pool-playing family, but they seemed to have disappeared.

The company's block of seats was located along the first base line. Greg bought a beer from a vendor, pushed down a row, and seated himself next to Royce, who was spouting David Ortiz's batting statistics over his shoulder to the couple seated behind him. "What a boob," Greg whispered to me. Three seats down from me, Daniella was wrestling Aspen back into her lap.

Royce and Greg got deep into a business discussion. They spoke a common language that was foreign to me: buy-in and buckets, paradigms and profitability scenarios. "Give it the elevator test," Royce advised Greg with a sagacious nod. "Don't try to boil the ocean."

The crowd stood for the seventh inning stretch. "I'm exhausted," Greg said to me in a low voice. "I've been going balls to the wall all week. Let's leave now. Royce will understand. He knows I've got a breakfast meeting tomorrow."

I was glad to go. Greg made his apologies, and we squeezed past a row of knees, trying not to upset cartons of popcorn and plates of sausage sandwiches. "Early meeting," Greg kept repeating with a rueful shake of his head. The bigwigs nodded knowingly, and the support staff rolled their eyes at each other as they twisted their legs aside to let us pass.

"Thanks for being a good sport, Jeanie," Greg said on the drive home. "I would've liked to ride the bus with you, but duty calls sometimes. You enjoy the game?"

"Yes," I said. I hadn't, really, but I was trying to keep things on a positive note. I had disliked all the brown-nosing and the superficial small talk, and I didn't care for Royce and his fake-boobs trophy wife.

"I had a good time too," Greg said. "But I stuck out like a sore thumb in my dress clothes when everyone else was going casual.

You should've brought me some clothes to change into."

Something inside me began to smolder. "How was I supposed to know?" I said. "You called me at the last minute, and you never said you needed anything."

But then his words echoed in my head: *I don't love you anymore. We need some time apart.* I snapped my mouth shut. I had to let this go. If I picked a fight now, I'd mess everything up. We needed to go home, check on the kids, have some mechanical sex, and go to bed. I would keep on being a dutiful wife, and our marriage would trundle along. It wouldn't be great, but at least we'd keep it together.

I bowed my head. "Sorry, Greg. I should have thought of it." I summoned an apologetic smile. He patted my leg, and everything was okay again.

"I'm glad I got the chance to touch base with Royce tonight," he said. "If I play my cards right, I'll be up for that promotion to partner before long. Royce offered to grease the skids for me."

Was he trying to win a cliché contest or something? "Really, Greg?" I said, feigning interest. He was already earning a very nice salary, so what did he need to make partner in such a hurry for, especially when the promotion would mean more business travel for him?

"Yeah," he said, nodding to himself. "It was a good night."

At home after the sitter left, I began to tidy the kitchen. Someone had slopped juice onto the floor by the stove, and a bag of potato chips was spilled open on the counter. Greg looked in from the living room. "I mentioned to Royce that I read *The Millionaire Next Door* a few months ago, and he asked if he could borrow my copy. Have you seen it anywhere?"

"It's probably in the closet, with a bunch of books that I couldn't fit into the bookcase."

I heard the closet door open and some shuffling around. I

scooped the spilled potato chips back into their bag and secured it with a clip. "It's not here," Greg called from the other room.

"Did you check the shelf?"

"Yeah. I don't see it."

"Check again, I'm sure it's there." I shrugged and ran water over a washcloth. He'd find it if he looked carefully enough. I bent to wipe the sticky juice on the floor. I heard a thump and a scraping sound from the living room and guessed he was searching through the packing cartons in the back of the closet. I rinsed the washcloth, draped it over the faucet, and went in to him.

He had dragged one of the boxes out of the closet and was squatting in front of it. "There's no point looking through that, Greg," I said. "It's only a bunch of stuff from the old house that was supposed to go to storage."

I noticed a thick paperback book lying open on the floor, and saw that Greg was holding a small square of paper in his hand. I saw the grainy black-and-white image and the bottom dropped out of my stomach.

Greg raised his hand. "What is this?"

I tried to speak but my mouth had gone dry.

"It says Jeanette Flanagan. From 1993." He looked up at me, bewildered. "You had a baby, Jeanie? Before I met you?"

My hands flew to my chest. "No. I didn't."

"Then what does this mean?" He shook the picture at me. "Tell me."

Chapter 17

My brain wouldn't work. Greg pushed the box aside and got to his feet. He stared down at the picture again, then at me.

"It's a long story," I said. "Let me explain."

He followed me to the couch. I clutched my knees to my chest at one end, and he sat at the other, and I let the story spill out of me: the mono, my failing grades, begging Professor Asner for help. I began to cry as I stammered through the positive pregnancy test, the missed clinic appointment, my change of heart, my unexpected miscarriage. When I finished, I sucked in a shuddering breath and waited for Greg's reaction.

He had remained impassive throughout my confession, and he took his time responding. He tapped his fingers on his knees and leveled a cold look at me. "Why didn't you say no?"

"What do you mean?"

"When that professor started putting the moves on you, you could have said no."

"I *did* say no. He wouldn't stop."

One side of his mouth puckered. "Really, Jeanie? You expect me to believe that? You went home with him, you got drunk with him. Sounds to me like you wanted to sleep with him."

"No, I didn't! It wasn't like that at all."

He linked his hands behind his neck and stared down at his

knees. "I cannot believe you never told me. I don't know what to make of it. It's a total shock." He slowly shook his head. "I never thought you were that kind of girl."

I held my hands out to him, pleading. "Please, Greg. You've got to understand."

He inclined his body away from me and stood up. "I need some time to process this." I tried to go to him, but he waved me off. "Alone," he said. "I want to be alone." I heard him in the kitchen, putting on his coat and taking out his keys, and the sound of Ginger's nails clacking on the floor. He went out the door, leaving her behind. The Audi's engine whined as he backed very fast down the driveway.

My entire body was leaden with anguish. I sank onto the couch. I had just destroyed my marriage.

We lived a fragile coexistence throughout the remaining weeks of the summer. Greg buried himself in work. He went to and from the office without saying a word to me, and he spent most of his time traveling on business. When he was away, he rarely phoned home except for an occasional five-minute call in the evening to check in on the children. I kept quiet and went about my household and family duties, hoping patience and the passage of time would heal the wound I had inflicted upon us.

I didn't blame Greg for being angry with me. I would have been angry too, and deeply hurt, if he had kept such a big secret from me for so long. I had to have faith that he would eventually forgive me for these years of deceit, and for blindsiding him with the sordid truth.

Nate started kindergarten that fall. On the first day of school he was up before I was, and I found him at the kitchen table, fully dressed in his new school clothes and eating a bowl of Cheerios he'd poured for himself. I helped him and Becky with their backpacks and posed them for a photo that I'd e-mail to Greg later. He was working on a project in Baltimore and hadn't told me when he'd be back.

I pushed the screen door open, and we clambered down the steps into the beautiful September morning. It was funny how a sunny day could still surprise me after I'd become so used to the endless gray skies of Seattle. Children and parents were streaming past our house, heading down the street toward the path that led to the school. Mothers carried coffee mugs and conversed with one another over their children's heads, and I noticed a handful of fathers walking along as well. I took Becky and Nate's hands, and we joined the animated throng.

At the edge of the schoolyard I gave Becky a hug and a gentle push toward the meeting place where the third graders were lining up. I spotted Nate's teacher near the side entrance to the school, holding up a sign that said *Kindergarten*. We waded through a lively group of older students and joined the gathering of wide-eyed kindergartners and their parents. Nate was clutching my hand so tightly that my fingers were going numb. I pried him loose and switched him to my other hand.

When the young teacher said good morning to everyone, Nate burst into life. "Hi, Mrs. Brodowski!" he cried, mangling her name, even though we'd practiced at home.

"*Do*browski," I whispered. "*Miss* Dobrowski."

Miss Dobrowski was a natural. She motioned the children into a semicircle and dismissed the parents with a furtive hand signal. Her pupils followed her single file into the building. I waited to see if Nate would look back at me, but he trotted inside without another glance in my direction.

I walked across the schoolyard and came upon a cluster of mothers standing by the fence at the edge of the softball diamond.

They were engaged in a heavy discussion about their children's room assignments. We exchanged friendly nods as I passed, but I didn't stop. I didn't have it in me to walk up to a bunch of strangers and introduce myself. I'd have to make myself join a volunteer committee or something, I thought, so I didn't keep feeling like such an outcast.

Melancholy filled me as I walked up our empty street. I was going to miss having my little Nate with me today. I entered the quiet kitchen and Ginger was there, waving her tail. I knelt and hugged her. The house felt dull and cheerless without the children in it, even with the morning sunshine streaming through the windows. I almost picked up the phone to call Greg but then thought better of it; he was likely busy with his clients or in a meeting. He wouldn't want to talk to me anyway. I turned on the computer instead, to e-mail the first-day-of-school picture to him.

There was a message from Perla in my inbox. She was full of news about her Girl Scout troop and the Disneyland vacation she and her husband were planning. She mentioned Ed briefly at the end. He had completed his associate degree and gotten a good job at a Seattle hospital, and Perla didn't see much of him or Lindsay anymore. I typed a paragraph in reply and didn't say anything about Ed.

An e-mail from Greg had arrived in the meantime. I opened it eagerly, hoping he was writing to say he was missing me down there in Baltimore, but I found only a list of the things he wanted me to take care of this week: auto maintenance, insurance paperwork, dry cleaning, prescriptions to refill. Same old, same old. No *I love you*, no *I'll call you tonight*. He was treating me like I was one of his staff, good for nothing but checking items off a list. I logged out of my e-mail account and shut the computer down.

I moped awhile. My friends back in Seattle were lucky. Perla's family actually did things together, and they seemed to be enjoying their lives; Ed had followed through with his school plans, and now he had a career he enjoyed. And what did I have? My children, of course. I was thankful to have them and thankful they were healthy, but my relationship with my husband was in shambles, and my career was nonexistent. There didn't seem to be much I could do about my marital problems at this point, but I could at least do something about my unfinished education. Maybe it was time I went back to school.

Greg's stay in Baltimore was extended by several days, so I had to wait till the following weekend to talk to him. He was working on his laptop at the kitchen table when I worked up the courage to broach the subject. I picked up a dish from the drainer and pretended to wipe it dry with a towel. "Greg? What do you think about me going back to school now that Nate's started kindergarten?"

He looked up and shook his head. "Uh-uh. Not now."

"Why not?"

"I've got too much going on."

I put the dish down and clasped my elbows behind my back, wondering how hard I should press for this. "I wouldn't start right away," I said, "since the fall semester's already begun. But I could enroll in January. That would give us time to figure out a schedule and arrange after-school care for the kids."

Greg sat back and crossed his arms. "I need you here to keep the home fires burning." The cliché contest was apparently still on. He gestured toward his laptop. "I've got a lot on my plate at the moment."

"I wouldn't have to take classes full-time," I said. "Two days a week would be enough. I've only got one semester to make up, you know, so it wouldn't take too long for me to finish. Then I could get a part-time job at the library in the mornings and be home with the kids in the afternoon."

"Jeanette, I have a lot of work to catch up on, and I don't have time for this discussion. Why do you want to go back to work anyway? We don't need the money. Royce's wife doesn't work. She belongs to some charity organizations around town—maybe you could join too and get to know her. It'd look better for me if you did that instead of being a librarian." I heard the trace of a sneer in his voice. He turned back to the computer screen.

I picked up the dish again and rubbed it until it began to feel warm. "You told me you wouldn't have to travel with this new job, but you've been out of town every week for the past two months." I was veering off topic, but I couldn't help it. The words pushed themselves right out of my mouth.

"You know I've got to jump on every opportunity that comes my way," Greg said. "That's how I'll advance my career."

"Maybe your family should be your priority for a change, instead of your career."

He glowered at me. "By advancing my career, I *am* making my family a priority. I'm earning the money to support you."

Weeks of pent-up frustration tumbled out of me. "I don't care about the money. I care about us raising our children together. We can't do that with you working all the time, can't you see? You're traveling just as much now as you did when we were in Seattle. Nothing's changed."

Greg got up and yanked the power cord from the wall. "You're wrong about that. Everything's changed. It changed when you told me how you slept with your college professor in exchange for a passing grade."

I really, really didn't want to go there again, but I had to defend myself from his accusation. "That's not what happened, Greg," I said as evenly as I could. "I told you it wasn't like that."

He coiled the cord tightly around his fist. "You can forget

about going back to school and getting a job. You're staying right here at home." He went into our bedroom and shut the door, and I cursed myself for not keeping my mouth shut.

| 151 |

Chapter 18

Greg came home on a Friday night two weeks later, bursting with news: there was a prospective client in Charlotte, North Carolina, and Royce had put him in charge of landing the account. "This is a major one," he said. "A potential gravy train. It could make my career." He was booked on a 6:00 a.m. flight on Monday, and he'd be gone for the entire week.

I walked Becky and Nate to school as usual that morning and returned home to start my weekday chores. I went upstairs to clean their bedrooms first. Nate's floor was covered with a colorful heap of Legos, and in Becky's room, a herd of plastic horses galloped across the throw rug. I stripped the beds, tidied up, and dusted. As I worked, I reflected on the point that my life had come to: Greg would probably land this client in Charlotte, and then he'd land the next one, and another one after that. He'd keep on chasing his vision of success, and he'd leave his family behind in the process. He was a workaholic, and nothing I could say or do was going to change that. I needed to accept that fact and resign myself to living without a voice. I could still find fulfillment in being a good mother and maintaining a stable home for my children. That strategy had worked for plenty of women back in my mother's day, so why shouldn't it work for me?

I finished cleaning upstairs and carted the vacuum down to my bedroom. As I ran it across the hardwood floor, I bumped something beneath the bed. I reached under and pulled out the bathroom scale that I'd stashed there months ago because there was no room for it in our cramped bathroom. I wiped off the dust and stepped onto it, and the number surprised me. I hadn't been this thin since my wedding day. I hooked my thumb into the waistband of my jeans and saw a two-inch gap between the denim and my skin. I knew I'd been losing weight because of worry and marital stress, but I hadn't paid attention to how much. I caught the hem of my shirt beneath my chin and looked down at my stomach. It was—*amazing!*—practically flat.

I went to the closet and surveyed my outdated clothes: pleated pants, jackets with padded shoulders, tailored blouses—all from my nineties library days. I looked through my dresser drawers. They were filled with the comfortable sweatshirts and sweatpants that I slouched around the house in every day. I had nothing the least bit stylish or sexy.

The Capable Mom look had to go. If Greg was so bent on spending his every waking hour traveling and working, then I was going to enjoy the fruits of his labor with some passive-aggressive clothes shopping.

The upscale boutiques on Main Street had pretentious, lyrical names: Lotus, Peppermint Stick, Aria. I'd never ventured into any of them before because they were so expensive, but high prices weren't going to get in my way today.

The first shop I went into offered a sparse inventory of tony clothing. I peeked at the tags and the prices shocked me. Eight hundred and fifty dollars for a scarf. Two thousand dollars for a handbag! The anorexic saleswoman walked up and cast a skeptical eye over me. I gave her a polite nod and zipped out the door.

Next door was the Gap, which was much more my style. I picked out shorts and fitted T's from the sale rack, but I paid full price for two pairs of boot-cut jeans and some cute sweaters. I studied my figure in the dressing room mirror and was astonished by how good I looked.

Emboldened, I walked with confidence into the next shop. I tried on a beautiful sheath dress in spring-green silk and spun myself before the three-paneled mirror. I could pair the dress with a pashmina shawl and wear it out to dinner with Greg some evening. We could have a date night like those women's magazines at the pediatrician's office were always harping about. I allowed the polished salesclerk to talk me into opening a store account, and I threw in a matching clutch and a crazy expensive pair of shoes to go with my pretty dress.

I dropped my shopping bags off at the minivan and crossed the street to Wayfield Books. Carla had recommended I do some reading. I gravitated by discreet degrees toward the Self-Improvement section in the back, looked around to be sure no one was watching me, and side-stepped over to the Marriage and Relationships shelf. I scanned the titles as fast as I could. I came to a book called *Salvage Your Marriage*, plucked it from the shelf, paid for it, and stuffed it into my purse. I'd start reading it tonight after the kids were in bed.

There was a beauty salon next to the bookstore. I paused on the sidewalk and studied my reflection in the glass. My hair was dull and limp from neglect. I could get it cut shoulder length for a change, maybe try some highlights. I went inside and made an appointment.

On the way home, I stopped at a traffic light, and the white steeple of Saint Rita's Catholic Church glared at me from the opposite street corner. The inescapable flood of guilt rushed in. I'd been putting a ton of effort into getting us settled in Wayfield, but I hadn't given church a single thought. I'd pretty much given up on it in Seattle, when Greg started spending his weekends on the golf course. Trying to get two small children to behave themselves through a long Sunday Mass was a weekly trial that I'd grown weary of dealing with on my own.

But Becky and Nate were older now, and taking them to church would be a lot easier than it used to. As long as I was on this self-improvement spree, I might as well throw some religion in there too. It certainly couldn't hurt. Nate would be due to make his First Communion before long. I needed to get my children's religious education back on track.

I checked my watch to see how much time was left before school let out. I had ten minutes to spare, to dash inside Saint Rita's and square myself with the Church.

The inside of the building was hushed and dim and smelled of polished wood and candles. The sanctuary lamp glowed red on the altar. I knelt in a pew at the back, crossed myself, and closed my eyes. I dredged up the prayers I'd been taught in grammar school: the Our Father, the Hail Mary, the Memorare, the Act of Contrition. As I recited the words, a peaceful feeling settled over me. When my allotted time was up, I crossed myself again and rose to leave.

In the vestibule, I picked up a church newsletter from the wooden rack, and the whoosh of guilt returned. When Carla and I were teenagers, we'd sometimes stop into Blessed Sacrament on Saturday afternoons, grab the weekly bulletin, and bring it home to our mothers as false proof that we'd gone to the four o'clock Vigil Mass. It was our ticket to sleeping in on Sunday morning.

I smiled to myself and put the newsletter into my purse. I would call the parish office tomorrow and register the Mercer family, and then I'd tell Greg we were going to church this weekend. Tell, not ask. It was going to be our routine from now on. And after we'd been to Mass, when he was still feeling virtuous, I'd revisit the subject of marriage counseling. I was tired of walking on eggshells around him, afraid to say anything that might upset our fragile truce.

– – –

Greg's answer was an emphatic *No*. "I already told you, I do not want to discuss my personal business with anyone." He opened the paper bag of bagels we'd picked up on the way home from church and poked his hand into it. "Do you want plain or sesame?"

"I don't care."

"Pick one."

"Whatever. I don't care."

"It's a simple question, Jeanie. Just tell me what you want." He waited for me to answer, a bagel in each hand.

"Hello, are you deaf or something?" I said. "Or do you not understand what 'I don't care' means?" I peeled the wrapper off a stick of butter and flipped it onto a dish. Why was I bickering over a stupid bagel? I didn't seem able to stop myself. "Since when do you care what I want anyway?"

"Oh, I see. I see what this is about now. You're pissed because I won't go to marriage counseling."

"That's right, I am pissed. It isn't fair that you won't even give it a try."

"I keep telling you, we don't need it. We're fine. Paying a total stranger to listen to us gripe about a bunch of petty stuff is a waste of time and money. You're getting all worked up over nothing."

I wanted to slap the complacent look off his face and tell him to shut the hell up. I clenched my fists to stop myself from acting on the impulse. That was something a crazy woman would do. I was losing it.

"You're an asshole," I said, "and I'm sick of it." I snatched the plain bagel from his hand and stomped out of the kitchen.

The elementary school was holding a Family Night on the second Friday in October. Becky read the flyer out loud to us: "Pizza and soda will be served in the cafeteria at six o'clock, followed by a screening of *Shrek* in the gym."

Greg smiled at her across the dinner table. "Sounds like it'll be fun."

"If you're even here for it," I said and splatted mashed potatoes onto his plate.

His face twitched in annoyance. "Was that really necessary?"

"You're never here for anything, so why would this event be any different?"

Becky's face fell. "You have to come, Dad."

Nate smeared a blob of mashed potato across his plate with his pinky finger. "Yeah, Dad, you have to come."

"Of course, I'll come." Greg took the sign-up form from Becky and filled it out: Mercer, family of four.

Dusk was falling that Friday evening when Greg called from Charlotte to say he'd been bumped to a later flight. I hung up on him. I took a flashlight from the closet and called upstairs to the kids: "Come on, it's time to go."

Becky came into the kitchen. "Where's Dad?" She had brushed her hair and put on her sparkly purple headband.

I didn't want to disappoint her just yet. "He's on his way home," I said. "He'll meet us at school as soon as he can."

The cafeteria was abuzz with children and parents. I spotted a woman named Ann whom I had gotten to know from volunteering in Becky's classroom. The kids and I wove our way around the crowded tables to sit with her and her family. When everyone had finished eating, the principal flickered the lights on and off, and we all moved into the gymnasium. I checked my cell phone before the room went dark, but there was nothing from Greg.

I checked twice more during the movie, but still no word from him. My irritation faded and was replaced by worry. There might have been a mechanical issue with his plane, or maybe the flight had been rerouted due to weather, or perhaps he was mad at me for hanging up on him. There was always the fear of another terrorist attack, but I wasn't going to think about that.

The Shrek in the Swamp Karaoke Dance Party reached its boisterous finale, and I felt around on the floor for Becky's and Nate's jackets. The lights came on, and I herded the kids toward the exit doors, anxious to get back and check the home phone for a message.

The cold night air felt good after the stuffy gym. We cut across the ball field, leaving dark footprints on the frosty grass. The stars were out but there was no moon. I clicked my flashlight on when we got to the wooded path. The beam shone strong for a few seconds, then began to fade, then died. "Oooo, it's dark," Nate said and reached for my hand.

There was another family several yards ahead of us, and the father had a giant Maglite that lit up the trees around them. I pulled Becky and Nate along, and we followed close behind them to where the path forked at the footbridge. The family veered off to the right, leaving us in the dark again. We shuffled through the fallen leaves until we came out of the woods and stepped into the bright pool of the streetlight. Down the street, I could see lights on in our living room. Greg was home.

We found him sitting in front of the television, scrolling through messages on his Blackberry. Becky and Nate ran to him. "How was the pizza and movie?" he asked.

"You missed *Shrek*," said Nate. "It was really good."

I set the dead flashlight on the coffee table. "When did you get home?"

"Couple hours ago."

"You mean you've been sitting here this whole time?"

"I was on the phone wrapping up some loose ends. Got a lot going on."

My inner bitch surfaced. "Yeah, me too."

He locked his Blackberry and dropped it into his shirt pocket. "Why are you giving me this attitude?"

"Why do you think?"

"For chrissakes, Jeanie, would you quit it? I come home in a fantastic mood with good news to share with you, and you've gotta be a total buzzkill."

The kids were staring at us. We needed to stop arguing in front of them. "Sorry," I mumbled. "I'll go up and get them ready for bed. Then you can tell me about your week."

When I returned to the living room, Greg had poured himself a scotch and was stretched out on the couch. He'd taken his dress shirt off and draped it over the back of the couch. His arms looked muscular, and his chest was well-defined beneath the thin fabric of his undershirt. The yoga was definitely making a difference. He moved his legs aside so I could sit with him. "Your hair is different," he said. "Looks good." He took a swig from his drink. "Well, babe, I did it. I landed the client."

"That's great. Congratulations."

"I've already got a team in place, and they hit the ground running yesterday. We're gonna do a full-scale analysis of the company's ops and develop a series of workstreams to actualize the deliverables. There's a ton of work in the pipeline, and the client's already talking about expanding our scope."

I didn't have a clue what he was talking about. "Wow," I said, for lack of anything more intelligent to say.

He rattled the ice in his glass. "I really hit a home run when I nailed this one. It's the talk of the firm. Everybody wants a piece of me now."

I was sure they did. So did I. "How often will you have to go down to Charlotte now?"

He looked at me like I was some kind of moron. "Every week. This is a full-time deal for me."

"Full-time as in Monday through Friday?"

"Well, yeah. I need to stay on top of my team so they don't go off the rails."

Ah, yes, his team. "How long will the project go on for?"

"I don't know. Several months at least. Maybe a year."

I felt my blood pressure shoot up. Was he out of his mind? "We just got settled in Massachusetts, and now you're going to be spending all your time in North Carolina?"

He raised his chin, defiant. "It's my job. What do you expect me to do?"

Warning lights flashed and buzzers blared in my brain, but I went on with it anyway: "You lied to me. You said this job wouldn't require any travel."

"It's always the same old shit with you, isn't it? I didn't lie to you. That's what the firm told me when I was hired. My situation has changed since then. Royce is fast-tracking me to partner, and I need to do whatever it takes."

"You told me things would be different here. Look at us—we have no friends because you're never around for us to do anything with anybody. I thought this move would be a good thing for us, but it's turned out to be a huge disappointment instead."

He banged his glass onto the table and stood up. "So, I'm a disappointment now?"

"No, that's not—"

"I work my ass off for my family, and you're disappointed in me? What kind of a wife says that to her husband?" He got in my face. "*Huh?*"

I shrank from him. "I didn't mean it like that, Greg! I know how hard you work."

He gave his desk chair a shove, and it glanced off the wall in a crazy spin. "I don't want to hear it. I'm a businessman. I travel. Deal with it, Jeanette. I'm sick of your fucking complaints."

I positioned the chair between us and stabbed my finger at him. "There you go again, avoiding the issue. We're not going to solve anything if we don't talk about this. If you'd agree to go to counseling like I keep asking you to, we might get somewhere instead of arguing all the time. We can't go on like this, Greg. We're not communicating."

"You should talk about not communicating. You're the one who's been hiding secrets from me for all these years. You're the one who screwed your professor—"

"*Stop saying that.*" My fingers clutching the chair were a bloodless white. I was so furious I thought I might pick it up and hurl it at him.

He eyed me for a long, cautious moment and seemed to be weighing something in his mind. At last he threw his hands up. "Okay, okay, enough of this. We'll go to counseling, all right? But if it turns out to be a whole lot of useless happy talk, I quit. I don't have time to waste on bullshit."

Chapter 19

The Mercers flew up to Boston over Columbus weekend, to view the fall foliage and do some sightseeing. Florence booked a two-bedroom suite at the Marriott on the wharf, and we met them there on Saturday morning.

Becky and Nate ran to their grandad, but they shied away when Florence descended on them in her voluminous Chico's caftan. I gave them both a look, and they submitted to her embraces, but then they edged back over to Howard.

He gave me a warm hug. "It's good to see you, young lady. I hope y'all brought your walking shoes. Flor's been busy as all get out, making a list of landmarks for us to visit."

Gordon and Ricki came out of the adjoining room and greeted us. There was no sign of their son. "Where's Preston?" Greg asked.

Ricki stuck her nose in the air. "He's attending Brandon Hall now. He's playing in a junior football tournament this weekend, so he had to stay at home with a sitter."

Florence went over to the writing table and picked up a laminated map of Boston and a guidebook that was bristling with Post-it Notes. "We need to get going, people," she singsonged. "We've got a lot on our agenda today. We're going to walk the Freedom Trail from Quincy Market to the Public Garden."

Howard patted his grandchildren's shoulders and winked at me behind his wife's back. "All right, Flor, we'll do our best to keep up."

The day was overcast and chilly, so I made Becky and Nate put their hats and mittens on. We followed Florence and Ricki out of the hotel, the three men trailing behind us. Our first stop was the statue of Samuel Adams outside Faneuil Hall. Florence raised her hand for attention and began to read aloud from her guidebook. Gordon's cell phone rang as she was enumerating the colonists' objections to the loathsome British, and he took the call without stepping away from us. Florence left off reading in mid-sentence and moved on in a huff.

We proceeded to the Old State House. Florence produced her guidebook once again and told us of the Crown's treachery at the Boston Massacre. Howard and his sons stood off to one side, quietly conversing. I noticed Gordon was going prematurely gray and he'd put on a good deal of weight. "New England sucks," I heard him say to Greg as we crossed the cobblestones, heading for the Old South Meeting House. "Too friggin' cold here. Why don't you come back down south?"

I turned around. "We just got here a few months ago, Gordon. We wouldn't want to move again so soon."

He ignored me. "You've got a big client in Charlotte now, right?" he said to Greg. You should ask the firm to relocate you."

I saw Greg and his father exchange a glance. "It's a short-term project," Greg said. "I won't be working there that long. Relocating wouldn't be worth it."

"Suit yourself, bro." Gordon turned up his coat collar. "Enjoy freezing your balls off this winter." I shot a dirty look at his wide rear end. *Shut up, Gordo. Mind your own business.*

We ate a lunch of hotdogs from a street vendor and walked to the Common. Becky and Nate were tired and in agonies of boredom, but Florence insisted we finish her tour. Howard promised them a ride on the Swan Boats, and we pushed onward to the Public Garden. Greg took a turn watching the kids, and I deliberately lagged behind the group, wanting a break from Ricki's incessant chatter.

Howard slowed his pace so he could walk beside me. "How have you been, Miss Jeanie?"

"I've been fine, thanks. Keeping busy with the kids and learning my way around the area."

He smiled at me, and his expression was kind and gentle. He went on in a lower voice: "I know you and Greg went through a rough patch a while back. Is everything all right with you two now?"

I hesitated a second before answering. "Not exactly. I did manage to persuade him to go to marriage counseling, but he keeps putting it off."

"And why is that? Is he unwilling to go?"

"No, he agreed to it. It's work that keeps getting in the way. He's always so busy."

The Swan Boats came into view; Becky and Nate shrieked with joy and raced ahead. Howard looked thoughtful. "I'll have a talk with him if you like. I'll encourage him to make this a priority."

I hugged his arm. "I'd really appreciate that."

We reached the pond. I sat on a bench with Greg while Howard took the kids to get in line for the boats. Florence removed another travel guide from her shoulder bag and announced the plan for tomorrow: we were all going to take a scenic drive up the coast. I disguised my pained sigh with a cough.

Ricki called me early the next morning. "Just to let you know, we can't make the drive today. Gordon's got some work to catch up on, so I'm staying here at the hotel to keep him company. He's going to treat me to a mani and pedi this afternoon."

Shoot. Ricki was a crucial buffer between Florence and me. "Anyway, I hope you have a great time today!" she said in the same singsongy voice as our mother-in-law. "And I'd better tell you, Mom's in a mood today. Just warning you."

We met Florence and Howard in the Marriott lobby at ten o'clock, climbed into the roomy Chevy Suburban that the hotel concierge had procured for us, and drove out of the city, heading northeast toward Cape Ann.

Howard drove, and Greg sat up front with him. Florence was in a mood all right, and she had it in for her husband. She leaned into the front seat, barking directions and finding fault with his driving. When we reached the vicinity of the Cape, she ordered him onto the back roads in search of obscure landmarks that she'd read about in her guidebook. She railed at him for driving too fast one minute and too slow the next. When he made a wrong turn, she erupted. "Not *here*, numb nuts! I said the *second* left." I hoped Becky and Nate couldn't hear her from their seats back in the third row.

Every few miles, Florence made us get out of the vehicle to investigate historic markers and falling-down barns and piles of rocks. Her bitchiness increased with each stop. Howard muttered under his breath and turned up the radio. He appeared to develop hearing loss and didn't pull over the next time he was ordered to.

"Why don't you listen?" Florence carped. "Howard, did you hear me?"

Greg glanced over his shoulder at me, and I gave him a questioning look: *What is up with your mother today?*

He shrugged. *Beats me.*

We stopped for lunch at a roadside diner, then resumed our pilgrimage. Howard turned the Suburban onto a sandy road, and we drew up in front of a lighthouse, the first place of interest to the kids all day. Florence referred to her guidebook as we climbed out. "This is the famous Straitsmouth Light."

"It's the Annisquam Harbor Light, dear." Howard elbowed Greg and pointed to a placard affixed to the fence.

"You're actually correct." Florence clapped her guidebook shut. "That's the first time today. How does it feel to be right for a change?"

I pulled Becky and Nate through the gate and up the walkway, to get away from her. Florence trotted off to photograph the lighthouse from every possible angle, and the kids and I explored the grounds by ourselves. Greg and his father had stayed behind in the parking lot, and I looked back at them several times. They were deep in conversation, with Howard doing most of the talking and Greg occasionally nodding. *Thank you, Howard,* I thought. *Thank you for caring and trying to help us.*

We climbed back into the Suburban, drove a few more miles to a state park on the northernmost tip of the Cape, piled out, and followed a seashelled trail along the shore until we came to a high outcropping of rock. Greg boosted the kids up, then extended his hands to his mother and me. We stood on our windy perch, taking in the broad sweep of water and sky. The ocean breeze whipped Florence's hairdo into disarray; she took a light scarf from her coat pocket and tied it over her head. She circled her arms around Becky and Nate and drew them close, and the hard set of her mouth softened. Howard moved over to stand with them.

I forgot myself for a moment in the dazzle of shimmery sunlight, but then Florence was on the move again with her damned guidebook. "There's a historic marker at the end of this path," she shouted to us over the wind. "Just another quarter of a mile or so." I groaned. Becky and Nate were tired and thirsty, and I'd left the backpack with our water bottles in the Suburban.

I followed Florence down the path, and a few minutes later, Greg came up beside me and handed me a plastic bottle. "I ran back to the car and got us something to drink."

"Thank you," I said, surprised. We paused to share the water with Becky and Nate, and then they skipped ahead of us on the sandy trail, giggling at the silly story their grandad was telling them. Florence bestowed a rare smile on her husband. Greg fell in step with me, and his arm brushed against mine. He took my hand as we came up to the historic marker, and I caught a glimpse of a smile on his father's face.

I made an appointment with a marriage and family therapist named Suzette who had a small private practice over in Cambridge. Greg agreed to take that Friday afternoon off from work, and he flew home from Charlotte for our first session.

We sat side by side on the love seat in Suzette's office, and I listened attentively as she gave us a practiced marital pep talk: "Don't despair. It took a long time for you to get to this place in your marriage, and it will take a long time for you to get out of it. You're going through difficulties now, but if you're committed to doing some hard work, you'll get through this, and your marriage will be stronger for it."

She explained her objectives: First, she wanted to hear the history of our relationship—how we met, what our courtship was like, why we decided to get married. Second, she wanted to learn about us as individuals—what were our childhoods like? How did we get along with our siblings? What values did we learn from our parents?

"The families we grow up in have a major influence on how we relate to other people as adults," she explained. "And they particularly influence our interactions with our spouse within the marriage."

A light blinked on—I'd heard this before. Family of origin. All of a sudden, I was back at our Pre-Cana class in the church basement. Suzette went on talking but I wasn't listening anymore. If only I had paid better attention back then and taken more time to think things through. I might not be sitting here in a therapist's office with my emotions all in a twist. I might not even be married to Greg.

Forty-five minutes passed, and Suzette began to wrap things up. "In our next session we'll explore the subconscious roots of your conflict, and then we'll begin to rewrite the narrative of your relationship." She sounded like Carla with all the jargon. I looked sideways at Greg and his face was a blank. Suzette marked us down in her Day-Timer for the same time slot on the following Friday and walked us out to the waiting room.

Greg waited until the elevator doors had slid shut. "That's it for me," he said, punching the button for the ground floor. "Exactly what I expected. Nothing but bullshit."

Chapter 20

After all the fun we had on our weekend with the Mercers, I insisted on spending Thanksgiving with my family in Adams Mills.

My sister Marian called me the week before. "I'm at Mom and Dad's house. It turns out Dad had a doctor's appointment last week that he didn't tell anybody about. His prostate was enlarged, and his PSA was elevated, so Mom drove him up to the VA for a biopsy. He'll get the results next Wednesday."

"I had no idea," I said.

"Me neither. I only just heard about it tonight. Hold on, Dad wants to talk to you."

My father's gruff voice came on the line. His speech was a little thick, a permanent effect of his stroke. "Don't worry, your sister says she'll go to the doctor with me, so I'll have another pair of ears. Your mother doesn't hear so well these days."

Marian took the phone back. "Just a sec, I'm going outside." I heard the porch slider open and close, and then she came back on. "Memory loss is more likely Mom's problem, not her hearing. Dad keeps covering for her and thinks we don't notice."

"Really? How bad is it?"

"Hard to say. She's asked me twice when his follow-up appointment is, even though it's written right here on the calendar, and Dad said she got lost on the way back from the VA. After we find out what's going on with him, I'm going to take her in for a checkup."

I let this news register. Dad might have cancer and Mom might have—what? Alzheimer's? I shuddered.

"I thought you'd better know about Mom before you came," Marian said. "We've all gotten kind of used to her forgetfulness, but it's been a while since you've seen her, and I didn't want you to be shocked. Eileen thinks it'd be better if you stayed at her house instead so there's less stress on Mom and Dad. I'll call you next Wednesday, as soon as Dad gets his test results."

Wednesday was a half day of school. I packed the minivan in the morning, and we were on the road by twelve thirty, but the Turnpike was already clogged with traffic. Greg had work to take care of, so I drove. He plugged his laptop into the power port, donned his headset, and gave us all a stern warning to be quiet if his phone rang.

The congestion on the Pike opened up after we passed the I-84 interchange, and I pressed my foot to the accelerator, glad to be free of the bumper-to-bumper crawl. I checked the time and saw it was after three, which meant Marian would be calling soon. I prayed silently: *Please, God. Please don't let it be cancer.*

Greg lifted his eyes from his computer screen. "Jeanie."

My mind jerked back into the van. "What?"

"You're speeding."

I looked at the speedometer and saw I was doing eighty. "Whoops." I eased off the gas and set the cruise control.

My cell phone jingled in the cupholder; Greg opened it and handed it to me. Marian laid it out without any preamble. "Dad has prostate cancer. It's already spread. He has to start chemotherapy and radiation treatments right away."

The lines on the road blurred. "I'm driving," I said in a shaky voice. "We're on the Turnpike. Can I call you back after we get to Eileen's tonight?" We said goodbye, and I clapped the phone shut and handed it back to Greg. I gulped for breath, trying to compose myself.

"Bad news?"

"Marian says Dad has prostate cancer."

"Prostrate? Isn't that one pretty easy to treat?"

I didn't bother to correct his pronunciation. "She says it's spread." A speeding car cut in front of me without signaling, and I stomped on the brakes. The luggage in the back shifted with a bump, and Ginger's head popped up in the rearview mirror.

"Dickhead," Greg said and flipped the bird. "Are you okay?"

I swallowed hard and nodded.

"Hang tough, babe."

What the hell did that even mean, *hang tough*? Why couldn't he say something normal, like *I'm sorry* or *I'm here for you*? I loosened my death grip on the steering wheel and checked Ginger in the rearview. She turned around three times and disappeared. We crossed into Connecticut, then New York, then Pennsylvania. The interstate receded into darkness.

It was late when we arrived in Adams Mills, so we went straight to Eileen's house instead of stopping at my parents' first. Eileen and her husband, Todd, lived two miles outside town in an added-on ranch house with their four homeschooled teenagers, two foster kids, and three slobbery rescue mutts. "You can bring your dog with you," Todd had said. "One more won't make any difference around here. You could leave one of your kids behind when you leave, and we probably wouldn't even notice we had an extra."

Becky and Nate disappeared with their cousins into the warren of bedrooms at one end of the house, and Greg carried our bags to the spare room at the other end. The room held a beat-up metal desk that was piled with schoolbooks and dented art projects. A girl's ice skate with a rusty blade weighed down a sheaf of papers that looked like last year's tax return, and a basket of unfolded laundry was wedged between the arms of the chair. Proudly overseeing it all was an eight-point buck's head, mounted on the wall above the desk.

"Is that locked?" Greg asked, pointing at Todd's glass-fronted gun cabinet in the corner.

"Yeah, of course it is. Eileen says Todd's going to take you trap shooting at the Fish and Game Club on Saturday."

"Fish and Game? Are you serious?"

"Yeah, all the guys are going." I poked him in the side. "It's fun, you'll like it. I used to go all the time when I was a teenager. My dad taught me to shoot there."

"I think I'll have to pass on that one." His gaze shifted from the Winchesters and Remingtons to the fold-out couch that had been made up with a worn set of flowered sheets that I recognized as hand-me-downs from my parents. He set our bags on the floor with a sigh.

Marian and Debra came over after dinner, and we stayed up late, discussing Dad's medical situation and what we could do to help as he underwent his treatments. They left around eleven thirty, long after Greg had gone to sleep. I eased into the squeaky bed in the dark, felt for the hard frame beneath the flimsy mattress, and curled up in a hollow between the bars. Greg stirred, gave my shoulder a quick double pat, and whispered, "Sorry about your dad." I squeezed my eyes shut and cried into my lumpy pillow. My parents' lives were falling apart, and the best my husband could do was pat me on the shoulder.

Mom and Dad came over in the morning. Dad looked pale and tired, and he was leaning heavily on his cane, but he made an effort to be cheerful for the kids. Mom gave big hugs all around but stayed mostly by Dad's side, letting her daughters take charge of the cooking.

"It's better if she stays out of the kitchen," Debra said as she peeled the sweet potatoes and I thickened the gravy. "She served us an awful coffee cake after church last Sunday. I think she forgot the baking powder."

When the meal was ready, we gathered around the kitchen table. Todd had extended it with plywood leaves that Eileen had camouflaged with her calico tablecloths. None of the chairs matched, and Becky and Nate were sitting on cushions on top of an old piano bench. Todd said grace, and then we went around the table as we'd always done, taking turns saying what we were thankful for. The kids mostly copied one another: they were grateful for apple pie, the drumstick, WrestleMania. The grown-ups were all grateful for their children. No one mentioned their health.

Greg's turn came last. "I'm thankful to be here this weekend with my wonderful extended family." My sisters beamed and raised their glasses of Cella Lambrusco, and Todd and the other guys held up their beers. I looked at Greg and thought, *You phony.*

"Amen," said Dad. "Let's dig in."

Greg wanted to leave on Saturday instead of Sunday, to avoid the traffic and the trap shooting. I faked a stomachache from too much pumpkin pie so that he would have to drive this time. I slumped in the passenger's seat with my arms wrapped around my middle and closed my eyes so I wouldn't have to talk. I was worn out from pretending to my family that everything was all right between us. We were definitely not okay. Something was pulling my husband away from me, and I didn't know what to do about it.

When we got home that evening, I took a long hot shower and went to bed. I was feeling genuinely ill now—whether from the pie or anxiety, I wasn't sure. Greg got in bed beside me, and I curled away from him. We lay there for a while without speaking, but his breathing sounded funny. He moved closer to me, and I felt his hardness pressing against the small of my back. I pushed up on one elbow and looked at him. He lay flat on his back. "Come on, babe," he said. "I need some action."

The last thing I wanted to do tonight was service Gregory Mercer. I covered my mouth with my hand. "Ew, I'm feeling sick again." I jumped out of bed and ran to the bathroom. When I was done faking sick, I went to the living room and spent the rest of the night on the couch.

Greg flew to Charlotte on Sunday and said he'd be gone for the week. I called Carla after the kids were asleep that night. "Greg acted like he didn't even care what's going on with my parents," I said. "He hardly talked to anyone the whole time we were at Eileen's, except to brag about his job. When I told him my sisters and I are planning to take turns helping out my parents, he was like, 'Fine, but only if it doesn't conflict with my travel schedule.'"

"Wait a minute," Carla said. "I read something the other day. It's in this issue of *Psychology Today* somewhere." I heard pages flipping. "Here it is. Narcissistic Personality Disorder." She named the defining characteristics: "A sense of entitlement." *Check.* "Excessive need for admiration." *Check.* "An inability to empathize with other people's feelings." *Check.*

What had happened to the Greg I'd fallen in love with? The sweet, caring guy who had proposed to me on Peachtree Street? "That sounds like Greg all right," I said, "but what am I supposed to do about it, Carla? I can't change him."

"No, you can't, but this article says if you try to understand the underlying reasons for the person's behavior, you can change how you respond to him." She read aloud: "'The narcissist believes he is a superior being who deserves to have his needs taken care of by others.' Your needs are important too, Jeanie. Greg has got to treat you with respect and allow you to tell him how you feel about things."

"Believe me, I've tried, but he doesn't seem to care. I'm not sure if I care anymore either. Every discussion we try to have turns into an argument unless I give in to him."

I told her how I'd faked sick to avoid an argument about sex. "That's not right," she said. "You need to stand up for yourself." I could hear cupboards opening and closing and the clinking of cutlery and glassware. "You've got to grow some backbone. Stop being a doormat."

"I know," I said miserably. "But how?" What leverage did I have? I had no family nearby to turn to for emotional support and hardly a friend here besides Ann, who was really no more than an acquaintance.

"You could tell him you're leaving him." Carla's words were garbled, like she was chewing on something.

"Are you kidding me?"

"I don't mean you really would leave, but you could threaten to if things don't change."

"I can't do that."

"Why not?"

"He might not care. He might call my bluff, and then what would I do? I have no job and nowhere to go except back to Adams Mills, and I can't face that. You know what it would do to my parents if I left Greg, especially right now, with all their health problems. And what about my kids and what it would do to them? I don't want a divorce, Carla. I want things to get better."

"It doesn't mean you'd get divorced. It would shake him up. Make him realize what's at stake."

My insides wobbled. I couldn't risk it. The whole thing would probably backfire on me. *The Boston Globe* had recently run a story about a state representative who was proposing legislation that would phase out alimony in divorce settlements. If Greg and I got divorced, I'd have to get a full-time job to support myself. The reality of that had hit me like a shock. The world had gone digital and my skills were obsolete. My lack of a college degree and my pitiful scraps of experience as a library assistant had left me way behind the times.

"Just think about it." Carla chewed some more and swallowed. "You can't do anything until after Christmas anyway. You wouldn't want to do that to your kids."

She was right about that, but I was so tired of being trapped in this life. Greg and I were woefully out of sync—he was the privileged boss, and I was the lowly hired help. We didn't have a marriage; we had a business arrangement. If we split up, I'd be forced to find some way to make things work for me. I'd have to become my own person.

"You know what, Carla?" I said. "I've had enough of this shit."

"That's right, and you're not gonna take it anymore!" A utensil rang against china on her end. "You deserve better, Jeanie. You're emotionally starving. You've been a good wife all these years, taking care of Greg and his home and his children while he traipses all over the frigging country doing God knows what with God knows who. Are you sure he's not cheating on you? With someone he works with, maybe?"

A trap door in my stomach swung open, and all my courage dropped out. "I can't even think about that."

"The signs are there, Jeanie. You can't keep sweeping this under the rug."

I didn't want to think about it, but I knew I had to. The anxiety and uncertainty were gnawing away at me. I had no appetite at all, and the clothes I'd bought not so long ago were becoming loose on me. I'd have to push through the next few weeks until Christmas, and then I'd reassess my situation. Whatever I decided to do, it would have to wait until the new year. I couldn't ruin Christmas for my kids.

"I know what," Carla said. "Why don't you have yourself a little fling while His Royal Gregness is out of town? Find yourself a hot guy out there in Wayfield, maybe a volunteer fireman or one of those Revolutionary War reenactors that go around in those tights—"

I had to laugh. My girl Carla did know how to lighten things up. "Stop it," I said. "You know I'd never do anything like that."

I dreamed of Ed that night. We were alone together and he was kissing me, and then things blurred and shifted the way they do in dreams, and we were in bed, naked, and we were *so close*—and then the image evaporated.

I couldn't go there, even in a dream.

Chapter 21

Greg was hungover from the first class upgrade he'd been given on his flight back from Charlotte the night before, but after he'd had his coffee, he went into the living room where Becky and Nate were watching cartoons, turned the TV off, and clapped his hands at them. "Who wants to go pick out a Christmas tree?" The kids leaped from the couch with joyful shouts.

The parking lot at Saint Rita's had been turned into a snowy Christmas market. Spruces and firs were arranged in long rows, and evergreen wreaths and bunches of holly were displayed on the wooden cafeteria tables. A Christmassy scent filled the air, and Bing Crosby crooned from the speakers that had been rigged on makeshift light posts. The kids whirled through the maze of trees, pointing and shouting.

"Look, Mommy." Becky pulled me down a row and stopped in front of a perfectly shaped tree that was about as high as my head.

Nate stamped his rubber boots on the frozen asphalt. "It's too small!" Greg stood behind us, smiling vacantly. He was wearing his overcoat and wool scarf, and his gloved hands were jammed into his armpits. Nate dashed away and I jogged after him, trying to keep him in sight. He skidded to a halt three rows over and jumped up and down in a frenzy. "This one, this one!"

Greg and Becky caught up to us, and we all gazed up at a big blue spruce tree. I reached out to touch it, and the sharp needles poked through the fingers of my knitted gloves. "Ouch," I said. "I'm afraid this one's too big, guys. It won't fit in our house."

Greg turned over the price tag and winced. "Kind of steep." He shrugged, turned his collar up, and signaled to one of the volunteers.

"Wait a minute," I said. "It's too big."

"It's fine." He spoke to a burly man in a Carhartt jacket. "We'll take this one." Becky and Nate cheered.

We drove home with the huge tree hanging over the windshield of the minivan. Greg scissored through the yards of twine and untied it from the roof. Becky and Nate watched, barely able to contain themselves. "Stand back, kids," Greg said as we got into position. We each grabbed hold of a branch. "Ready?" he said. "Go."

The tree started to slide, and I lost my grip on it. Greg jumped out of the way, and the full weight of it struck me in the chest and knocked me backward. I hit the icy driveway square on my tailbone, and a flash of pain shot up my spine.

"Mom! Mom! Are you okay?" the kids yelled.

"I'm all right," I gasped. The enormous tree lay across my lap. I peered through the mass of branches. "Greg?" I could see him standing there, his hands hanging at his sides. "Can you get this off me?"

He pushed his coat sleeves up, grasped the trunk, and began to pull. Branches snagged my hair and scratched my face. "Stop," I shouted. "Don't pull it like that. You're hurting me. Try standing it up."

With a grunt he levered the tree upright, and Becky and Nate fell on me and began picking twigs out of my hair. Greg dragged the tree around the side of the garage and let it drop on the ground with a thump. The kids pulled on my arms, and I got slowly to my feet and brushed the needles off the front of my coat. My lower back was throbbing.

"You okay?" said Greg.

"I think so, except for here." I rubbed my tailbone. Becky wrapped her arms around my waist, and Nate hugged my leg.

Greg inspected his gloves for blemishes. "Let's go inside. It's freezing out here."

"What about the tree? We need to bring it inside and put it in water."

"It can wait."

Becky spoke up. "The tree needs water, Daddy. The man said."

Greg held his ground. "We'll do it this afternoon."

After lunch, Becky and Nate clamored to put the tree up, but Greg said he had a headache and went into the bedroom to take a nap. I went down to the cellar to bring up our Christmas decorations. As I bent to pick up one of the bins, I felt another shot of pain in my back. I ended up pushing the three bins with my feet, across the dusty concrete floor to the stairs, and boosted them up the steps one at a time.

Nate occupied himself with a stack of Christmas books, and Becky got to work setting up our nativity set. She arranged and rearranged the little figurines, trying to position the cows and the donkeys for optimal viewing of the Baby Jesus. I swallowed an Advil, filled a Ziploc bag with ice, and sat with it wedged behind my lower back, waiting for the pain to subside.

It began to grow dark around four o'clock, and I turned on the living room lamps. Greg had been napping for quite a while. I went to our bedroom door and listened; I didn't hear anything, so I turned the knob and went in. The lights were off, and Greg was sitting hunched on the bed with his Blackberry to his ear. He jumped when he saw me. I mouthed "Sorry" and backed out of the room.

I got dinner started. I heard Greg in the other room a few minutes later, speaking to Becky and Nate. "What's up, kiddos? Who's got a hug for Dad?" I turned the heat down on the stove and went in to join them. Greg's eyes were unnaturally bright, as though he might be running a fever.

Nate tugged at his father's sleeve. "Can we put up the tree now? Can we, can we?"

"We'll have to do it tomorrow," I said. "When Daddy feels better. He needs to rest right now." I felt Greg's forehead. "Do you think you're coming down with something?"

"Nah," he said. "I'm just beat is all."

He said he felt fine the next morning, so we went to church, then picked up our dozen bagels on the way home. He measured coffee and water into the coffee maker while I got out the cutting board and the knife to slice the bagels. "By the way," he said casually, "I'm gonna have to catch an afternoon flight to Charlotte. The client wants to meet with me first thing in the morning."

I felt a familiar sinking feeling. I carefully worked the point of the knife into a bagel. "How long will you be gone?"

"Can't say. It'll take most of the week to sort things out. The company's overloaded with holiday orders, and things are getting all fucked up."

Nate looked up at his dad. "Fugged up," he repeated.

Greg frowned at him. "That's enough, son." He got out mugs and spoons, avoiding my eye.

We'd been planning to go Christmas shopping for the kids this week, and I already had a babysitter lined up. I pictured the knife slicing through my hand, blood gushing to the floor. What would Greg do? Probably stand there staring while I bled to death. I set the knife down and stepped away from the counter. I was definitely going nuts.

– – –

Greg called from Charlotte on Monday night to tell me he needed to stay there through Thursday at least, and on Thursday he said he couldn't possibly get away till late on Friday. Becky and Nate continued to pester me about putting up the tree, but I held firm: Christmas was supposed to be the season of family togetherness. We would wait to put the tree up when their father got home.

I picked up a DVD of *Santa Claus Is Comin' to Town* and made Becky and Nate their favorite macaroni and cheese casserole for supper that Friday night. Greg had said his flight was due in at five, but at six thirty he still wasn't home, and I didn't have a flight number to look up. I lit the candles on the Advent wreath, and we sat down to a quiet meal, and I let Becky blow the candles out as soon as we finished eating. I let Ginger outside and stood at the back door waiting for her. My breath floated away in frosty puffs, and the smell of snow was in the air. From the next street over, the sound of Christmas carolers floated through the trees. A crushing loneliness fell upon me.

The phone rang during the movie, but I didn't get up to answer it. Greg would be home sooner or later, and it didn't make any difference if I knew when to expect him or not. I put the kids to bed after the movie ended and went to check the phone message. "Hey," Greg said. "Things ran long with the client, so I had to switch to a later flight. I'll be home around midnight." That figured. I turned the ringer and the sound on the answering machine off and went to bed.

I awoke the next morning with the sensation that something was amiss. The house was unusually quiet, and the light seemed funny. I thought I'd slept through my alarm and we were late getting up for school, then remembered it was Saturday.

I went to the kitchen and saw the light blinking on the

answering machine. "Flight was canceled," Greg's recorded voice said. "Can't rebook, everything's full. Gonna stay put here for the weekend. No sense coming home for one day when I've gotta be back down here on Monday anyway. I'll call you tomorrow." *Click.*

I erased the message. No Daddy this weekend. Well, fine. I would bring the Christmas tree in and put it up myself, and Becky and Nate could finally decorate it. I pushed the kitchen curtains aside and looked out at the fresh snowfall. We could go outside and play too. Maybe go sledding on the hill behind the school. We'd have hot chocolate afterward and sit by the tree and play games. We'd have fun, just the three of us.

When we'd eaten breakfast, I put my coat and mittens on and walked around the side of the garage. The tree was buried in a snowdrift. I scooped the snow away and tried to lift it, but it wouldn't budge. I crouched down and saw that the bottom branches were frozen to the ground, so I kicked them loose and heaved the tree up. It was godawful heavy, and the effort caused another painful spasm in my back. I leaned the tree against the garage wall and caught my breath. One side of it was flattened, and there were clumps of ice and dead leaves sticking to it. I dragged it in spurts across the driveway and wrestled it up the steps. I pulled the storm door open, straining to keep the tree from falling, but I couldn't get it over the threshold.

I called out to the kids for help. They came running to the door and stopped short when they saw me and the tree. I butted a branch out of my face. "Can you guys hold the door open for me, please?"

"I'll help." Nate lunged, tripped over the doormat, and almost toppled me off the steps.

"Don't!" I barked. He picked himself up, chagrined. I softened my voice. "Let Becky hold the door, okay, Nate? You can be in charge of . . . of making sure Ginger doesn't get out, all right?"

The dog was standing behind them, watching me with a baffled expression. "Okay, Mommy," Nate said. He wrapped his hands around Ginger's collar and dragged her away from the door.

Becky squeezed herself underneath the prickly branches and popped out on the stoop, clad in her parka and boots. She pushed the storm door wide and held it for me.

I pushed and pulled and cursed under my breath as needles stabbed me and clumps of ice worked their way up my sleeves. My lower back was on fire. I forced the tree into the house and let it crash onto the kitchen floor.

I kicked and pushed it into the living room, leaving a trail of needles and melting snow. Becky and Nate went ahead of me, pushing chairs and rugs out of the way. I tried to figure out how I was going to maneuver the tree into its place by the window. It was much too tall, for one thing. I'd have to chop at least a foot off the trunk first.

I got the saw from the garage and began to hack away at the trunk, stopping every minute or two to rest my arm. Becky and Nate hovered nearby, cheering me on. After twenty minutes of sweaty effort, I had managed to cut off a good-sized section of trunk.

"Stay out of the way, kids," I said. I pulled the hood of my sweatshirt up to protect my head, plunged my arms through the branches, and got hold of the trunk. I counted—"One, two, three"—and muscled it into the tree stand. I got down on my hands and knees and tightened the screws as fast as I could, crawled out from beneath the dripping boughs, and stepped back. My back was killing me, but the tree was up.

Becky and Nate ran to me, and we admired our beautiful Christmas tree. It was still quite flat on that one side, but I could rotate it toward the wall so it wouldn't show. If I dared touch it again. I got out the broom and dustpan to clean up the spilled needles, and the kids went around with a wad of paper towels, wiping up the puddles. The house smelled piney and festive.

I realized it was nearly noon and we were all still in our pajamas. I sent the kids upstairs to get dressed while I showered. As I was toweling my hair dry, I heard Becky shout. "The tree is falling!"

I ran into the living room in my bathrobe and saw the tree leaning precariously, about to come crashing down onto the coffee table. I thought fast—what would Dad do? I ran to the kitchen, dug the remnants of twine out of the garbage can, and ran back to the tree. I tied one end of the twine around the tree trunk, made a big knot in the other end, and opened the window. I hauled the tree upright, stretched the length of twine over to the windowsill, and lowered the sash over the knot. The line held tight, and the tree stood erect once again.

Becky clapped her hands, and Nate looked up at me in awe. "Mom, you're the smartest lady."

To hell with you, Greg, I thought. *I did it without you.*

Chapter 22

It was one week till Christmas, and our house and the Koppelmans' next door were the only ones on the street without any lights up. I brought our four strings up from the cellar and went out to the garage for the ladder, but when I tried to lift it off its hook, the weight was too much for my injured back. I had intended to hang the lights along the edge of the roof, but instead I improvised by draping the shortest string over the scraggly yew bush by the front door. Then I went inside to take another couple of Advil.

I made a fresh ice pack for my back and thought about the Christmas shopping that still needed to be done. The chances of Greg freeing up the time to go with me were pretty much zilch at this point, and I really needed to get it done today, before the stores ran out of everything.

I disliked the mall under normal circumstances, but Christmas shopping was different. My spirits lightened up as I blended into the crowds of shoppers, enjoying the jolly piped-in holiday music and the twinkling snowflake decorations. I dawdled in toy stores, dithering over Matchbox cars for Nate and craft supplies for Becky.

As I was heading toward the food court to grab a quick lunch, the Brooks Brothers window display caught my eye. I went inside, and a salesperson showed me a set of men's onyx-and-gold cuff links and studs that I knew Greg would love. I handed over our credit card and asked to have the set gift wrapped in silver paper.

I toted my packages out to the parking lot, and my happy mood fizzled when I saw a long line of cars backed up at the mall exit and traffic at a standstill on Route 9. I was going to be late picking up Becky and Nate from school.

When I finally made it back to Wayfield, I zoomed through the quiet side streets, determined to get home in time. I screeched into the driveway and took off running down to the path. I ran into the school building, rushed through the halls, and found Becky waiting with Nate outside his classroom door. It was six minutes past dismissal. One of the Botoxed mothers that I always tried to avoid strutted past me with her daughter, looking cool and composed. I gave her a casual wave and held my breath so she wouldn't see that I was panting.

"Where were you?" Becky asked.

I exhaled. "Christmas shopping," I answered with a mysterious air.

"Oh boy!" said Nate. "What did you get?"

I laughed and zipped his coat. "I'm not telling."

We walked down to the footbridge and stopped to look over the railing at the icy creek. It was frozen solid along its banks, but a dark current flowed in the center of the creek bed. The kids slid their mittened hands along the lower rail, pushing a ribbon of snow over the edge and into the frigid water below. It started to flurry as we continued our walk home. Nate hopped from one foot to the other, chanting lines from *Green Eggs and Ham*, and Becky skipped and hummed a tune to herself.

I was surprised to find Greg home when we got back to the house. He had his parka on, and he was coming out of the garage with the ladder under one arm and the remaining strings of Christmas lights looped over his shoulder. He set the ladder down. "I lucked out and got a seat on an earlier flight," he said. "Thought I'd put the lights up before it gets dark out."

He finished as the afternoon was fading. The kids and I were frosting cookies when he came back inside. "I'm all done," he said. "I put one string around the doorway and the others along the roof, and I set the timer so they'll turn on at five o'clock every day." He looked at me expectantly.

"Kids," I said, "let's put our coats and boots on quick and go look at the lights Daddy put up." We all went outside and oohed and aahed, and Greg looked mighty pleased with himself. The snow had meanwhile turned to a sleety mix.

We went back into the house, but Greg kept his parka on. "I think I'll take the dog for a walk," he said. "She could probably stand to stretch her legs." Ginger came running when she heard the jingle of her leash. Greg's Blackberry was sitting on the telephone table by the side door, and I saw him slip it into his pocket as he went out.

I opened a package of ground beef, put it on the stove to brown, and chopped up some onion. I turned the gas higher and began to break up the meat with a wooden spoon. I stopped, my hand hovering over the frying pan.

He never walks the dog.

He took his Blackberry with him.

He didn't come home last weekend.

No, I thought. *No.*

I stirred the onion so it wouldn't scorch, drained the fat off the meat, dumped it all in a pot with a jar of sauce, and left it to simmer.

Greg returned with Ginger. "You won't believe what happened," he said. "I walked down to the footbridge, and the whole thing's turned into a sheet of ice. I took one step and fell right on my ass." He rubbed his left butt cheek to prove it. "I somehow lost my key ring when I fell. I looked all over for it, but I couldn't see anything in the dark. I'll have to go back and look again in the morning." He shook his head ruefully.

"Why did you have your keys with you?"

"They were in my coat pocket from this morning."

He'd brought his parka with him to sunny North Carolina? We stared at each other for a few beats, and then I looked away, ashamed of my suspicions. He couldn't be making this up. It sounded so ordinary.

He was up early the next morning. "I've got to go find those keys before it snows again," he said. He was gone for a long time but returned triumphant. "They landed on the ice at the edge of the creek. One more inch and they would've disappeared into the water."

I spent the next few days baking, wrapping presents, and cleaning the house so everything would look nice for Christmas. Greg went to the office each day and was home in time for dinner in the evening. On Christmas Eve morning I ran to the store to pick up ingredients for enchiladas, Greg's new favorite meal, and two bottles of red wine. We hadn't had a single argument all week, and I wanted to keep him happy.

That evening I surprised the kids with new pajamas—Power Puff Girls for Becky, Bob the Builder for Nate. They hung their stockings from the mantelpiece and set out a plate of cookies for Santa. Greg read them *The Night Before Christmas*, and then we tucked them into their beds and kissed them goodnight.

"I'll finish cleaning up the kitchen," I said. Greg nodded, went into the living room, and turned on the computer. As I scraped at the sticky residue in the bottom of the rice pot, I had a sudden feeling of foreboding. Were Greg and I simply going through the motions? Things appeared to be okay on the surface of our marriage, but what exactly was going on underneath? I was too afraid to look.

I needed another drink. I uncorked the second bottle of wine, then poured myself another glass and one for Greg. He had his e-mail open, but he clicked out of it when I set his wine on the desk. "It's Christmas Eve," I said. "Did you really need to be checking your e-mail?"

He shut down the computer without responding, picked up his glass, and went to stand by the Christmas tree.

"Come sit with me," I said. We sat on the couch without touching and tried to make conversation. *The kids are excited, aren't they? Yes, I hope they don't get up too early. Looks like it's snowing out again.*

I caught myself counting the lights on the tree—*thirteen, fourteen, fifteen* . . . I stopped and looked at Greg, who appeared to be counting lights himself. I finished my wine and got up for more. Maybe I could drink myself happy.

We waited till we were sure Becky and Nate were asleep, then Greg helped me get their presents out from under our bed. He had no idea what was inside the brightly wrapped packages that I piled into his arms. He'd be as surprised as his children tomorrow.

In the morning, Nate's feet hit the floor with a thud. It was still dark out. He and Becky conferenced in loud whispers in the upstairs hall, then came pounding down the stairs and fell on their presents. I put my robe and slippers on and curled up in the armchair to watch them. Greg hovered with a trash bag to dispose of the wrapping paper the second it was stripped from the gifts.

Becky was in raptures over the American Girl doll that I'd picked out for her. "She looks just like me," she said as she stroked Molly's brown hair and adjusted her wire-rimmed eyeglasses. Nate went bonkers over his new scooter. He traveled a wobbly circuit from the Christmas tree, through the kitchen, and back to the living room, running over everything in his path.

Becky sat Molly on the arm of my chair and smoothed her felt skirt. "Where are your presents, Mommy?"

I looked at Greg. "Who should go first, you or me?"

"You can open yours first. I'll go get it." He went into the bedroom and returned with his hands behind his back. "I didn't wrap it. I'll explain why in a sec." He handed me a paper department store bag.

"My goodness," I said, "whatever could this be?" I reached into the bag and pulled out a hot-pink bra that was clearly too big for my modest chest, and a pair of matching panties in size large. Both were trimmed with bands of tacky purple lace.

Becky convulsed into giggles. "Daddy gave you underwear!"

I stared at the ugly lingerie. I'd look like a three-dollar hooker in this getup.

"They didn't have your size in stock," Greg said. "That's why I didn't wrap them. You'll have to exchange them."

"I sure will." I stuffed the items back into the bag and set it aside.

Now it was Greg's turn. I drew the silver package out of the pocket of my bathrobe. He peeled the paper off and opened the box, and his eyes widened in surprise, as though he hadn't expected me to get him anything this good. "Wow," he said. He removed the cuff links from their velvet nest and held them up to admire them.

Nate squeezed himself between us, holding his Trouble game. "Can we play, Daddy?"

"Sure, son." Greg helped Nate set the game up on the coffee table, and we played two rounds. We let Nate win the first one and Becky the second, then put the game away so we could get ready for church. Greg offered to take Ginger for a quick walk, and I took the kids upstairs to get dressed.

At church, Greg puffed his chest out like a proud patriarch. He sang "Hark, the Herald Angels Sing" in a deep voice, and when the collection basket came around, he bent his head in modesty and dropped in a couple of folded bills. We went up to receive Communion, and afterward I knelt and prayed a fervent prayer: *Please help me keep my family together.*

Afterward, we called both sets of grandparents and all the aunts and uncles, and we ate a quiet dinner that evening. Nate was wiped out. I put him to bed early, and he went right to sleep. At Becky's bedtime, I watched her make Molly comfortable with a small pillow and an old baby blanket on the floor next to her bed. She gazed at her doll for a moment, then looked up at me and whispered, "I think she's asleep." She climbed into her bed and pulled the covers up under her chin. "Why are you crying, Mommy?"

I wiped my cheeks with my sleeve. "I'm not crying, honey. Time for you to go to sleep now." I kissed her and turned out the light.

Greg was separating Becky's and Nate's toys and games into two small piles beneath the tree when I came back down. I went to the bedroom to get my sweatshirt, then helped him finish tidying up. He placed a set of Crayolas on top of Becky's pile. "You didn't get them very much."

My restraint flew out the window. I was going to let him have it this time. "You have got to be kidding me." I pointed at the tree. "See that? I put it up by myself after you left it frozen in the yard. I went Christmas shopping alone, I went to the school play alone, I went to Family Night alone. I have to do everything by myself, and I'm tired of it."

Greg's face darkened. "I don't have time for all that stupid crap. I have important work to do, important clients. I'm under a lot of pressure here, in case you didn't notice. You have no idea what I deal with on the job every day. No idea."

"No, I don't, because you won't tell me anything about it. You don't want to talk to me, and you don't want to listen to me either. You don't care what's going on with your children, and you don't care about me." I tried to keep my voice low so I wouldn't wake Becky and Nate. "We are not a family. This is not a marriage. We do nothing together, and you're practically a stranger to your children. Do you even know who their teachers are, or who their friends are? I feel like I'm a single parent, raising them alone. And you know what? It sucks."

Greg fired back, practically shouting. "Spare me, Jeanie. You have it easy here at home. You don't have to travel all over the fucking place and negotiate with assholes every day. Seriously, how hard can it be for you to take care of this tiny house and a couple of little kids?"

I threw Nate's Power Ranger to the floor. "You're so caught up in your corporate world you're blind to everything, including your family. Your kids are growing up and you're missing out on it. What kind of a life is that?"

He snorted. "Give me a break. Look at yourself." He regarded me with undisguised contempt. I stood there in my flour-dusted sweatshirt with my hair falling out of its clip. I knew my roots needed touching up, but I'd kept forgetting to call the salon, so I hadn't been able to get an appointment in time for Christmas. Greg gestured toward my head, and I tried to slap his hand away, but he caught my wrist and forced my arm down. I struggled against him but couldn't break free. "God damn you, Greg," I hissed. He flung my arm back at me, releasing his grip.

I jumped away from him. "That's it, I've had it. I've had enough."

"What's that supposed to mean?"

Energy surged through me. "It means I'm through with you and this lousy marriage. I'm taking the kids and going home."

"Home?" His voice dripped sarcasm. "To Adams Mills?"

I couldn't believe I'd actually said it. "Yes, home. I'm going home."

He let out a long, low chuckle, and his eyes bored into mine. "You're not going anywhere."

"Yes, I am. I'm leaving."

He shook his head. "No, you're not. I'm not gonna let you ruin my image with the firm now. You're going to stay right here by my side until I make partner."

I had started to shake, and I struggled to keep my voice even. "No," I said. "I won't."

"Yes, you will, or you know what I'll do? I'll tell your whole family your dirty little secret." He put his hand on my chest and pushed me backward, out of the living room and down the short hall to our bedroom. "I'll tell your parents and all your sisters what a sleaze you were in college. How you fucked your professor so he'd pass you, and how you got pregnant and had an abortion."

"*I did not.*" I grabbed for the doorframe, but my fingers slipped over the molding. "I didn't have an abortion. You know that, Greg." I tried to dodge around him, but he kept pushing me until the backs of my legs pressed the edge of the bed.

"You're nothing but a slut, Jeanie. You slept with that guy Ed back in Seattle too, didn't you?"

"*No.*" I twisted away from him, and pain streaked through my lower back and down my legs. I fell backward onto the bed with Greg on top of me.

"This is what you want, isn't it?" He mashed his mouth against mine, his lips hard and insistent, and an image flashed in my head: my college English professor, pinning me down on his bed. *You want it, don't you? That's what you came here for.*

Greg fumbled with my sweatshirt and tried to yank it over my head. "You need me, Jeanie. You're nothing without me." My ponytail holder got snarled in my hair, and he jerked it loose. He peeled my sweatpants down to my ankles and flipped me onto my face. I gave in to him. I was twenty years old again—weak, afraid, intimidated.

"Mmmm," he groaned. He worked me hard, shoving my face into the pillow. I craned my neck, gasping for breath between his thrusts. It lasted a few seconds more, and then he was done. He rolled off me and onto his back.

I clutched my arms to my chest. My eyes were open wide, staring at nothing. After a while I heard Greg's breathing slow. He was asleep.

I crept out of the bed and fumbled for my bathrobe on the hook behind the bedroom door. I went into the bathroom and let the shower run over me until the hot water ran out. I put clean clothes on, went upstairs to Becky's room, and curled up on the floor next to her doll.

Chapter 23

The sound of Becky's voice woke me in the morning. "Mommy, what are you doing down there?"

I lifted my head from the rug. She was hanging over the side of her bed with a puzzled look on her face. Next to me on the floor, Molly snoozed peacefully under her baby blanket. Becky reached down for her doll. "Is Daddy mad at us?"

She must have heard us arguing last night. I pushed myself up to a sitting position. My back ached, and I was raw between my legs. I hugged Becky. "No, honey, he's not mad at us."

She straightened Molly's pinafore. "I'll draw him a picture with my new crayons."

"That's a good idea." I hid my face in my hands. *Help me, God. Please help me.*

It had snowed during the night, as predicted. "Dad, can we go sledding today?" Nate asked as he shook Cheerios into his bowl.

Greg was standing at the counter, drinking coffee. "We'll see. Dad's got some work to do today."

I moved around the house in a daze, trying to keep busy and avoid Greg. I emptied the dishwasher, took out the trash, started a load of laundry. Becky and Nate went off to play with their Christmas presents, and Greg disappeared into the bedroom. I took pork chops out of the freezer to defrost, checked for potatoes in the pantry, swept the kitchen, and mopped the floor. Each thrust of the mop was a reminder of what my husband had done to me last night. I crashed the mop head into the sink, wrung it out, and whacked it back to the floor. I was furious and terrified at the same time.

I couldn't let my parents find out what I'd done in college. Dad was fighting for his life, and Mom's memory was more than likely in an irreversible decline—senility ran on her side of the family. My parents needed love and support right now, not sordid stories about their youngest daughter's past.

I looked up and saw Greg standing in the doorway. The mop slipped from my hands and clattered to the floor. I backed against the counter and hugged my arms around my middle.

"I'm flying to Charlotte on the three o'clock flight."

Relief flooded through me. *Good*, I thought. *Go.*

"I might be gone for a while this time. But I'll be calling home every night to talk to the kids." His eyes daggered into mine. "And you."

I squeezed myself tighter and willed myself not to cry. This was so messed up. So completely, totally messed up.

Nate skidded into the kitchen. "Dad, Dad, can we go sledding now? Can we?"

Greg hesitated. "I'm kind of busy now, son." He glanced my way, and I looked back at him but didn't say anything. Something seemed to shift in him, and he turned back to Nate. "All right," he said. "We'll go sledding. Go tell your sister."

I stuffed Nate into his blue snowsuit and helped him and Becky put on their boots. They waited by the door for their father, puffy and clumsy in their snow gear, their faces flushed with heat. "You can go out to the garage and get your sleds," I said, and they bolted out the door.

I roamed the house after they'd gone, in search of a vigorous task to throw my nervous energy into. I opened the oven and inspected the insides. It wasn't really dirty, but I mixed up a paste of baking soda and water anyway, donned my rubber gloves, and began to scrub.

I was finishing up some time later when Becky and Nate clomped into the kitchen. Outside the window, I saw Greg trudging through the snow from the mailbox, carrying a bundle of forgotten newspapers. I sat on the floor and helped the kids remove their snow clothes. Their cheeks were glowing, and they chattered away, telling me all about the sledding hill and the friends they'd seen there. Greg came in, and his nose and ears were red from the cold. I laid hats and mittens on top of the radiator to dry and didn't speak to him.

He stayed shut in the bedroom while I made lunch. My mouth was dry as dust, and it felt as if I couldn't swallow. After a while, Greg came out and set his things by the door. He had packed a large suitcase in addition to his regular traveling bag. He came to the table and squatted between Becky's and Nate's chairs. "Daddy has to go on a trip, kids."

Nate was concentrating on peeling the crust off his sandwich. Becky took a gulp of milk. "Okay, Dad."

Greg went to get his coat, and Becky slid off her chair. "Wait, Daddy." She ran out of the room and came back with a crayoned drawing in her hand. "I drew this for you." It was a picture of the four of us standing in front of a small house. The windows were heart-shaped.

I couldn't bear any more. I ran blindly up the stairs to Becky's room and sank onto her narrow bed, clutching at her flowered bedspread with both hands. *Oh my God, how am I going to live like this? I have no one here to turn to. I have nothing.*

The stairs creaked and Greg was at my side. "My taxi's here. I'm leaving now."

I couldn't look at him. Tears dripped down my face.

"Can I get a hug before I go?" He sounded so sure of himself, so certain of my acquiescence.

I shook my head, *No*. He hauled me to my feet and pulled me to him. I hung limp in his arms and turned my face away. "Let go of me."

I watched the taxi drive away from the house, leaving black lines in the slushy street. The corners of Becky's window were white with frost, and a cold draft seeped through a crack in the warped frame. I heard the TV turn on downstairs and SpongeBob babbling to his friend Patrick. It grew dark outside. I got up and went to check on my children.

My hand shook as I dialed Carla that night. I should have programmed her number into speed dial a long time ago, but I didn't know how to do it. "Holy crap," she said when I told her what had happened the night before. "It's like he was banging a prostitute. His latent need for control has manifested in aggressive behavior."

I shuddered and wiped my running nose. The kids were asleep, and I was in my bed in a sweater, long johns, and wool socks. I was cold as ice and I couldn't stop shaking. "Why is he treating me like this, Carla? Why does he act like he hates me?"

"It's not you, Jeanie, it's him. He's got serious issues. Probably has a little something to do with that freight train mother of his. This is a toxic relationship that you're in. You need to separate your identity from his and remind yourself that you're still a good person, no matter what he says or does. And you should talk to a lawyer."

"A lawyer?"

"You need to protect yourself. Know your rights. You have no idea what he might be planning, so you need to be prepared."

"But he doesn't want me to leave him. He said so."

"Listen to yourself, Jeanie! You're deluded. He's a controlling, emotionally abusive man, and he's trying to take you for a ride. You need to do some sleuthing and find out what's going on. I'm sure it wasn't work that dragged him from his home on the day after Christmas. There's got to be another woman involved."

I might have vomited that very second, but there was nothing in my stomach to bring up. I hadn't eaten a thing since our Christmas dinner.

"Make sure you call that counselor too," Carla said. "You're going to need someone to talk to."

"But I can talk to you."

"I'm five hundred miles away, hon. You need someone close by who knows how to help you through this. A professional."

I actually almost laughed. "I thought you were a professional."

"Very funny. Listen, I have to run. I hear the boys fighting again. Be sure to make those calls, and let me know what the lawyer says."

I pulled a blanket over my head and curled back into my protective ball.

Ann invited Becky and Nate over to play with her kids the next day. While they were gone, I rattled from room to room, desperate for something to keep my mind off the disaster my life had become. I paused in front of the Christmas tree. The length of twine I'd rigged up was still in place, but the tree was listing toward the window now. I decided it would be safer to take it down. The kids would be disappointed, but I'd have a huge mess on my hands if the thing collapsed to the floor in the middle of the night.

I brought the empty bins up from the cellar and began taking ornaments off the tree. I removed the white ceramic fawn that Greg had given to me the year we were married and tossed it into a box, not caring if it broke. I yanked off the ostentatious Augusta

National Golf Club ornament from Florence and Howard, and the sappy "Our First Christmas Together" ornament from Ricki and Gordon, and chucked them as well. It was cathartic.

I wondered where I'd be a year from now—still mucking along with Greg, cooking and cleaning for him and putting up a false front for my children? I wished I could replace him and start over with someone else, someone who actually wanted to be a family man. A man who preferred being at home with his wife and kids to sleeping in hotels in strange cities night after night.

I tugged the string of lights off the tree, balled it up, and flung it into a bin with a satisfying shattering of bulbs. I tipped the tree onto its side, crammed it through the front door, and dragged it through the snow to the curb.

Carla's advice to do some sleuthing was nagging at me. I sat down at the desk and riffled through a stack of bills. Gas and electric, phone, cable, internet. I'd fallen behind on everything in the weeks leading up to Christmas, and half of these were probably overdue. At the bottom of the pile, I found Greg's unopened corporate American Express bill.

I stared at the envelope. "I can't do this," I said out loud. I stuffed the envelope back beneath the pile, pressed my sweaty palms to my cheeks, and told myself to get a grip. I stood up and went to look for the phone. I'd call the marriage counselor instead.

I got Suzette's answering machine and I immediately disconnected. What was I supposed to say—My husband's holding me hostage in our marriage? I've got a deep dark secret that I'm afraid my mom and dad will find out? It sounded like a made-for-TV movie. She'd think I was a whack job.

School resumed on January second. When I returned home from my walk that morning, the windowpanes were dripping with condensation and the house was overly warm, which meant the boiler was on the fritz again. I adjusted the thermostat and the hissing radiators gradually quieted. The sun came out from behind a cloud, lighting up the dust in the air. I'd been cleaning like a madwoman for days, but somehow the house still looked dirty to me.

I couldn't put it off any longer. I went to the desk, pulled out the American Express envelope, and forced my thumb under the flap. I unfolded the pages and checked the balance due: $5,748.72. How on earth did Greg manage to spend that much in one month?

I scanned the first two pages. There were multiple charges from airlines, hotels, restaurants, taxi services. Page three stopped me cold: *Dogwood Floral.* One hundred and seventy-five dollars, charged on December 13. I checked the calendar tacked to the wall. December 13 was the night Greg hadn't come home from Charlotte.

My hands trembled, scattering the pages. My thoughts raced. Was it someone's birthday? A special occasion of some sort? My mind pushed back against the obvious. I looked up the florist's address on the internet. It was two blocks away from Greg's client.

Son of a bitch.

I dialed the florist's number and a young woman answered. "Good morning, Dogwood Floral. How may I help you?"

I wedged my other hand under my thigh to stop it from shaking. "Hello, my name is—" I cast my eyes over the desk, and they fell on a computer ad on the back page of Greg's *Men's Health* magazine. "—Dell. I'm the personal assistant for a Mr. Gregory Mercer with Carbide Equity in Boston. I'm preparing his December expense report, and there is a charge to his American Express account that he's having difficulty recalling. I wondered if you might be able to tell me the details of the transaction?" I marveled at my sudden ability to detach myself emotionally. Carla would be so proud.

I told the woman the date and the dollar amount, and she was quite willing to assist. "Just a moment while I look that up. Oh yes, I remember this one. He came in and ordered a dozen long-stemmed roses, and we delivered them to the recipient's office." She gave a tinkly little laugh. "He said he was taking her to dinner at the Four Seasons that evening. It was their first date."

I could hardly draw air to speak. "Uh huh."

"I can fax you a copy of the order if you like. It might help jog his memory."

"I'm sure it will."

I recited the number for Greg's fax machine. "Thank you for your help, Miss," I said and slammed the phone down. "Son of a *bitch*."

The fax machine whirred and spit out a sheet of paper. The receiver of the roses was a woman named Veronica, and she worked for Greg's client. The order form included the message that had accompanied the delivery: *There is something about you . . . Greg.*

I felt as if my lungs had collapsed. Greg was having an affair. I was overcome with nausea, and I couldn't still my shaking hands. I tried to rise from the chair, but my legs wouldn't move.

The queasiness passed and was replaced by a cold sweat. Greg was cheating on me with this woman in Charlotte, this fucking *Veronica*, and he expected me to just sit here and take it. I straightened up. I needed to check his cell phone records too. I needed to find as much proof of his treachery as I could.

I logged into the T-Mobile website, pulled up Greg's call log, and scanned it rapidly. Veronica's number showed up repeatedly. There were dozens of calls between them, incoming and outgoing, at all hours of the day and night. I looked back through the dates and times. There was an outgoing call on the afternoon of December 23, when Greg had lost his keys while walking the dog, and another the next morning, when he'd miraculously found them. He'd placed a twenty-minute call to this woman on Christmas morning, when I was busy getting our children ready to go to church. I was boiling with fury. I twisted my wedding rings off my finger and threw them into the trash can beneath the desk.

In an odd way I felt better now, knowing without a doubt that Greg had cheated on me. It put the blame for our problems squarely on him instead of me. How could I have been in denial for so long, in the face of so much damning evidence? I'd been a gullible fool, willfully ignoring the signs of my husband's betrayal.

I opened every one of his drawers and files and ripped through them like a woman possessed. I found a photo of Greg at a cocktail party, standing in the center of a group of stuffed-shirt investment bankers. A sheaf of handwritten notes fell out of a binder, but it was only something to do with a conference he'd attended. I went to the hall closet and checked the pockets of all his coats, then to the bedroom to ransack his side of the dresser. I stretched my arm underneath our bed and unearthed the box where he kept his college memorabilia, but I didn't find anything useful in it. I rocked back on my heels, trying to think where else I could look.

His car. I scuffed my feet into my boots, ran out to the garage, and heaved the overhead door up. Greg's Audi gleamed in the sudden sunlight. There wasn't a speck of mud or road salt on it because he'd hardly driven it all winter.

I popped the trunk. It appeared to be empty at first, but then I spotted something in the shadows in the back. I reached in and pulled a black plastic case toward me, flipped the latches, and lifted the lid.

A gun. I tilted the case toward the light and saw that it was a .22 caliber Smith & Wesson Model 41—the same pistol my father used to use for shooting competitions in Adams Mills, before his right arm was weakened by the stroke.

Why on earth did Greg have a gun? He disliked anything to do with firearms, and he thought hunting was for morons, despite having three brothers-in-law who were avid outdoorsmen. Maybe he'd gotten bored with yoga and had taken up target shooting as his latest fad, and forgotten to mention it to me?

The wind blew a spray of snow up the back of my shirt, and I shivered. I picked up the gun and saw that the safety was off. I ejected the magazine, which was full, pulled back the slide, and saw there was a round in the chamber. Greg didn't know jack shit about guns, and here was proof. He had no business driving around with a loaded and unsecured handgun that he probably didn't know how to use. I cleared the round and emptied the mag, put the cartridges in my pocket, placed the gun back in its case, and shut the trunk. Whatever he was up to would have to remain a mystery until he came home again. Meanwhile, it was time for me to find a lawyer.

Chapter 24

I opened the Greater Boston phone directory and was instantly overwhelmed by the pages and pages of attorney listings. I had never in my life had any reason to call a law firm before, and I had no idea how to choose one or how to go about engaging an attorney's services.

Half-page ads blared *DUI! Criminal Defense!* Smaller ads offered counsel for every legal dilemma on God's green earth, from personal injury and medical malpractice to bankruptcy and labor disputes. I ran my finger down a page, reading the cumbersome compound names—Ludovico & Giacometti. Katzenburg Stanhope Bogdanowicz. I pitied the person who had to answer their phones all day long.

Most of the firms were located in downtown Boston, and there was no way I was going to drive into the city, where I had no clue how to get around. I swapped the heavy phone book for the slim Wayfield directory and found a listing for the Law Offices of Durand & Putnam, 12 Main Street.

I cruised down Main, past the commuter rail station and the town square, squinting at the numbers on the old buildings. Durand & Putnam was located in a four-story white brick building that had a barber and a shoe repair shop on the ground floor. I parked on the street out front, entered the tiny lobby, and took the elevator to the top floor. The doors opened to a small reception area of polished wood and dark carpeting. The receptionist looked up from her keyboard and asked how she might help me.

"I'd like to speak with an attorney, regarding a divorce?" I was appalled by the words coming out of my mouth.

"Do you have an appointment?"

"No, I don't." I had jumped in the car and driven straight here without calling first. It had felt good to finally be in motion.

The woman looked me over, but in a kindly way. "Have a seat, please. I'll see if Mr. Durand is available."

Mr. Durand was one of those hale-and-hearty New Englanders with a brusque manner and a wicked Boston accent. He had to be pushing eighty, or possibly ninety. He crushed my fingers in a firm handshake, seated himself behind an immense antique desk, and folded his spotted hands over the front of his suit coat. He leaned back, rocking and creaking in his leather chair, as I described my situation. I shared only what I thought was pertinent—I had uncovered evidence of my husband's infidelity, and I wished to file for a divorce. I said nothing about secrets, or threats, or pistols hidden in car trunks.

"Yes, yes," Mr. Durand said at intervals, nodding sagely. He'd heard it a hundred times before. Maybe a thousand, by the looks of him. When I'd finished my tale of woe, he rocked some more and studied the ceiling. "Every time I take one of these divorce cases, I swear I'll never do it again. It's the kind of work you don't want to touch with a ten-foot pole."

My shoulders drooped.

"But you seem like a good, level-headed woman." He paused to tip his chair back and consider the ceiling again. The crags in his forehead deepened. "Sometimes these things have a way of blowing over. It may be a passing fling that your husband will work out of his system and be done with." He raised his bushy brows at me.

I shook my head. "I don't think so. I can't stay with him any longer. I can't trust him. It's all so . . . it's disgusting to me."

"I see." He bobbed his head, and the chair creaked with him. He asked the name of Greg's firm and what his position and salary were. "Ah," he said when I told him. He considered for a moment. "All right. If you are convinced that your husband is conducting an extramarital affair and you therefore no longer wish to be married to him, I will take your case."

"Thank you, sir." Formality seemed appropriate, on account of his age.

Mr. Durand tapped a heavy hand on his blotter. "I want you to go home and get to work. Gather up every piece of financial information in the house—every document pertaining to bank accounts, stocks and bonds, life insurance policies, real estate holdings, income taxes, et cetera. I want you to make copies of these documents, but on the quiet, now." He shook his knobby forefinger at me. "You don't want to tip your hand. That would give your husband the opportunity to spirit his money away to a place where we can't find it." He raised an accusing eyebrow.

"However," he continued, "the goal here is not for one person to take the other to the cleaners. The goal is to be fair to all parties involved, particularly the children." He reached for the gold pen next to the legal pad that he hadn't made a single notation on. "Carbide Equity, eh? Rest assured, your financial settlement will be more than adequate for your needs."

I made out a check for $5,000 to cover the retainer fee and wrote *Life insurance premium* in the checkbook register. I thanked Mr. Durand for seeing me and left his office feeling better than I had in months.

I signed up for more volunteer hours in Becky's and Nate's classrooms, to help me keep my sanity. I came home from school on

Friday to find a phone message from Suzette waiting. "Hello, Jeanie," she said. "Greg called and set up an appointment for the both of you on Tuesday at ten thirty. He said he's been away on business lately, and he thought this would be an opportune time for the two of you to continue with your therapy. Please give me a call back to confirm."

What the hell? Greg wanted us to go back to marriage counseling, without even discussing it with me first? I wondered if I should agree to it. He might try to bad-mouth me to Suzette, to get her on his side. I'd have to think this over first.

I flipped through the mail, hoping for a friendly letter from one of my sisters to cheer me up, but it was all junk, except for our monthly bank statement. Wait a minute—the bank! I dropped the mail, hurried to the computer, and logged into our Citizens Bank account. The Account Overview page came up, and it said our last login was on January 5, which was yesterday. I hadn't been on the site in over a week, so that meant Greg had checked the account in the meantime and had guessed the real purpose of that "life insurance" check I'd written. The appointment he'd set up with Suzette was damage control. He wanted to stop me from filing for divorce.

I thought it through. I might as well keep the appointment with Suzette and confront Greg in a safe setting. That's what Carla would probably advise me to do. I dialed Suzette's office and got her machine. "This is Jeanie Mercer," I said after the beep. "Confirming for Tuesday."

I asked Ann if she could pick Becky and Nate up from school for me on Tuesday afternoon, claiming an urgent dental appointment. I looked up the Veronica woman on the internet and learned she was thirty-two years old and married. The bitch was as bad as Greg. I folded up the florist's fax and put it in my purse.

I practiced my positive self-talk (Carla's suggestion) as I rode the elevator up to Suzette's office: *You've got this. Stand up for your-self. Stay calm.* Greg was already in the waiting room, flipping through a magazine. He stood and came toward me with his arms open for a hug, and I took a quick half step back. He sat down again, looking a bit perturbed. "How are you, Jeanie?"

"I am just fine." I placed my coat on the coatrack and remained standing. I studied a framed print of Monet's water lilies, strategically placed to soothe Suzette's warring clients. I slipped my hand into my purse and touched the folded paper.

The office door opened and Suzette beckoned us inside. "Hello, Jeanie. Hello, Greg." She motioned for us to sit. I sat in the center of the love seat, crossed my legs, and placed my hands on my knee, left over right, so Greg would see that I wasn't wearing my wedding rings. He seated himself in one of the padded armchairs, and Suzette took the other.

"Hello, Suzette," I said. I kept my face averted from Greg, but I watched him out of the corner of my eye. He was looking at me curiously. I felt his eyes travel over me and pause at my hands. His features settled into a scowl.

Suzette gave us an expanded version of her pep talk and stressed the need for us to communicate openly and honestly with one another. Greg fidgeted and jiggled his foot. I concentrated on sitting still and faking a composure I didn't feel. Suzette broke off her monologue and looked at us with concern. "I must tell you, this lack of emotion is disturbing to me." Greg shifted in his seat and rolled his shoulders. I clenched my knee tighter.

"Jeanie," Suzette said. "Why don't you tell me what brought you here today."

I leaned forward to block Greg out of my peripheral vision. "We've been having problems for quite a while, as you already know. I didn't want to give up on our marriage. I wanted to keep working on it. But now he's gone too far."

"In what way?"

"He's having an affair."

Greg inhaled—*Ssssst*. His foot stopped jiggling.

"How do you know this?" said Suzette.

"I have proof right here." I pulled the fax from my purse and handed it to her. "He sent flowers to a woman he works with in Charlotte." I pointed at the paper. "You can read the message." I sat back and hugged myself. The shaking had started again.

Suzette studied the fax a moment, then handed it to Greg. He glanced at the paper and folded it over. He jutted his chin at me. "You told me I should find someone to talk to."

Suzette's voice was sharp: "Do you really think this was what she meant, Greg?"

His shoulders twitched. His eyes flickered from Suzette to me to the floor.

I turned on him. "I've looked up your cell phone records too. I know you've been talking to her constantly."

His foot started to jiggle again. "She's just a friend."

Blood roared in my ears. "I'm pretty sure she's married too."

He winced. He lifted his chin again, defiant, and crossed his arms.

Suzette's expression was severe. "I do not think this is an appropriate kind of friendship for you to have at this juncture, Greg."

I looked at Suzette. "I told him I was leaving him, and he threatened me. He said he—" I stopped short. I wanted more than anything to expose Greg as the self-serving, controlling bastard that he was, but the consequences suddenly came clear to me: flaying him open like that would only infuriate him, and I'd have nothing left to stop him from telling my parents everything, to get revenge on me.

I thought of my father and his brave effort to fight his cancer, and my poor mother, slowly losing her mind. It wasn't fair. Their last memories of me should be good and happy ones. I couldn't subject them to this.

Greg's eyes locked onto mine. *Go ahead and say it*, he dared me.

"Hold on a moment," said Suzette. "Greg threatened you, Jeanie? In what way?"

My mouth went dry. I couldn't speak. "Jeanie?" she prompted me.

"He didn't actually threaten me," I said in a whisper. "He only said he didn't want me to leave him. He doesn't want a divorce."

Greg sat back, a crooked smile on his lips. He rubbed his hand over his mouth, and the smile disappeared. "Yes," he said to Suzette. "I want us to stay together, and I'm willing to work on the marriage. It's just that I'm really behind the eight ball at work right now. I'm under a tremendous amount of stress, and I don't appreciate these insinuations about a valued colleague that I work with."

Something cracked in my core. I jabbed my finger at his face. "You have a lot of nerve to sit there and say this woman is just a friend! Guess what? I don't believe you. You're a lying, cheating prick, and you don't care about anyone but yourself. All that matters to you is your career and your income."

Greg stood up. "I think we're through here."

Suzette jumped to her feet. "Wait, Greg. Please sit down again. We've just uncovered the crux of your conflict."

He tossed his coat over his arm and stormed out. Suzette watched him go, flabbergasted, but collected herself after a moment. "I'm not supposed to speculate about these matters," she said, "but it seems quite likely, due to Greg's defensive posture, that he has indeed been unfaithful to you. I highly recommend that you see a medical doctor, to make sure you haven't contracted anything communicable."

"I don't have a doctor. I found one for my kids when we moved here, but I never got around to taking care of myself."

"I have a friend who's a family physician. She often helps me with cases like this." Suzette jotted some information on a notepad, tore the sheet off, and handed it to me. "I'll call her and tell her you're coming. I'm sure she'll be able to fit you in this afternoon."

A nurse led me to a plain white examination room. I undressed, put on the flimsy paper gown, and climbed onto the table. The doctor knocked and entered with a solemn expression. "I'm sorry you're having difficulties," she said gently. "Suzette indicated you'd be needing an STD screen. Is that correct?"

"Yes."

She pulled the stirrups out with a clang. "Lie back and put your feet up, please." Her latex gloves snapped. "Bend your knees and slide your bottom toward me. A little more. That's good." A drawer slid open and closed. "You'll feel pressure now." I felt the cold of lubricated metal, heard the click of the speculum as she adjusted it. I squeezed my eyes shut and tried to relax my muscles. I pictured my children playing in the snow—Nate in his blue snowsuit, Becky chasing snowflakes.

Chapter 25

ivorce, divorce. All night long, the ugly word echoed through my uneasy sleep. *Wake up*, I commanded myself. *Wake up and it will go away.* I opened my eyes to the thin light of dawn. Snow hissed against the bedroom window. Another day to face on my own.

I saw Becky and Nate off to school and returned home to pore over our files. Greg had set our brokerage account up for online access, and I didn't know the password. I'd always left our financial business up to him and trusted him to do what was best for us. Now I was kicking myself.

I called the brokerage house, but the account was in Greg's name, and they refused to divulge any information to me without his permission. I dug deeper into the files and found a statement from before he'd switched the account to paperless. Following Mr. Durand's instructions, I made two copies of everything—one for him and one for me to keep hidden in an envelope in the back of my closet.

The doctor's office called on Friday to tell me the tests had come back negative. Greg flew back to Boston that night so he could spend Saturday with his children. He stayed in a hotel and came over in the morning. He knocked at the side door and waited for me to let him in, as though he didn't consider it his home anymore.

"I need to get something from the files," he said. "HR needs a copy of my immunization records. I'm going to be traveling internationally pretty soon." He patted his briefcase to show me how important he was, then he went to the living room and opened the filing cabinet. I watched him from the doorway, worried I might have put something back in the wrong place. He removed a sheet of paper from a folder, read it over, and nodded to himself. He made a copy of it and examined the paper with a frown. He pressed the Copy button again but wasn't satisfied with that one either. "Copier's running out of ink," he called over his shoulder. I backed into the kitchen.

He went to the foot of the stairs and yelled up to Becky and Nate. "Let's go, kids. Dad's ready to roll." We both stood waiting in the kitchen. "I'm taking them out for lunch at Johnny Rockets and then to a movie," he said. He sounded congested. When he took a handkerchief from his pocket and blew his nose, I saw he was still wearing his wedding band.

The winter weeks passed slowly. Greg continued to come and see the kids on Saturdays and spent his nights at the hotel. I had no idea where he was during the week.

"He hasn't taken his wedding ring off," I told Carla. "Maybe he's not serious about that other woman. Maybe it was just a fling, like the lawyer said, and he really does still want me."

"Oh please, Jeanie. You've been his brood mare and housekeeper for all these years, and now he thinks he can have his cake and screw it too. Face it—*you* don't want *him* anymore. You've only stayed with him this long out of duty."

I heard the truth in her words, but I didn't want to accept it. I carried on with my solitary routines and tried to keep my focus on my children. So far, they weren't aware that anything was amiss. Their father came and went, which was nothing new to them. He sometimes called to say goodnight to them before they went to bed, and then I'd take the phone back, and we'd exchange a few sentences about their schoolwork. We didn't discuss anything personal or anything to do with our current situation.

I started running again, and I discovered a network of paths that wound through the town and the nearby woods. I labored up rocky hillsides and hurtled down into forested ravines, trying to lose myself in the physical exertion. At night I sat up in bed, drinking endless pots of tea and watching mediocre BBC adaptations of Jane Austen novels, until sleep overtook me. I heard nothing from any of the Mercers.

Greg called on a frigid night in early February. "I just wanted to see how the kids are doing."

It was ten thirty, and Becky and Nate had been in bed for two hours. "They're all right," I said cautiously.

"Do they miss me?"

"I suppose they do, but they're used to you being gone."

Several seconds passed, and then he said softly, "I miss you."

My hand went to my heart. It hurt to hope.

He called again a few nights later. "How are you doing, Jeanie?"

It had been a trying week. Becky was home from school with strep throat, and Nate had started having bad dreams. He'd woken up crying every night, and he had so much trouble going back to sleep that I'd been letting him stay in my bed, which inflamed Becky when she saw him there in the morning. "I'm stressed out, Greg," I said. "We need you here. The kids need you."

"I know. I know I'm making it hard on you." He sighed. "It's been hard for me too."

I felt myself crumbling. I was so tired, so lonely and pathetic,

sitting in this house all by myself. "Are you still . . . still seeing . . ."
That woman. I couldn't say it out loud.

"There was nothing to that, Jeanie. Like I said. She was just someone I used to talk to."

"Used to?"

"Yeah."

"But you work with her."

"Not anymore. She isn't part of the project team. She's administrative. She's a nothing."

Another stab of hope. If only he'd come back and give us another chance. We'd sunk so low, maybe we'd hit bottom. Things could only get better from here.

I had no pride left. "Please, Greg. Please don't give up on us yet. Suzette can help us work through this. We have to try."

He was silent for a long time, and I didn't dare speak. "Okay," he finally said. "I'll try."

On Saturday, he brought a movie for the kids to watch. He set up the portable DVD player in Becky's bedroom and instructed them to stay put upstairs until it was over; Mommy and Daddy had something important to talk about.

I made coffee and we sat down. Greg's executive diary lay open before him on the table. He consulted his notes, placed a pen between the pages, and folded his hands on top of it. "I had a counseling session with Suzette yesterday."

This was news to me. I waited for him to explain.

"I'm feeling optimistic that we can put our marriage back together with her help."

I folded my hands, mirroring his posture. "Go on."

"I know I've done a lot of things wrong, Jeanie. I've been a complete dick. You were absolutely right—I got caught up in my career, at the expense of my family. When Royce told me I was being considered for partner, that was all I could see. I was obsessed with getting that promotion." He compressed his lips the way Bill Clinton used to when he was trying to look humble. "I don't know what got into me when I threatened to hold your past over your head. It was wrong of me. Just plain wrong. I let my ego get the better of me. I never should have treated you the way I did." A flicker of a smile curved his lips. "I got it, by the way. I'm a partner now."

What did he expect me to say? *Congratulations, honey! You practically destroyed your marriage in the process, but it's all good now!* I simply nodded, and he went on. "The trouble was, when Royce gave me the news, it kind of rang hollow. It wasn't the same without you to share it with. That's when I realized how wrong I'd been."

He fingered his pen. "And then there was that other thing, you know, in Charlotte. I fully admit it was inappropriate for me to have that sort of, uh, friendship with that person. Suzette really took me to task for it. She says that kind of relationship is like a drug—it feels great while you're doing it, but the feeling doesn't last. There's no substance to it." His voice dropped to a whisper. "It was a huge mistake, and I cannot tell you how sorry I am."

I gaped at him. I was dumbfounded.

"I don't blame you if you don't trust me. Suzette says I have to work at rebuilding your confidence in me." His chair scraped the floor, and next thing, he was lowering himself to one knee. He took my right hand in his. "I'm asking you for your forgiveness."

The coffee maker let out a gurgling sigh, and somewhere outside, a snowblower blatted to life. I bowed my head and sent up a silent prayer: *Please tell me if I can believe him. Please tell me what to do.*

I opened my eyes and wiped them with shaky hands. Greg gazed at me in earnest and twined his fingers through mine. "Please, Jeanie," he said. "Please."

I had to forgive him. It was the only way forward, the only way to heal. I leaned into him until our foreheads were touching and answered him softly, "I forgive you."

I went to see Mr. Durand first thing on Monday. "My husband has had a change of heart," I said. "I want to put the divorce on hold."

Mr. Durand was rocking away behind his giant desk. "No one would be happier than I would to see you patch this up and put it behind you," he said, "but be prepared. You're going to hear all kinds of advice from people, telling you that your husband is a scoundrel, you should send him packing, and so forth and so on. Let that advice go in one ear and out the other. This is your marriage, and only you can make the decision as to what is best for you."

"For the love of Christ!" said Carla. "You're jumping right back onto the merry-go-round."

My sisters were more optimistic. I was doing the right thing, they said. I had to give Greg another chance.

My father had only three words for me: "Trust but verify."

Chapter 26

Suzette instructed us to start "dating" again. "Work on making each other your priority," she said. "Try to tap into those romantic rituals that you shared in the early part of your relationship."

Valentine's Day was coming up, so it was the obvious choice for our first night out since we'd gotten back together. Greg and I came up with a plan: I would arrange the babysitter, and he would fly back from Charlotte and take me to dinner at an Italian restaurant in the North End. But then he called to tell me the client was going ballistic and he needed to stay in Charlotte an extra day, "to put out some fires." We would still go out to dinner, but we'd do it a day later than planned.

Valentines were 50 percent off at the Wayfield Hallmark on the fifteenth. I chose a plain red heart-shaped one that said *Be Mine* on the front and was blank inside. I wrote *I'll be yours* and signed it simply *Jeanie*. I didn't want to overdo things.

Greg's flight wasn't due in until six, but I had the sitter come at four so I could take my time getting ready without Becky and Nate interfering. I dressed up in a maroon silk top, a short black skirt, and a pair of heels that were way higher than I was used to. I coaxed my hair into a fairly neat chignon, sprayed it in place with half a can of hairspray, and put on a pair of dangly earrings. I checked myself in the mirror and decided I looked good—sexy, even—and a thrill ran through me. I dabbed on a few drops of a new perfume I'd bought (no more Eternity for me), tucked the valentine into my handbag, and told the sitter I was leaving to pick up my husband from the airport. "We'll be home by eleven," I said, emphasizing the "we." Suzette had cautioned us to not "rush the intimacy," but if Greg wanted to stay overnight, I wasn't going to argue.

I kissed the kids goodbye and went out to the garage. I'd decided to take the Audi, because the occasion deserved a classier ride than the minivan, which was littered with Cheez-Its and Polly Pocket dolls. I turned the radio on to get an updated weather forecast. They were predicting three to five inches of snow this evening—all the more reason for Greg to spend the night.

I spotted him outside Terminal A, trim and handsome in his camel coat, and a thrill rippled through me again. It took me a minute to maneuver through the snarl of vehicles and pull up curbside. Greg walked around to the driver's side and opened my door. "I was expecting you in the van."

I got out to change places with him. "Hello to you too."

My skirt rode up as I slid into the passenger's seat; I didn't tug it back down. Greg shifted the car into drive, then back into park, and turned to give me a kiss. "You look pretty, babe. Happy Day After Valentine's Day. Mm, you smell good."

He said we would go for a drink first at a little wine bar he knew of. We crawled through the traffic jam on the Charlestown Bridge, turned onto Prince Street, then onto Salem. We circled the block twice, looking for a parking space, and ended up around the corner on a dark side street. I thought of the gun in the trunk, but this wasn't the right time to bring it up.

The bar was cozy and charming with its exposed-brick walls, candlelight, and moaning saxophones. The hostess called Greg "Mr. Mercer" and led us to a booth in a corner. My eyes skimmed the tabletop. I thought he might have arranged for a bouquet of flowers to be waiting for me, or maybe a box of chocolates, but the smooth wood surface held only a flickering candle and the wine list. I started to remove my coat, and Greg jumped to help me. "Whoa," he said as the deep V-neck of my top was revealed, and I felt a rush of heat on my face and neck.

Greg ordered champagne and a dozen raw oysters. He sucked them straight from the shell, which he said was the correct way to eat them. I forced one down and let him have the rest. He propped his elbows on the table and rubbed his fingers up and down the stem of his champagne flute. "I'm really glad we did this tonight."

"Yes," I said. "Me too."

He talked for a while about the project in Charlotte and told me about another client he might become involved with in Austin, Texas. Texas brought horses and cowboys to mind, which made me remember the gun. I told him I'd found it—by accident, of course, when I was looking for the first aid kit that was supposed to be in the minivan—and I asked him where it had come from.

"Royce loaned it to me. He's going to give me a few shooting lessons. Says it's a great pastime, thinks I'd enjoy it."

"What's wrong with him? You don't just give a firearm to someone who's never used one before."

"It's fine, Jeanie. He showed me the basics."

"But you don't even like guns. You blew off Todd when he invited you to go trap shooting at Thanksgiving."

"This is *marksmanship*, Jeanie. Way different from what y'all do up north, plinking away at clay chips and shit. Royce belongs to this classy shooting club out in Weston. He says they've got a board room for corporate events and—"

"Wait a minute. Did you get a Massachusetts gun license? They're pretty strict here, you know."

He did that annoying thing with his hand. "Please. I've got it under control."

"Just promise me you'll be more careful with it. You should always keep it unloaded until you're ready to use it."

"It is unloaded."

"No, it wasn't. You've got to clear the gun before you put it away. Or at least use the safety."

"Sure thing." He cocked his forefinger and thumb at me and made a clicking sound with his tongue. He yawned, stretched his legs out beneath the table, and nicked me in the ankle with the sharp sole of his shoe. "You know, babe, I'm pretty tired after dealing with everything that went down at work this week. Why don't we give dinner a pass tonight? I'll take you out on Saturday night instead, when I'm rested up."

I hid my dismay. "Whatever you want to do."

He poured the remainder of the champagne into my glass, and it frothed over the rim. When I went to drink it, the bubbles got up my nose and made me sneeze. I opened my handbag to get a tissue, and the valentine in its bright red envelope slid out. I quickly poked it back in. I had to get rid of that card. Greg obviously hadn't gotten anything for me, and I didn't want to make things more awkward between us than they already were. I slid across the padded seat of the booth. "I think I'll run to the ladies' room before we go."

A waitress directed me to a unisex restroom at the back of the bar. I stuffed the valentine into the trash can and piled crumpled paper towels over it, in case Greg came in after me. I applied more lipstick and smoothed my chignon.

Greg was waiting for me at the entrance. We left the warmth of the bar and stepped out onto the freezing sidewalk. We stood close together, and our breath wafted away in small puffs. Greg slipped his hand beneath my jacket and under my silk top. He kissed me and stroked the bare skin on my back. I quivered with longing and kissed him back, aroused.

The kids were asleep when we got home. Greg paid the babysitter and saw her out, and then he got down to it, right there in the kitchen. He lifted my skirt and pressed me back against the counter. My mind wandered during the one-minute act. I stared over his jerking shoulder at a reflection in the darkened window. I didn't recognize the woman staring back at me.

Chapter 27

The international business travel that Greg had been antici-
pating turned out to be a trip to Tokyo during the week of
Becky and Nate's spring break. He promised to bring us lots
of souvenirs and pictures. "We'll keep working on things when I
get back," he murmured in my ear as he hugged me goodbye. The
kids and I waved to him from the driveway, and then I went inside
and got to work. The house was in need of a good spring cleaning.

I carried a bag full of cans and bottles out to the minivan,
to bring to the town dump for recycling, and then I bundled up
Greg's *Wall Street Journal*s that had piled up on the coffee table.
As I was gathering the papers together, a story headline caught
my eye: *One Tough Day for Two-Timers*. It was subtitled *As Cheat-
ers Juggle Valentines, Private Eyes Work Overtime; The Feb. 14
'Business Trip.'* I sat down to read the article, which was about a
detective who had videotaped a woman's husband leaving a valentine on the windshield of his mistress's car. Valentine's Day is a
difficult holiday, the story said, for those who have both a spouse
and a secret lover to please.

I dropped the paper and ran to the computer. Our dial-up
connection was running slow, and it took a full minute for me to
pull up the T-Mobile website. I tried to log in. *Incorrect password*,
it said. I backspaced and typed it in again. *Incorrect password*. I
pounded my fists on the desk. Greg had changed it because he
was hiding something. What gall he had, what brazen, bald-faced

arrogance! He thought he could go right on merrily banging that little Southern wench, and I was too dumb or too timid to figure it out. What a total idiot I'd been, to be taken in by his scripted apology and his phony plea for forgiveness. I should have known I couldn't trust him.

I went for the phone. I would call him right this second, tell him what a shitheel he was. I'd tell him not to bother coming home; he could stay over there in Japan forever for all I cared. I dialed his number, and it went right to his voice mail. I cocked my arm and was about to launch the phone across the room when it rang in my hand.

It was Carla. "Oh my freaking *God*," I shrieked. "I can't take it anymore. *Aaaaagh!*"

When I regained a measure of control over myself, I explained what I was flipping out about. "Put the kids in the car and start driving," she said. "Come home for the week, and tell one of your sisters they need to watch Becky and Nate for you on Saturday night. You and I are gonna go out and have some fun for a change."

I stayed at Mom and Dad's house this time. Becky and Nate slept in the twin beds in Debra's and my old room, and I stayed across the hall in what used to be Eileen's room. Mom had converted it into a sewing room many years ago, but she didn't use it anymore. The Singer was hidden under a plastic cover, and bolts of fabric were stacked in a corner, collecting dust.

Dad was thinner and more easily fatigued than he'd been at Thanksgiving, but he was feeling optimistic about his treatments. His latest scan had shown that the tumor was shrinking. He napped after lunch every day while Mom bustled around the house, endlessly tidying and sneaking peeks at the reminder lists she'd written for herself in her graceful parochial school cursive.

She tried to keep them hidden from us, but I had found one taped to the inside of the kitchen cabinet where she kept her Centrum Silver. *Wash clothes on Monday*, it said. *Dust furniture on Wednesday.*

A wet spring snow fell. I took Becky and Nate over to Marian's house, where the ground was coated enough for sledding in her backyard. The cousins whizzed down the hill on their plastic sleds until the snow turned to mush and everyone was soaked. When they grew tired, they tumbled back into the house, and the kitchen floor became a mess of muddy boots and soggy snow pants. I helped Marian make lunch, and I cleaned up afterward as well, to keep my hands busy and my mind blank.

The kids went down to the basement to play, and Marian began mixing up a batch of cookie dough. I sat at the kitchen table, idly turning the pages of a week-old newspaper and wondering when Greg would call again from Tokyo. We'd spoken for a few seconds last night, but the overseas echo had been bad, and then the call had disconnected. I would need to be careful what I said to him when we finally did talk. I didn't want to say anything that might get him riled up before I had a chance to meet with Mr. Durand again.

Marian clattered a baking sheet into the oven and filled the teakettle at the sink. "How are things going at home?" she asked in her soft voice.

I didn't want to get into it. I was here to try and put my troubles out of my mind for a while. "Things are okay," I lied.

She didn't ask anything more. Of all the people in my family, Marian especially didn't believe in prying. She'd had her own set of troubles years ago, when her first pregnancy started showing only a month after her and Todd's wedding. She took the whistling kettle off the stove. "Well, we're glad you're here. You know you're always welcome." She set a box of tea bags and a cup and saucer in front of me. "You and the kids always have a place here if you ever need it."

Debra offered to have Becky and Nate sleep over at her house on Saturday night, and Carla came to pick me up in a dinky Ford Fiesta. I laughed as I got into the car. "This is so not your style."

She dropped her jaw in mock offense. "Don't diss my ride, sister. Bruce got us a good deal, no money down and low monthly payments." She was wearing a faux-leather jacket and boots, and her hair was piled in a crazy mess on top of her head. She'd gone from her natural blond to a deep chestnut, and the change was confusing. My mother waved to us from the front door. She'd been delighted to see Carla but couldn't remember her name. Maybe it was the hair.

Carla tried to gun the Fiesta's wimpy engine. The car spun backward into the street, swerving on the wet remains of the snow. Carla shook a cigarette from a pack of Marlboros; she offered one to me, but I declined. "I only smoke when Bruce isn't around," she said. "And he's always around. These cigarettes are stale as shit." Van Halen's "Jump" came on the radio, and she cranked the volume and high-fived me. "I've been dying for a girls' night out," she shouted over the music. "This is just like the old days!"

We drove up to Erie, where Carla wouldn't be likely to run into any of her students' parents. We bar-hopped all over the place, downing beers at every stop. Carla said she'd given up buying herself shots for Lent, and accepted them from any man who offered. The alcohol didn't have any effect on her. Music pounded, and we shouted to each other as we danced our way through the crowds, drinks held high so they wouldn't spill.

We paused for a breather at a relatively quiet sports bar that I remembered using Debra's driver's license to get into when I was a senior in high school. The bouncer waved us through without checking our ID. Three young men were sitting near the door at a table covered with beer glasses and empty pitchers. Their accents sounded Canadian. Carla, always intrigued by foreigners, pulled two chairs up for us to join them.

The guys grinned drunkenly and said they had come down from Toronto for an IT conference. They were attractive in a geeky way, with longish sideburns and Buddy Holly eyeglasses, and they seemed to be amazed at their luck: two apparent cougars had just delivered themselves to their table. One of them signaled the waitress and ordered two more pitchers.

Huge TVs were mounted on the walls around the bar, each one tuned to a different sports channel, and a Green Day song was blaring in the background. I had to strain to hear what the Canadians were talking about. The guy sitting next to me shouted something about broadband capabilities and began to explain the technical details of his work. I tuned him out. I was drunk. It felt good to not be plagued with worries about my husband, my home, or my kids. I pinched a french fry off the techie's plate, and he pushed the rest toward me with a "help yourself" motion. I thought he was cute. I bobbed my head in time to the music and grinned at him. Carla grabbed the tallest of the trio by the sleeve and hauled him outside for a smoke. The third guy excused himself and went to find a seat closer to a television. Hockey was on.

The techie was saying something to me again. "What?" I said. He leaned closer and repeated whatever it was, and I nodded as though I'd heard him. A thin stubble covered his cheeks and chin, and it looked awfully sexy to me. *I could kiss him.* The thought was appealing—a revenge kiss. Revenge on Greg. The guy put his hand on my knee under the table. I wondered if I could do it. Just a kiss, nothing more. But how could I make it happen? I couldn't kiss him right there in public; I was *married*, for heaven's sake.

Someone I knew from way back when might see me, and reports of my immoral behavior would undoubtedly work their way back to my sisters.

Carla and the tall guy breezed back in, bringing a cloud of cold air and cigarette smoke with them. The waitress set a foaming pitcher in front of me, and I felt suddenly sick to my stomach. I slapped Carla's shoulder; when she saw my face, she jumped up. "Gotta run, fellas." She grabbed me by the wrist, and we ran for the exit.

I threw up in the gutter next to the Fiesta and felt instantly better. "Just like college!" Carla cried with glee. For the first time all night, she seemed actually buzzed. She started the car, rolled her window down, and lit another cigarette. "Help me watch the road while I drive, Jeanie. Four eyes are better than one." She thought about what she'd said for a second. "Whatever." She put the car in gear, and we rolled back to Adams Mills.

My head was throbbing and my mouth was full of cotton in the morning. I found a bottle of my father's Doan's pills in the bathroom cabinet, stuffed three in my mouth, and gulped water straight from the faucet to wash them down. I forced out a bright "Good morning" for my parents when I went downstairs, in an effort to disguise my hangover.

It was Sunday, so we were meeting the rest of my family for Mass. I placed Becky and Nate between their grandparents to ensure their good behavior, then sat back and closed my eyes, pretending to be deep in prayerful meditation. The organ droned as the priest and the altar servers processed up the center aisle. I tried to recall the events of last night, but it was all so fuzzy. Drinking. Dancing. Puking.

The priest began the Introductory Rites, and the congregation responded in unison. I recited the opening lines of the

Confiteor: *I confess to almighty God, and to you, my brothers and sisters, that I have sinned through my own fault* . . . I had a blurry memory of the geeky Canadian guy and how I'd wanted to kiss him. My stomach lurched. *Did I?* No, I was sure I hadn't; I'd only wanted to. Thank goodness. It was a passing fantasy, I guess, or maybe just plain lust, since I'd been going without sex for so long. Lust was one of the seven deadly sins—I'd learned that right here at Sacred Heart. But I would never, ever give in to it. I would never sleep with another man, not as long as I was still married. But I was definitely guilty of the sin of Gluttony, for all that drinking. And Greed, I suppose, went along with Gluttony. And Envy. I was envious of Carla, who seemed, for the most part, to have her head screwed on straight, while I was such a hot mess. Come to think of it, I was guilty of Wrath as well, for wanting to get revenge on Greg. Well, that was five sins out of the seven. Good God, I was going to Hell for sure. I bowed my head and prayed for the Lord's mercy. It *had* been an awfully fun night though. More fun than I'd had in a long time.

After church, I packed up our things, said my goodbyes to everyone, and left for home. I stopped at a Sheetz in Wilkes-Barre for a large Diet Coke and a packet of Tylenol, and again on the Pike for coffee. I was nervous about seeing Greg again. I was dreading the coming confrontation over the changed password.

Perhaps I was making too much of it. He might have had to update it for security purposes and simply neglected to tell me. It wasn't fair for me to jump to conclusions. I called his cell each time I stopped, but he didn't answer. I kept checking my phone as I drove, in case I'd passed through a dead spot and missed his call. Nothing came up. We arrived in Wayfield around seven, and there was no message from him on the home phone either. I guessed he was still on his way back from Tokyo.

I grew increasingly anxious as the evening wore on. *Where was he?* By eleven, my hangover headache had intensified to a constant painful throbbing, and my mind was in a tangle of worry. Had something happened to Greg's plane, or to his taxi? I checked the TV news, but there were no reports of airline crashes or Turnpike fatalities.

I dialed him one last time at eleven thirty, as I was getting ready to go to bed. "Hello," he said. "I was just getting ready to call you."

"I'm so glad to hear your voice. I was worried about you."

"Worried? I'm fine. I just cleared customs in Atlanta."

That brought me up short. "Atlanta?"

"Yeah." He was breathing in a choppy rhythm, like he was walking fast.

"Are you heading for your Boston flight?"

A breathy pause. "No."

"What? Why not? Aren't you coming home tonight?"

Another long pause, filled with breathing. "No, I need to get back to work."

My throat constricted. "You're not coming home."

"I never said I'd come right home after Tokyo."

I fought for calm and tried to think. Hadn't he told me he'd be back today? I couldn't remember exactly what he'd said. "I thought you'd be anxious to see us, after being away so long."

"I have a lot of work to catch up on down here."

"You've got a lot of work to do up here too. We're supposed to be working on our marriage, remember? How do we do that if we're not together?"

"How are we supposed to *live* if I don't work? Listen, there's some people waiting for me. We can discuss this in our session with Suzette when I get back on Friday. I'm extremely tired, and I'm going to my hotel now. I've got to get some sleep."

- - -

I padded up the stairs to check on my children. They were both deep asleep, exhausted from their busy week with their cousins. Becky had Molly sleeping in her bed with her, and Nate was flopped diagonally across his bed with his feet hanging over the side. I eased his legs back into place and covered him up.

I closed both their doors and stood in the narrow hallway. I was wiped, completely spent. I pictured myself ten years from now, raising two teenagers on my own while Greg jetted around the globe, chasing other men's wives. Nate would grow up to be just like him, like in that Harry Chapin song that was so popular when I was a kid. And what about Becky? How would my example as a wife affect her future relationships? She was learning all the wrong things—that a man can treat his wife as though she's the hired help, and all the wife can do is keep quiet and endure it.

I stared into the dark stairwell and imagined throwing myself down the worn wooden steps, crashing to the floor below. I might break my leg or fracture my skull. I'd have to go to the hospital, and Greg would have to come home to take care of me. The urgency of my injuries would blot out the horror of my marriage slipping through my fingers.

I shook the vision from my head, flicked the light on, grasped the banister, and carefully descended the stairs. Hurting myself wouldn't solve anything. Nothing could solve this. I had married a man I hardly knew, in a desperate attempt to redeem myself from sins that I now knew I wasn't guilty of. The assault I'd endured at the hands of Professor Asner wasn't my fault, and neither was the violent sex that Greg had forced me into on Christmas night. I flashed back to our wedding day and how he hadn't been able to meet my eye as my father walked me down the aisle. I'd brushed it off as bashfulness at the time, but now I knew the truth: Greg hadn't been committed to me from the start.

I thought of Ed and how he'd opened my eyes to what was missing in my marriage. And Perla, who had taught me what a normal family was like. So had Eileen and Todd, and all the rest of my family. We were ordinary and traditional, and perhaps a bit behind the times, but we all genuinely cared about each other and looked after one another. I thought about the Mercers in comparison, and Florence in particular. She was the kind of mean-spirited, bitter woman that I was in danger of becoming.

I'd been trained since childhood to pursue a life as a devoted wife and mother, but now my sacred duty was slamming up against the hard, cold reality of my dysfunctional life with Greg. It was time to wrench myself free.

Chapter 28

G reg left me a message later that week, while I was volunteering at school. "I've got to stay here a few more days so I can circle back with the project team. You'll need to call Suzette and tell her we can't make our appointment on Friday."

"Screw you," I said to the answering machine. "Call Suzette and tell her yourself."

I sat down to think for a minute. I needed to tell Mr. Durand to proceed with the divorce. I tried to summon the energy to make the phone call, but I couldn't do it. It seemed so final. I gazed dully around the room and found myself staring at the blank computer screen. My eyes traveled from the computer to the bookcase, slid over the rows of books that I had arranged so neatly when we moved in, and stopped at the bottom shelf, where Greg's executive diaries were arranged in chronological order with the dates marked on their spines.

I went over and picked up the most recent volume. I opened it and skimmed the handwritten notes, not sure of what I was searching for. Greg had a system for labeling his entries: *P* indicated a phone call, *C* was an in-person conversation, *VM* was voice mail. Each entry had a date, followed by a person's name.

I paged through the diary until an entry jumped out at me: *Dad.* It was labeled with a *C* and dated the thirtieth of June last year. I thought for a second—that was when Greg had come to Boston to accept the new job, and then he'd gone down to

Augusta to play some celebratory golf with his father. The note read, *Divorce laws more favorable in Massachusetts. Stay together for time being. Too much $ involved. Don't purchase house.*

I slammed the diary shut and hurled it at the bookcase. "That's it," I said. "I'm done." Greg's show of remorse was a sham that he'd devised to pacify me and buy him more time until the state got around to passing the new divorce legislation. My father-in-law was nothing but a fake and a calculating schemer. And all this time I'd thought Florence was the one I had to watch out for.

Greg finally came home at the end of the week and acted like everything was just swell. The next morning, he said he was going to meet Royce at the shooting range for a couple of hours of practice. I took Becky and Nate over to Ann's for lunch, and when we got back around one o'clock, I saw that Greg had returned. I told the kids to play outside for a while and went into the house.

Greg was in the living room with the gun and a cleaning kit laid out on the coffee table.

"Did you clear it first?" I asked.

He made a face at me. "Yeah."

I sat down and watched as he clumsily ejected the magazine and set it down beside a second mag that I could see was fully loaded. He reached for the television remote and clicked on the World Cup soccer quarter-finals, England versus Portugal. David Beckham missed a corner kick; Greg scowled and turned his attention back to the tools in front of him. He picked up the bore brush and the bottle of cleaning solvent but set them down a second later to follow the soccer action until the broadcast cut to a commercial. He took up the bore brush again and tried to stick a cleaning patch onto the end of it. I didn't trouble myself to correct his faulty technique.

"Too bad we had to miss our session with Suzette yesterday," he said. "We'll have to catch up on things next Friday."

I crossed my legs and drummed my fingers on the arms of my chair. "Yeah, we'll have plenty to catch up on all right. If we even go."

He looked up. "Why wouldn't we go?"

"You tell me." I noticed his leg start jiggling. "It's pointless for us to keep going to counseling," I said, "if we're not committed to making this work."

"I'm committed."

"No," I said. "I don't think you are."

He played with the tools on the table, unsure of what to do with them. "I don't know what you want me to say, Jeanie. There's so much gray area here, you know? I don't operate very well in the gray. I like things to be black and white. All this counseling—" He gave one of his fake chuckles. "It doesn't seem to be getting us anywhere. It's so discouraging." He looked down and sighed.

I studied his profile. Was he for real, or was he acting? Either way, I was through playing his game. I saw his brow crimp as he peeked up at the soccer game. I reached for the remote and clicked the television off. "Greg," I said. "Answer me this, once and for all. Do you want to keep your family together, or do you want to be done with this?"

He spoke his answer softly, into his chest. "I don't know." He lifted his head and looked straight at me, and there was no anger or guile in his face this time. Only bare honesty.

I realized he genuinely didn't know what he wanted, and I couldn't wait any longer for him to figure it out. This life was killing me, and I had to stop the bleeding. I regarded him with something close to pity; he was throwing away the greatest gifts he'd ever been given, all because he thought the world revolved around no one else but him. I was through with his narcissism and his need for control. He could go ahead and tell my whole family my secret if he wanted to. I would face their questions and their disappointment, and I'd somehow find a way to deal with it. Greg didn't have any power over me anymore.

"What a sorry man you are," I said.

He bolted upright. "Fuck you," he said. "Go to hell." He picked up the gun and pointed it at me, and I froze. Had he actually cleared it? Did he even know what he was doing? A kick of adrenaline surged through my limbs, but I didn't move, afraid of setting him off.

He lowered his arm and put the gun down. "It isn't loaded, stupid."

I lunged. I grabbed the gun and the full magazine, smacked the mag into the grip, racked the slide, and took dead aim at my soon-to-be-ex-husband's heart. "Get out."

Greg's eyes went wide with astonishment. "You wouldn't dare."

"I said get out."

"This is assault. I could call the cops on you."

"It's self-defense. Now get the hell out of this house."

He rose with his hands open at mid-chest and backed out of the room. I heard him scrambling for his jacket and car keys, and the side door banged. I lowered the gun, set the safety, and shoved it into the back of my jeans like the Pennsylvania country girl that I was. Fuck *you*, Greg. *You* can go to hell.

I heard my children shouting outside, and I went to the window. I saw Greg's car stop in the street as he drew abreast of Becky and Nate, who were playing in a neighboring yard. He lowered the window and waved goodbye to them across the empty passenger's seat.

Chapter 29

called Mr. Durand and told him to proceed with the divorce filing. Then I started packing. As I was clearing out the few personal items that I had stored in Greg's desk, I came across a bundle of last year's Christmas cards, forgotten in the back of a drawer. I flipped through them and paused to look at the one we'd received from the Claytons. It was a photo card with a big picture of Ken and Paige and their eighteen-month-old son. He was chubby and towheaded, just like Nate had been at that age.

Just like Nate. I studied the picture more closely. This boy and my son looked so much alike you might think they were brothers.

I returned to Adams Mills and moved myself and the kids into my parents' house for the time being. The arrangement worked well for all of us—I would help take care of Dad as he finished up his radiation treatments, and he'd have help looking after Mom as her mind continued its graceful slide into oblivion. I convinced him to sign up for internet service, and I registered for evening classes at the community college in Butler. I got a job working in the media center at the high school (they didn't call it a library anymore), and I enrolled Becky and Nate at Blessed Sacrament so they could go to school with their cousins.

I drove the children out to Wayfield to spend their school vacations with their father, but Greg didn't ever come to Adams Mills, except for when he dropped them off at home at the end of their visits. He never did follow through on his threat of telling my family what had happened to me in college.

Our divorce was finalized in the fall. "Now that's over with," Carla said, "you need to get even with that asshole Asner. You've got to take back your power from him."

Wreaking revenge on people was not my thing. It was costing me enough heartache to gather the grace within me to forgive Greg. But Carla's suggestion did have a kernel of merit. I needed to let go of the blame and reclaim my right to a happy and purposeful life.

I went to my college website and looked up the English Department. There was no Steven Asner listed among the faculty, but there was a message on the homepage welcoming the new department chair, Professor Candace MacNamara. Asner's ex-wife. I typed his name into a couple of search engines, but I couldn't find anything. It was as though he had disappeared.

My family celebrated Thanksgiving at Mom and Dad's house that year. Eileen, Marian, and Debra came over in the morning to help with the cooking, and all the kids ran interference to keep Gramma away from the chaos in the kitchen. When the food was ready and everyone was seated, we went around the dining room table as we always did, sharing something from the preceding year that we were thankful for. When my turn came, the blessings I named were obvious ones: I was grateful for a home and a family to come back to.

My cell phone rang long after I'd gone to bed that night. Greg's voice was so hoarse I almost didn't recognize it. I turned the bedside clock toward me and saw it was a quarter to two. I wondered if he'd been up this whole time or if the weight of his conscience had pulled him awake.

"Jeanie," he said. "I have to tell you something." Several seconds passed, and I almost fell back to sleep; he cleared his throat and went on: "All those years, I thought I was doing the right thing. I was working hard so we could have a good life. I know you tried to warn me about what was happening to us, but I didn't get it. You weren't saying it in a way that I could understand."

So, it was my fault that our marriage fell apart. Right. I raised my eyes heavenward in the dark and sent up a thank-you to Blessed Mary, ever virgin, and all the angels and saints, for helping me to free myself from this man's narcissism and manipulation. I yawned into the phone. "It's late, Greg. I can't talk to you right now. I've got to get some sleep."

THE END

Acknowledgments

am grateful for the many talented teachers, fellow students, and writing group friends that I have had the privilege of working with at Writers & Books, a literary arts center in my current hometown of Rochester, New York. Your enthusiasm, encouragement, and helpful suggestions have inspired me to persevere.

About the Author

Regina Buttner is a registered-nurse-turned-writer from Upstate New York. *Absolution* is her first novel. Learn more about her at www.reginabuttner.com.

SELECTED TITLES FROM SPARKPRESS

SparkPress is an independent boutique publisher
delivering high-quality, entertaining, and engaging content
that enhances readers' lives, with a special focus on
female-driven work. www.gosparkpress.com

Charming Falls Apart: A Novel, Angela Terry, $16.95, 978-1-68463-049-3. After losing her job and fiancé the day before her thirty-fifth birthday, people-pleaser and rule-follower Allison James decides she needs someone to give her some new life rules—*and fast*. But when she embarks on a self-help mission, she realizes that her old life wasn't as perfect as she thought—and that she needs to start writing her own rules.

Child Bride: A Novel, Jennifer Smith Turner, $16.95, 978-1-68463-038-7. The coming-of-age journey of a young girl from the South who joins the African American great migration to the North—and finds her way through challenges and unforeseen obstacles to womanhood.

That's Not a Thing: A Novel, Jacqueline Friedland. $16.95, 978-1-68463-030-1. When a recently engaged Manhattanite learns that her first great love has been diagnosed with ALS, she is faced with the impossible decision of whether a few final months with her ex might be worth risking her entire future. A fast-paced emotional journey that explores whether it's possible to be equally in love with two men at once.

And Now There's You: A Novel, Susan S. Etkin. $16.95, 978-1-68463-000-4. Though five years have passed since beautiful design consultant Leila Brandt's husband passed away, she's still grieving his loss. When she meets a terribly sexy and talented—if arrogant—architect, however, sparks fly, and neither of them can deny the chemistry between them.

The Opposite of Never: A Novel, Kathy Mehuron. $16.95, 978-1-943006-50-2. Devastated by the loss of their spouses, Georgia and Kenny think that the best times of their lives are long over until they find each other; meanwhile Kenny's teenage stepdaughter, Zelda, and Georgia's friend's son, Spencer, fall in love at first sight—only to fall prey to and suffer opiate addiction together.